THE LIES YOU TELL

MEL SHERRATT

1

Monday, 17 July

I hardly dare open my eyes, but I must. I don't even know how long I've been here. An hour, perhaps? Two hours? A minute? Why is my watch broken?

I'm sitting on the floor, my back against the wall. My knees pulled to my chest, my hands wrapped around them. The kitchen tiles are cold on my feet. A metallic smell is in the air.

There is a sound to the silence; it's ringing in my ears. I can't hear anything else. Not the traffic on the street below. Nor the noise of the neighbours arriving home after a hard day's work. Nor a murmur or a groan from ...

One, two, three. Come on! I can do this.

I lift my head and open my eyes. Sheer horror rushes through me and I force myself not to close them again.

It's real.

It wasn't a dream.

I can't believe there is so much blood.

A spasm in my stomach and I retch. Please, no. Don't let me be sick. I can't leave any trace of me behind, not even that. It could be vital evidence against me.

I hold my right hand out. It shakes violently, more blood drying under my fingernails.

To my right is a chair. It usually sits under a small pine table. My black dress is strewn across it, my heels beneath it, one fallen over on its side. Flashbacks of what I did come rushing at me.

I removed my dress to wash away the blood.

The urgency of the situation catches up with me. I slap my palm against my forehead. What am I going to do? I mean, I never intended this to happen.

It could have been so much better. But he ruined it. And now there will be no going back.

I open a cupboard, looking for detergent. I must clean the place up. Make it look like I wasn't here, and then get rid of all the evidence.

As I race around, I do my best to ignore the body slumped in the opposite corner of the room.

2

Friday, 26 May

Tamara Parker-Brown sipped her coffee as she stood in the window of her office. She was expecting Esther Smedley in ten minutes and, even though they had met briefly, she wanted to see her again. There was a lot to be learned from how a person walked. Shoulders held high while taking large strides might denote a confident person. Someone wiping sweaty palms and fidgeting with hair could come across as nervous. Doing a bit of both would seem to be natural, she assumed, and what she would most probably do.

Above the rooftops of the buildings across from her, the trails of several aeroplanes criss-crossed a clear blue sky. She sighed, wondering if today would bring a dash of rain, a hint of a thunderstorm; anything to take a break from the incessant heat. London was heading for its hottest May in decades. Even a drop in temperature to the twenties would be bliss instead of the early thirties of the past two weeks.

Tamara wished she didn't have to have someone so close to her home, but, in the same vein, knew she couldn't afford the office prices of central London when she'd refused any more financial help from her family. Besides, living in Westminster was a bonus as it allowed her to be near everything. If she got the pitch, it would mean a walk rather than a tube journey, which was the cheaper option.

Ever since she had received a proof copy of *Something's Got to Give*, she knew that Dulston Publishing was on to something. The book had such an interesting premise, told in alternative chapters from the kidnapper and victim, and was gruesome but voyeuristic. As soon as she had read the first chapter, she'd been hooked and had done nothing else that whole day and evening until she'd read it through to the end. Then she'd read it again, disappointed that she'd finished it so quickly.

Over the past week, she had interviewed several people, having finally decided that she couldn't do everything single-handedly. She'd been nervous during the first few, but after a while she'd settled into it. She hadn't expected to get through so many candidates though – all of them useless so far.

Unable to afford a recruitment agency to sort out the wheat from the chaff, the choice of candidates hadn't been ideal. Some of them didn't seem to have ever worked in an office. One woman said she didn't know how to type but could handwrite everything. Another mentioned she could only work certain hours because she had a child at nursery and a sick mother, which would have been fine if Tamara had stated that the position was part-time.

There had been a man who had seemed a good candidate at first, but after careful consideration, she'd thought it best to settle for a female. She never voiced that, though, because she wasn't sexist. She just hadn't felt comfortable when he'd been there.

She spotted a woman with auburn hair walking along the pavement, and took a step back to hide behind the heavy embroidered curtains, while still keeping her in view. Tamara liked Esther already. She had chosen to wear a jacket despite the temperature already creeping up. Dressed in a plain, navy skirt suit and a white blouse, her stride seemed confident. Under her arm was a small, zipped case.

As she drew closer, Tamara watched the woman pause for a moment at the bottom of the steps, before taking a deep breath and bouncing up the stairs to the front door.

The intercom buzzed.

'Hello.'

'Hi, this is Esther Smedley. I have an interview at ten o'clock with Tamara Parker-Brown.'

'Come on up. I'm on the first floor.'

Tamara buzzed her in and then went to the vestibule. She checked over her appearance one more time in the oak-framed mirror that had been passed down from her grand-parents. She definitely hadn't got long legs and a svelte figure, or hair to die for like her interviewee, but she was passable with her brown wave and stout motherly figure, even though she had yet to have children.

'Wish me luck with this one, Grandma,' she said to her reflection, before taking a deep breath and throwing open her door.

'Hello, again.' She held out her hand as Esther appeared, trying not to be startled at how stunning she was up close.

'Hi.' Esther's grip was firm and positive.

'Come on in and we can get started.' Tamara closed the door and showed her through, urging her to take a seat at the large table, which until recently, had been piled high with paperwork, books, and work paraphernalia. It had taken her a good hour to remove everything from it so that she had somewhere to interview prospective people.

'Would you like anything to drink?' she asked, hoping not, as she wanted to get to the questions. 'Tea, coffee, a glass of water?'

'A glass of water would be lovely, thank you,' Esther replied. 'And would you mind awfully if I removed my jacket?'

'Of course not.' Tamara smiled. 'No need for airs and graces at Parker-Brown PR.'

Esther Smedley placed her manicured hands on the table and clasped them together while she answered the questions Tamara threw at her. She'd had plenty of practice during role-play in the adult education classes she'd been made to attend.

Yes, she was reliable, punctual and keen to learn. Yes, she was able to work on her own initiative as well as being an avid team player. Of course she was a good organiser and had excellent project management skills. Blah, blah, blah.

Customer service was of great importance to her. No, she didn't have experience in everything required, but she was a fast learner and always open to constructive criticism if it helped her to become a better employee. Yawn, yawn, yawn.

After what seemed like a lifetime, Tamara scanned the piece of paper in front of her. From where she was sitting, Esther could tell it was a list of things she needed to pass muster. She hoped she'd ticked enough of the boxes to satisfy the woman.

'Do you have your references to hand?' Tamara asked.

'Yes.' Esther unzipped the leather folder she'd placed on

the table beside her and pulled out a sheaf of papers. 'I also have some examples of my work that I'd like to show you.'

She could see excitement in Tamara's eyes as she perused the rest of the paperwork. Of course, there wasn't anything there that Esther had done. All the samples had been sourced from the internet.

While Tamara listened, Esther talked in great detail about the experience she had gained working on several media campaigns. None of that was true either, but it made her sound *so* interesting that she almost wished it wasn't a pack of lies.

'These are very impressive,' Tamara said, after looking through the first few.

'Thank you!' Esther smiled widely.

Tamara read the fake references next. Esther sat and twiddled her thumbs before moving her hands out of view. She didn't want it to seem as if she was nervous. It was more that she was irritated the interview was taking so long.

Finally, Tamara looked up again. 'You'd be able to start immediately, you say?'

'Yes.' Esther nodded. 'The reason I am out of work at the moment is because I've moved areas. I've enjoyed working on small campaigns so much that I wanted to expand my knowledge. I'm sure it will be of great value to me if I'm continually around central London. The rent for my flat is extremely high but I feel it will be worth it, and it isn't far on the District line from Earl's Court to Victoria. It's very handy for early starts and late evenings.' Esther smiled shyly.

When Tamara smiled back at her, she knew she had won her over.

'I'm very impressed with what I've seen so far.' Tamara leaned forward and gave the paperwork back to her. 'I think we might get along well together. Would you like to do a month's trial for me?'

Esther left the office, her steps light as she made her way back to Victoria Street. She glanced up at the window to see Tamara watching her. She smiled and waved. When the wave was returned, she laughed to herself as she walked away.

Well, that had been easier than she'd imagined. Of course, Parker-Brown was a means to an end, but Esther hadn't expected her to bow down so easily. Maybe she would do more checking now she had left. Only the next few days would tell. If she didn't get a phone call, or an email to discuss things further, or to tell her the decision had been overturned, she was home and dry.

Esther had been watching Dulston Publishing for some years now. She had a Google alert set up for whenever a mention of Jack Maitland's name came online too. She'd come to London in the hope of getting a job in publishing, but everyone wanted references or previous experience and she had neither until she'd thought to fake them. Wait-ressing had been her next option and a few cash-in-hand gigs, where the pay was appallingly low, had got her to a few publishing events handing out champagne and canapés.

She'd done this for two months, and was wondering if she needed to change tactics when she'd overheard Tamara talking about Dulston Publishing, and some of the prospec-tive employees she had interviewed with no joy.

Not wanting to miss out on a golden opportunity, she had approached Tamara as she was leaving, and blagged her way to an interview. She'd been disappointed that Dulston Publishing themselves hadn't been hiring directly, but this had been the next best thing. A bit of mundane day-to-day working would be worth it to get closer to him, and what better way to utilise the skills she had learned recently.

And Parker-Brown wouldn't suspect a thing because of Esther's acting skills. That was the beauty of her act – she could fool people, make them feel at ease with her, trust her. It was the same with all the men she'd fleeced over the years. One-night stands were great because she could keep up the pretence enough for that. Once she'd left with their cash and whatever she could lay her hands on to sell, then she could return to her usual self.

No one ever got to see the real person underneath the delightful persona she had created.

Well, not unless she wanted them to.

3

Friday, 16 June

Tamara smiled to herself. Here she was again, standing in the window of her sitting room, watching the world go by. Although London was always busy, she at least got a chance to see her neighbours as they left for work. Not to talk to, obviously. *One does not do that kind of thing on her street*, she mused. But she knew most of their routines: who came out at what time, who took the children to school on certain days, and who, like she, worked from home.

If she stared across into the bay window of number twenty-seven, the house directly opposite her flat, she would see Sarah Fitzpatrick trying to cajole her youngest two children into getting dressed. Her husband went to work before Tamara took her coffee. Sarah and her children always left by 7.45 a.m. Sarah would then return until 2.00 p.m. and then she would rush out to collect the children again.

Tamara wouldn't say she was a nosy neighbour, but she

was a stickler for routine. She only looked out of the window while she drank her first coffee every morning. After that, no one would see her for the rest of the day, unless she was using the laptop to work from rather than her big screen. But even then, she wouldn't be spying. It was routine that she liked.

The first cup of coffee was always the best part of the day. Despite the restless sleep she'd had the night before, she knew it would invigorate her – take away her nerves around the plans for the day ahead.

Even at 7.30 a.m., she was trying to feel excited rather than apprehensive. Today was pitch day. Everything was ready, yet it had come around far too quickly. She prayed that she wouldn't let herself down this time.

It would be a dream come true to work on the new campaign with Dulston Publishing. Winning the pitch could be fabulous news for her. Maybe then she could move on from the 'episode'.

She sipped at her coffee as she watched the couple from two doors down rush their children out into the car, strapping them into seats with military precision before driving off. Tamara wanted to have her own family one day but for now she was content to work. There was plenty of time to find someone to trust again. First, she needed to win this pitch.

She had never been good at public speaking, despite starting her own PR company and having to present pitches all the time. It was something that pushed her beyond her comfort zone and it was challenging, some days more than others. At times, she had wanted to give up, but the fact that she would have to admit defeat to her parents was enough to spur her on again.

Sometimes the pitches were in front of a handful of

people; sometimes they were in rooms holding around two hundred delegates.

Sometimes she was great at it. Sometimes she would fail miserably and someone else would end up with the campaign.

The pitch today was extremely important. She had to be noticed soon or things would go to the wall. The small projects she'd worked on since starting the business were great to keep it afloat but she was hardly surviving. This job could be the start of something better for her; where she was respected, in demand and able. It could further her career, helping her to impress people and gain more work.

Yesterday, Tamara had been talking through her fears with Esther. She had been working with her for three weeks now. Tamara felt extremely lucky to have found her, even though she had been the only person who came forward with anything about her.

Esther said that she was going to nail this pitch and Tamara was determined to prove her right. She had been repeating affirmations and practising positive scenarios in her mind, where she saw herself standing up in front of everyone, word perfect, calm, and confident.

But then the old anxiety would return and she would feel a rush of heat to her cheeks as she remembered the last time. She had told Esther how terrible it had been but she hadn't elaborated because it was too embarrassing. She had gone completely blank, dropping all her cue cards and generally making a fool of herself. She hadn't been able to get out of there quickly enough, hence not having much work since. It had been a complete disaster.

At thirty-three and single, Tamara always felt as if she had let her family down. Her parents were old-fashioned and wanted her to find someone with money, marry him, and be dependent for the rest of her life. But she wouldn't be happy doing that, even more so after what had happened with Michael.

Her two elder brothers and one younger sister were all married, with six children between them. She seemed to be the black sheep of the family. She wasn't attractive, but neither was she ugly.

And coming from a wealthy family had its disadvantages. To get people to notice her she had to constantly show that she was successful and sought after, but it was expensive to keep up appearances. She had to dress up what she had in the best that designers could offer, and groom herself impeccably.

Luckily, her job meant that she was sometimes wined and dined throughout London. She told everyone she employed a cleaner and her food was delivered weekly to her door, but in reality, she did her own shopping, cooking, and cleaning. Her one saving grace was her car, although it was usually stationary outside her flat for most of the week. It was a Mercedes-Benz C-Class bought by her father. She'd had it since it was new in 2009, and it was only worth about five thousand pounds now. But even if it had been more valuable, she didn't have the heart to sell it to make ends meet.

She picked up her cue cards and read the words aloud from the first one.

'We at Parker-Brown PR know a good book when we read it. We absolutely adored *Something's Got to Give*.'

Tamara held her shoulders high. She could do this.

4

Esther let herself out of her flat and popped her keys in her handbag. Unlike Tamara's block of flats, whose neighbours were either quiet, out at work, or the homes were empty during the week, she could hear the baby from the first floor screaming out his lungs, and the beat of the music from the flat across the way. No matter what time, the noise never stopped.

She was glad to get out during the day, but at least she had a roof over her head, and felt fairly safe when she returned, which had been quite a change.

In the dimly lit hallway, she opened the front door, the sound of the street bursting in. As she stepped down onto the pavement, she wondered if she was the only one from the flats who was earning a wage. Thank goodness it wouldn't be forever. She'd managed to grab a great haul last night. One unexpected man, the bar emptied in his room, a quick sex session and once he'd fallen asleep, she'd been out of his hotel with his wallet and laptop two hours later. His laptop she would pawn; it was the money she was more interested in.

If the buildings weren't so tall, Esther was sure she would have been blinded by the sun, which was high in another cloudless sky. It had been hot for several days now, the heat unbearable on the tube as well as in the office where she worked. The noise from the traffic was even more intolerable than the dust that seemed to hang around in the air, yet the fan she had on the desk wasn't equipped for a heatwave.

She was quite enjoying her time temping at Parker-Brown PR, even though she didn't really want to be there. Tamara didn't seem to have many return clients and was depending on this new pitch hitting big. Through her knowledge of social media, Esther had come up with a few ideas to get her started – even if it was a double-edged sword at times because people are so stupidly open – and knew she could create a buzz around something.

After calling for takeaway coffee, she joined the throngs of people pushing to get through the barriers at Earl's Court tube station. She saw the same faces day after day: the woman with her hair in a bun and a red jacket who always had her head in a magazine, the men in their slinky suits, holding briefcases assuming it made them look important, and several groups of teenagers competing to make the loudest noise.

On the platform, she squashed herself into the crowd as she waited for the District line to arrive. Already she could feel a headache forming, the exhausting heat wafting towards her. It would be hot and stuffy on the tube. She would be drenched in sweat before she got to work.

While she waited, she rehearsed everything in her head again. She was determined nothing would stop them from winning the pitch for Dulston Publishing, so she had put together some thoughts of her own, surprising herself that she was quite creative when she could be bothered.

At Victoria, she jogged up the escalators out into the open air on to Victoria Street. Tamara's office was only a five-minute walk. That was probably a blessing in wet weather but a curse when the sun was shining as it was today. Lunch in St James's Park would have been good if they hadn't got the meeting that afternoon. No doubt Tamara would want to run through it all a couple of times that morning, whereas Esther felt she could do it in her sleep.

Finally she reached her destination, looking up to the sky one more time. After relishing the feel of the sun on her face, she walked up the steps and punched her code into the door entry system. She had been given access to that and the office, but not to the main door of the flat on the second floor where Tamara lived. She had to gain Tamara's full trust first. She was working on that.

The door opened into a hallway, a row of post boxes to her right. Two bicycles stood next to them and a large, potted plant revealed itself as she closed the door. She stepped onto a Minton tiled floor, a staircase at the far end of the hall.

Raj Patel, the old man from the flat downstairs, was in his doorway. He greeted Esther with a smile, his hair slicked back from his face, eyes shining from within crow's feet and hooded lids. As far as she knew, no one seemed to have a bad word to say about him. Tamara had told her he had become the building's unofficial caretaker since losing his wife a year ago; said it kept him fit and active. To her, he was another busybody, probably sticking his nose into other people's business whenever he could.

'Morning, Raj.' Esther smiled back as she collected Tamara's mail from her box and tucked it under her arm.

'Morning, Esther. Looks like another hot one. I swear I'm going to faint if it gets any warmer in here.'

'It's fine by me. You know I like my men hot.' She giggled coquettishly.

'You are a cheeky one.' He wagged a crooked finger at her.

'Always.'

Raj's laughter followed her up the stairs. Once alone again, Esther let out a huge sigh, her shoulders drooping heavily. Although Raj was inoffensive, sometimes it was hard to be affable all the time. She played along to ensure everyone thought she was a nice person. Over the months, it had been something which she'd become extremely good at.

Still, her nerves ratcheted up to full, she would kill for a boost from some speed right now, even though she had been clear of amphetamines for a while.

And even she knew it would be dangerous to go back there again.

5

'I'm *so* glad to see you!' Tamara ushered Esther inside quickly. 'I had my morning coffee, then sat down to go over everything again and my mind went completely blank. I can't remember anything about the presentation we prepared. I've forgotten all the figures I need to know. I'm so nervous I'm sure I'll forget my name, or worse, the title of the book! I ... I need a good talking to.'

'Don't worry,' Esther replied. 'You have this covered.'

Tamara sighed. Esther's manner was always so confident. It was just as well because all the positive thoughts she had been thinking earlier had vanished, only to be replaced by abject fear.

She was talking herself into doing the exact opposite of what was required. The more she thought about the pitch, the more she watched herself stumbling over the words and messing it up completely. She took a deep breath in an attempt to relax.

'What you need is another coffee.' Esther turned her around and gently pushed her towards the open door in front of them. 'Go and sit down in the control room while I make it, and then you can run through everything again with me.'

Tamara walked forward, almost feeling as if she had taken some sort of drug to make her high. It would take her ages to come down from this afterwards. That was if she ever got through it in the first instance.

The control room Esther referred to had originally been Tamara's sitting room. The flat was in a row of three-storey Victorian townhouses, all with airy rooms and high ceilings. Tamara's grandfather had died ten years back and when her grandmother passed away, almost two years ago now, she had left it to her, much to the annoyance of her family.

The will had stipulated it was because Tamara was the only one of her siblings to be unmarried and without children, so the flat was deemed a good starting point for her. Tamara could still remember her cheeks burning as the details had been read out in the solicitor's office, with all her family present. Talk about rubbing salt into her wounds.

She had the top two floors of the building. When she'd moved in, she'd sectioned it off into office space on the first floor and used the area above as her living area. A locked door had been fitted at the top of the stairs, ensuring her privacy. It wasn't ideal but neither was it too much of an issue.

She had really enjoyed having Esther there. She was always self-deprecating, fun to be around, and bubbling over with ideas. She had brightened up her working days so much already and Tamara herself had become far more productive. It was good to have someone around to brainstorm with, or chat to in general over coffee about last night's TV. Working alone, she had missed that.

She reached for her cue cards as Esther came into the room with two mugs, both handles in one hand. She watched her move aside a pile of papers and place them down on coasters, surprised she had been able to find them among the paraphernalia.

'I'm really looking forward to this,' Esther said, a huge grin lighting up her face. 'It's going to be amazing.'

'I wish I had your confidence.' Tamara sighed, shoulders sagging at the thought of what was to come.

'I'm not confident.'

Tamara raised her eyebrows quizzically at Esther.

'I'm not! I fake it. You need to do that too. Visualise yourself standing tall, talking like a pro, and everyone listening intently to you. You have to see yourself winning that pitch and imagine how you will feel when you do.'

'I've been trying that and failing miserably.'

Esther giggled. 'You could visualise the audience without any clothes on. It's a method that works, apparently, but I think I would laugh too much at the thought.'

Tamara picked up a copy of the novel and pretended to swipe Esther around the head with it. 'You're supposed to be encouraging me, not making me even more nervous.'

Esther pulled out a chair and sat down, crossing her legs and smoothing down her dress. She looked up at Tamara with such encouragement that she couldn't help but smile back.

'You will never be readier,' Esther insisted. 'Besides, it's natural to be nervous. Have you met anyone from Dulston Publishing before?'

'I've known Jack Maitland – he's the company director – since I was in my teens but I haven't had much to do with him since then. I've seen him around at a few launches, but I don't think I know any of his staff, although it's possible I've mixed with them. I go to so many events.'

'What's he like?' Esther sat forward and rested her chin in the crook of her hands. 'Is he good-looking?'

Tamara thought back to the last time she had seen Jack. It was at a book launch that had been heavily attended. There had hardly been room to stand, let alone mingle. She had only seen him because he stood out above the crowd.

'Tall, dark, and handsome, if you like that kind of thing,' she told Esther.

'But you can still think about him with no clothes on?'

'Esther!' Tamara looked horrified, then laughed at the thought.

'You see, that's what you need to do. You'll be fine. Although ... I do have another idea, if you'd be interested in hearing about it?'

Tamara checked the time once again. 'Yes, of course. You can tell me all about it on the way.'

6

Tamara buttoned up her jacket while she stood waiting in the reception area of Dulston Publishing. It was a tiny space, but bright, with a staircase leading to another floor in front of them. Behind the receptionist, rows and rows of hardback and paperback books were stood with their covers facing out.

A poster displaying their non-fiction title of the month was standing prominently in the window, next to a pile of the books. The bright blue font stood out from its yellow background. It looked arty, something Tamara knew her father might like. She made a mental note to check it out for Father's Day that coming Sunday.

Discreetly, she wiped sweaty palms down her skirt and thought better of pouring another cup of water from the cooler. If she wasn't careful, she would be running to the bathroom in the middle of the pitch and that wouldn't do at all.

'Are you sure I have everything ready?' she asked Esther yet again.

Esther nodded, swinging side to side on the round chair she was sitting in. 'Remember, you got this.'

'Says the woman who seems as cool as a cucumber. You look amazing, by the way.'

Esther was wearing a pale blue shift dress and navy sandals with a mid-heel. She had curled her hair so that it hung down in coils.

'Thanks. So do you.'

Tamara sniggered. Her recently straightened hair had turned into a frizzy mess in the heat. She sat down next to Esther, hoping that the wetness she could feel under her arms wouldn't seep through her white shirt.

'Is that your natural hair colour?' she asked.

Esther nodded. 'I used to hate it as a child but I quite like it now.'

'It's an amazing colour. Better than boring brown.'

A door opened to their right and Jack Maitland came out. His bio on the company website said he was thirty-seven and he unquestionably wore his years well. As she'd mentioned to Esther, he was tall, with a slim build that was obviously kept in shape with some sort of rigorous exercise regime. Short, dark hair showed flecks of grey around the roots. He wore black, slim-legged trousers and a white shirt, sleeves rolled up, dark hairs showing on his forearms.

'Good afternoon, ladies.' He strode across the room, his smile widening as he held out a hand to them in turn. 'How nice to see you again, Tamara.'

'Likewise, Jack.' His eyes were so blue that Tamara wondered if he was wearing coloured contact lenses. She pointed to Esther. 'This is my assistant, Esther Smedley.'

'It's good to meet you.' He clapped his hands together. 'Come on through.'

Tamara waited for her stomach to settle before standing

up. She grimaced at Esther behind his back as they followed him.

They were shown into a room with a large, oval table that would easily seat twelve. Tamara gave silent thanks when she saw there were only four people sitting at its far end. Two men, in shirts open at the neck and sleeves rolled up, stood as they approached. They both looked to be mid-thirties but that was where the similarity ended. The one closest to them had a plump face, a receding hairline but a cheeky, infectious smile. The one next to him had a sharp chin and strong Roman nose, slicked back hair and shifty, deep-set eyes.

'Let me introduce you to Oscar and Ben, part of my team,' Jack said. 'Oscar is one of our editors and worked on *Something's Got to Give*. Ben is our communications manager.'

'Pleased to meet you,' Tamara said, completely forgetting to introduce them both. She glanced at Esther discreetly and wondered if she sensed her trepidation. Esther gave her a reassuring nod as she felt her hands shaking.

A woman in her mid-fifties with bouffant, blonde hair, wearing a suit that was clearly too tight, closed her diary and gave them a smile. Next to her sat a younger woman with white-blonde hair cut in a choppy style and wearing the brightest shade of pink lipstick. It was stereotypical of Tamara but she assumed she was the author. She had a rabbit-in-the-headlights look about her whereas the older woman held her shoulders high.

'This is Simone Byatt, our extremely talented author, who we were so fortunate to sign last year,' Jack said, pointing to the younger woman. 'And this is her agent, Arabella Smythe.'

There wasn't enough room to shake hands across the table, so Tamara continued to smile.

While Esther sat down across from Arabella and Simone, Jack sitting across from her, Tamara moved to the head of the table in front of the drop-down presentation screen. She pressed a few keys on the laptop. Thankfully the presentation had been loaded before they had gone into the room.

She lifted her shoulders as everyone looked expectantly at her. Esther gave her a discreet thumbs up. She took a breath and began.

'We at Parker-Brown PR know a good book when we read it.' She smiled at Simone, trying to recall the words she had rehearsed earlier. 'We absolutely adored *Something's Got to Give*. We loved the mystery woven in between the psychological suspense. It was a truly remarkable book that got under my skin and I want to share it with everyone.'

So far, so good. Tamara relaxed a little. She said a few more things, running through several slides. But then she began to flounder.

'We know that ... er.' She looked at the cue card and then at the one underneath it. 'I ... er.' She turned to the presentation on the wall behind, but all the words seemed to be bouncing up and down. A rush of colour flooded her cheeks as she felt all eyes on her. She opened her mouth but nothing came out. Again, she looked at her cue card. Think, Tamara, think!

'We did extensive research,' she heard Esther say. 'Online, we targeted reading groups on Facebook and posed questions on Twitter. People who will enjoy this book come from any generation, male and female. Women who like psychological thrillers tend to have families of their own so the emotions play on them, because they can relate to them.

They love to delve into the psyche of modern friendships, toxic marriages. And everyone enjoys a sense of justice. So it's a wide demographic and an excellent market, but extremely broad.'

'I've heard all this before.' Arabella waved a hand, dismissing their research. 'How are you going to sell the book?'

'Our aim is to pitch it to a market and only target the best group,' Esther continued.

Arabella rolled her eyes at Jack and sat back, her arms folded across her chest. 'I know that but how?'

'Well ...' Tamara flicked through her cue cards again, feeling her skin heating up once more. The room was quiet except for the sound of the air conditioning struggling to cope. The patches of sweat underneath her arms must have grown to huge pools by now.

This wasn't looking good. If she didn't recover this soon, it would be lost.

In desperation, she looked across at Esther, seeking out her help.

7

'It's Royal Ascot next week.' Esther stood up as all eyes fell on her. 'Each year there are three thousand extra staff employed to help cater for the deluge of spectators that will visit the event. For the people of Ascot, I imagine it's both a huge money maker and a terrible nuisance as their village is lost to others.' By then, she was by Tamara's side. 'Yet Royal Ascot is somewhere everyone likes to be noticed. From the women in their elegant outfits, the men in high spirits, horse trainers willing their riders to win, to the colossal amount of money being placed on each race. Well, we want *Something's Got to Give* to have the same impact too. Our plan would be to concentrate on one place for a short time before then going wider.'

'You're talking poster campaigns around the city?' Arabella butted in again. 'And adverts in tube stations?'

'No, I don't feel those kinds of big adverts work particularly well, unless you're a best-selling author with a new book out. I see them and I move on, although one theory in marketing is that you have to see something seven times before it piques your interest enough. Personally, I think the money for that kind of thing, because ads like that are so expensive, can be better utilised. Instead of going for as many places as we can to get the book seen, I'm talking about going hell for leather for one supermarket and one group on social media. Make them your *lead* players. Make them feel they have been *chosen* to represent your book.

'Book bloggers would be our first port of call. If they like the book, their reach can be phenomenal. But because they are so good at what they do, many of them will be booked at short notice. So, we would have to make them our second major priority. The hit list we'd compile would be elite, based on Alexa data on traffic to websites. Some of the popular sites get hundreds of thousands of hits per year.'

'How would you target them?' asked Jack.

'We would handwrite letters and deliver print copies to our chosen group. We could also arrange a pre-launch event, where—' Esther looked over at Simone '—if you're up for it, you can meet all the main buyers. You could stand up and talk about the book. No one is more passionate about it than you.'

'Oh, I'm not sure about that,' Simone piped up. Esther watched as she slipped down in her chair.

'Don't worry.' She held up her hand. 'We can get you through it, again if it's necessary. Because I have another idea.'

Esther clicked a further button and the blurb for the book came up on screen. She pointed to it before addressing them all again. 'Your novel has two female characters. One has committed murder and the other one knows. Hashtag campaigns are a really great way of getting the book seen in many places, so, as well as one or two large-scale advertisements, my suggestion would be to print two hundred books and send two each out to the top bloggers. Let them read one book and run competitions to give away the second book – i.e. make them feel special because they have been the first and only group to read it.

'But we do this after the elite list has read it. That way readers in the book industry will be crying out for it then. And there will be no other free copies given away. Make it become their priority that they have to get a copy.'

Esther realised she had everyone's attention as she continued.

'We can also use something catchy that isn't necessarily the book title. It has to be short and snappy, quick and easy to type. We can send teasers through the post, with a hashtag printed on them too.'

'Teasers?' Arabella's brow furrowed.

'Something like a photograph of two women that has been cut in half, with a jagged edge as if it's been torn in temper. Reviewers photograph this, with their copy of the book, and share these images everywhere.

'It could have a huge impact on visibility,' Esther continued. 'Concentrate all this on the two weeks before publication day and your sales could soar. *Then*, when everyone is talking about it, we get you slots on radio and TV, and in magazines. I know review slots have to be booked months in advance but as time is of the essence, we want to see if we can get the journalists to come to us. Once everyone has the hashtag firmly in their head.'

'Which is?' asked Jack.

'#DidSheDoIt. It's intriguing, right?' She looked at them all in turn. 'Now *Something's Got to Give* has a whole new meaning. You hear about the elevator pitch where you sell a book in a sentence. Well, I think "did she do it" sells the book in a hashtag.'

Arabella smiled. 'I like that.'

'Also,' Esther went on, 'print and digital sales are two very different platforms and if you price the e-book low at first – which I know seems counter-productive – it can gain momentum in sales, and, by using the hashtag, the number of units you shift will make it worthwhile.'

'But if people are talking about which one did it,' queried Oscar, 'won't this lead to spoilers if they guess?'

'Readers and reviewers often leave spoilers regardless, so I really wouldn't worry about that too much.' Esther turned to look at Tamara. She would either be as mad as hell that she had stolen her thunder or relieved that she had saved her from dying on her feet. She held her breath until she was rewarded with a smile.

Both Simone and Arabella were now sitting forward, and so too were the men from Dulston Publishing.

'Any questions?' she asked.

Tamara was happy to join in then and swiftly came into her own. The facts and figures she had forgotten came pouring out of her.

Twenty minutes later, Jack showed them out of the building.

'Thanks for coming, ladies.' He smiled as he held the door open for them. 'We'll be in touch on Monday to let you know how you got on. But I have to say, I'm really impressed with your campaign.' He lowered his voice slightly. 'I'll be honest with you. I messed up on this. I should have seen it wasn't working months ago.'

'Well, rest assured, you'll be in safe hands with us,' Tamara told him. 'It does rather depend on your budget, but

I'm sure you'll be pleased with the outcome if you hire us, Mr Maitland.'

'Please, call me Jack.' He shook their hands again.

They exited the building and once they were out of sight, Tamara turned to Esther, shoulders drooping. 'How could I have lost my nerve again? What an idiot I made of myself. If it weren't for you, I don't think Parker-Brown PR would have stood a chance.'

'It was something I came up with only last night. I hope you didn't mind but I knew how important this pitch was for you.'

As Tamara paused, Esther wondered if she had gone too far. She dug her nails into the palms of her hands, not stopping until it became too painful.

But then Tamara's smile was back. 'You're right. You rescued me – you did an excellent job in there. I think Jack was impressed.'

'It seemed that way!'

'Simone didn't say much, did she?'

'I'm not surprised with that battle axe of an agent speaking on her behalf.' Esther put a hand to her mouth. 'Whoops, sorry. Just thinking aloud.'

Tamara giggled. 'She reminded me of my old dorm mistress.'

'You went to boarding school?'

'Yes, and I hated every minute of it.' She sighed loudly. 'I really hope we're successful with the pitch. It will be so much fun working with him – and you.'

Esther smiled through gritted teeth as Tamara put an arm through hers. She didn't like anyone invading her space. It was bad enough having to shake Jack's hand for the first time. She'd wanted to throw up on the spot.

And she didn't do touchy-feely either. Tamara seemed to

be really big on it, alas, so she would have to learn to accept it.

Especially if she was to fool her into thinking they were going to become good friends as well as work colleagues.

Think of the plan, Esther. Think of the plan.

8

Saturday, 17 June

Esther waited until it was dusk before setting off on her journey. It wouldn't do to go too early; it would spoil everything and she wouldn't be allowed to have as much fun.

The change in the weather that evening had worked in her favour, the promised storms finally breaking after another hot day, sending people scuttling indoors. The night air was still warm, but the darker clouds meant she couldn't be seen as easily.

The tube clattered along and she scratched her leg absent-mindedly, the plaster on her cut not offering enough protection. She'd have to be careful or it would get infected again and she'd need another prescription. But the urge to take her razor blade and slice at the already open wound was enough to get her out of the house that evening.

She had so many scars on the top of her thigh now. A criss-cross of anger and pain and disgust. Some she would leave to heal over; others she would pick at, slice at until they were open again. It was more painful to go over old wounds, but it energised her, made everything calm again. It meant she wouldn't have to go in search of amphetamines.

Out on the street, twenty minutes later, all was quiet. Puddles glistened under the street lamps and she almost tiptoed to avoid them. The houses on this side were large and set back in vast gardens. Some had closed gates, some open driveways. The road itself was lined with every make of expensive car you could think of.

She stopped in front of her destination. There was a light on in the large bay window downstairs. So far, the curtains had always been open, allowing her to see right in. She walked past the driveway for a few metres. Well hidden now that it was dark, she still checked in either direction to see if the coast was clear before shimmying up and over the wall.

She dropped on to the lawn on the other side with a small thud. Her hands stopped her fall and she stood up slowly, even though she knew they couldn't hear her from there. Security lights didn't reach her hiding place.

On one occasion, she had crept in and damaged his car. But the lights had illuminated her and she hadn't been comfortable with that. She could bet there were cameras around the property too, so after that she had been warier of being seen.

She stepped forward three steps and hid in her usual place behind an oak tree. She'd been here so many times now that it was so familiar. Whenever she felt the need, she would come and rid herself of her anger by watching.

Sometimes it worked and she could fight her resentment without having to inflict pain on herself. Other times, it inflated her emotions and made things worse once she was back at her flat. But either way, it was a risk she had to take.

There was something about being here that made things right.

Watching him, when he didn't know she was there.

The man who had made her life a living hell.

The man she would take great pleasure in bringing down.

She could see straight into their sitting room. They were both at home. She was sitting on a settee. There was a paperback in her hands; her head was down, engrossed in its pages.

He was slumped in an armchair, his head leaning to one side as he dozed. He faced right out on to the garden and yet he had never seen her.

Sometimes she stayed there minutes and it was enough. Other times, she would be there for an hour, even when it was clear they had gone to bed and she wouldn't see them.

Watching was all she needed.

It never failed to amaze her how peaceful their lives were. How they got on with ordinary things while she suffered in silence. He had no idea of the train wreck he had made of her life that day. That day when she was fifteen, helpless to resist him, powerless to stop him.

Fury boiled inside her and she banged a fist into her thigh. The wound under the plaster began to tingle. If it started to bleed, she would get out her blade. If it stayed intact, it would be deadened for a while.

Like her. She'd been dead inside since that day.

Soon this would all be over. She would feel no hatred towards him, only contempt. Satisfied she was in control now. Angry no more.

But for now, she was content to sit and watch. Bide her time, pick the right moment. She wanted to take him by surprise.

9

Carley Evans was eating supper when the phone rang. Her husband, Owen, stretched across the sofa for it but she got to it first.

'Please don't answer that,' he said.

She knew he was joking but equally he would be annoyed if she had to go in.

'DC Evans.' Listening to the caller, she felt herself roll towards Owen as he moved further along the settee towards her. He began to nibble at her ear.

She squirmed, trying to slap him away playfully but he continued. She stood up, stepping away before his hand slipped underneath her top.

Carley heard an exaggerated sigh over the voice of the caller.

'I'm on my way.' Her expression was serious as she disconnected the call. 'There's been a shooting in Shoreditch.'

Owen shrugged and reached over to her plate, grabbing for the last piece of naan bread.

'Hey!' She raised her eyebrows in protest.

'Well, you won't be here to eat it, will you?'

'I'll make it up to you when I get home.'

'Not in the early hours, you won't.'

'You mean you don't want to be woken for sleepy sex?'

'Not after you've had your hands all over a corpse!'

She stepped towards him, leaned over and kissed him on the lips. 'You taste of rogan josh.' She smiled before grabbing her jacket and then her car keys.

Driving across the city on a Saturday evening was always a time loser. The streets of London had never been paved in gold but they never failed to draw Carley in either. The noise, its busyness, so many people and the bright lights – even the traffic. She had lived in Clapham all her life, and had joined the Met, eight years ago now, straight from university. There was something about policing a city you knew so many parts of like the back of your hand, while other parts you had never visited. So many communities, nationalities, neighbourhoods around every corner. So many crimes, no matter which area she worked.

Carley drove on to the Manston Estate and along the main road. Silverstone Avenue was the third on the right according to her satnav instructions, then it was first left. She turned into Barnham Road, and was greeted by lights from several emergency vehicles and flashes from fluorescent jackets. One uniformed officer had cordoned off the scene; another was moving the public back.

Carley parked her car as near as she could to the scene, looking round as she locked it, cackles of laughter from behind adding to the chaos. A group of women walked along the bottom of the street, their heels clattering on the tarmac.

'Ooh, what's happening here?' one of them said, stopping in her tracks. Carley felt relieved when a woman seized hold of her arm and shouted, 'Never you mind, Ms Bride-To-Be. We're going to the next pub. I need another drink.'

Several onlookers stood with their phones high in the air, filming the police's every move. Carley hated social media for that. Everyone was so nosy nowadays. They wouldn't be able to see anything for several hours until all forensics had been carried out. She hoped their batteries were flat by the time it came to removing the body.

Carley surveyed the area quickly. It wasn't a place she'd like to live. Even without another murder to add to their statistics, there seemed a desperation about it. Boarded-up properties shared the street with houses in disrepair. Bags of rubbish were piled high outside a takeaway; one had been ripped open, its contents spewing out on to the pavement. Graffiti scrawled across several windows made everyone aware whose territory they were in. Yet again she wondered if her car would be safe.

DI Max Stanway was already at the scene and came walking towards her. Max had been Carley's line manager in the Murder Investigation Team for five years now, and she had a great deal of respect for him. His positive attitude got his team through many a bleak day; he was known at the station as Twilight, a nickname because of his likeness to the actor Robert Pattinson. He had the same floppy hair, strong chin and nose. But he wasn't sinful in any way, his placid nature getting him out of many scrapes. Carley had learned so much from him over the years they had worked together. She was pleased he would always have her back.

She showed her warrant card to the first officer and signed the clipboard to mark herself presence at the scene.

'Sir.' She nodded as Max finally drew level with her.

'Well, well, well!' he exclaimed, looking her up and down. 'I don't think I've ever seen you in anything but a suit.'

'Sorry. I thought it best to get here as quickly as I could.'

Carley was dressed in jeans and a black leather jacket, a white T-shirt underneath, and red Converse boots. Her feathered blonde hair, which was usually tied back in a ponytail, hung loose to her shoulders, a thick fringe framing brown eyes.

'I'm joking. Nice to see you relaxed for a change.' Max pointed back into the alley. 'Our victim is male. Gunshot wound to the chest. Beaten about a bit too.' He paused slightly. 'It's someone we know.'

'Oh?' He'd had her full attention at gunshot wound, but now they knew him, her senses heightened.

'It's Jamie Kerrigan.'

Carley raised her eyebrows. The amount of times both she and Max had arrested Kerrigan must have stood in double figures. Kerrigan was into money lending, drugs, thieving – you name it, and they were sure to have charged him for it. He had been in and out of juvenile detention, and later prison, since he had been fifteen.

'He's just been released after that two-year stretch for burglary, hasn't he?' Max said.

Carley nodded. She'd been working on a complaint that Kerrigan had viciously assaulted his girlfriend again, so she knew his recent movements. 'He came out six weeks ago, and went to ground. His parole officer says he hasn't been back to his bail hostel for two weeks so there's a warrant out for his arrest.'

'Well, we won't be needing that!'

They dressed in forensic suits and shoe covers before stepping into the alley. Floodlights lit up the area like a fairground attraction, a tent erected to shield the body. A team of CSIs was already on the scene, two uniformed officers carrying out house-to-house enquiries.

Inside the tent, Terry Simpson, the head CSI, was kneeling over the torso.

'Carley! How're things?'

'It's Saturday evening and I was halfway through my curry and on a promise afterwards.' She rolled her eyes but her tone was cheery. Of course, no one wanted to be present at a murder scene any time of the day or night, but either early mornings or weekends were the worst.

'Ah, how is married life treating you?' Terry smiled too. 'Being in my twenty-fifth year, I can't quite recall the flushes of young love.'

'It's good, thanks.' Carley was relieved when he added nothing else. Having only been married for six months, the first thing everyone wanted to know now was when they were planning a family. But not every couple wanted to conform to tradition. She was twenty-nine, and Owen thirty-one, giving them ample time to have children.

She looked down at the body. Max was right. Even without ID and with bruising, she could tell it was Jamie Kerrigan. The tattoo of an eagle in flight was partially showing on his neck, a scar still visible through the swelling of his left cheek where he had been glassed in prison a few years ago.

He was fully clothed, lying on his side. Carley surmised he had dropped to his knees when shot and fallen to his right, an open denim jacket offering no protection at all. Blood was visible over his hands. She would hazard a guess it was his own as he had tried to quell the bleeding.

She stooped down to Terry's level.

'He's taken quite a beating to the torso,' Terry pointed out, 'and a couple of punches to the face before he was shot in the stomach. I can't be confident until the post-mortem is completed but it does seem to be that wound which is the most likely cause of death.'

'Anything found on him?'

Terry nodded and pointed to a table. Carley saw a wallet inside a plastic evidence bag. She went over to investigate.

'There's still a few notes inside it,' she said, rifling through it. 'A driving licence: DOB 15 January 1983. His phone is here too.'

'It's obviously not an opportunistic attack, although the gunshot might have been unintentional,' Max said.

'Do you think it's revenge for something?' She looked at the body again before standing up.

'Always possible with Kerrigan.'

They walked slowly out of the alley, removed their protective wear and popped them into a bag. Carley stood waiting for instructions from Max while he made a call to the control room.

'I know it's late but we have a few officers going door knocking,' he said once he was finished. 'Can you supervise that and then we'll get going again in the morning? Timeline can be established after the post-mortem, but see if there are any cameras in the vicinity that can catch inside the alley, and get on to the council first thing for CCTV footage of the street. It's a hotspot area so there might be a way of tracking them.'

'Unless they went along the back.' Carley pointed to the row of railings at the far end.

Max squinted, seeing the shadows of several large trees and a privet hedge. 'Yes, they could easily have disappeared that way. We need to do a search for the weapon too.'

'I'm on it.'

Before moving, Carley studied the crowd that had grown in size since she had first arrived. It was a mixture of young and old, male and female. One woman even had a toddler clinging to her waist. They looked to be normal people, nosy, inquisitive, perhaps concerned it had happened close to their home.

She stared at every one of them for a while, trying to remember tiny details, distinguishable things. It was always possible that one of them could be their killer.

10

Monday, 19 June

Tamara tried to put the pitch from her mind that weekend. Saturday morning had been spent catching up on administrative tasks as so much time had been spent on the Dulston Publishing work. She'd then joined her parents for lunch at The Ivy, and had managed not to clash with her mother too much.

Elizabeth Parker-Brown had been praising Tamara's sister, who was helping with the latest charity gala dinner she was organising. It always stung Tamara to see her face light up when she mentioned her youngest daughter, and her children, and her home and anything else she saw fit to throw at her to make her feel inadequate. On more than one occasion, she had felt her mind wandering.

On Sunday, she'd cleaned out the spare room, hopefully in readiness for preparation for the launch of *Something's Got to Give* but then sat down on the floor in a heap, after convincing herself she had failed miserably to make a good impression.

She thought back to Esther stepping in for her. She had done a tremendous job, surprising her with her ability. The analogy about Royal Week at Ascot had been brilliant and quite unique, yet it all seemed too well rehearsed.

Or maybe that was because *she* had made such a mess of things.

Whatever it was, Tamara chose to move her embarrassment to one side and be grateful. And she *was* pleased. At least she could hold her head up high this time, whether they won the pitch or not.

So when the phone call came, she was prepared for both responses, even though she knew she would be disappointed if they hadn't got the job.

It was a few minutes before 9.00 a.m., and Esther had yet to arrive when Tamara saw Jack's name come up on her phone. For a moment she didn't dare answer it.

'Don't be silly,' she scolded herself. 'Like Esther said, "you've got this".'

'Morning, Jack,' she sing-songed to him. 'Lovely day again. Did you have a jolly weekend?'

'I did, thanks. Nothing better than spending time relaxing with my family after a hard week. How about you?'

'Oh, you know. Busy, busy.' Tamara crossed her fingers as she waited to hear the news.

'Right, then. I won't leave you in suspense. I was extremely impressed with your pitch last week. More to the point, so too were my team.'

'That's great to hear.' Tamara held her breath, waiting for the 'but'.

'Of course, the final choice wasn't really down to me. We

needed to ensure Simone and Arabella were on board too. We've had some pretty impressive pitches.'

'Ah.' Tears pricked her eyes. Her one chance to prove herself and she had blown it again.

'I'd be delighted to offer your company the job.'

Tamara frowned. Did he say ...?

'Hurrah. That's marvellous news!' The tension in her body melted away and she knew she would be wearing a smile for a good few days to come. She couldn't wait to tell her parents. Let her mother try and put her down now.

'Like I mentioned,' Jack continued, 'everyone was really impressed with the ideas to go small and personal to get a much larger reach out of a curiosity impulse buy. Simone and Arabella can't wait to hear more of what you have planned. Personally speaking, I can't wait to talk things through with you more too.'

'Let us know where and when and we'll be there.'

'Great. I'll be in touch to arrange another meeting for later this week. Do you have time?'

'Of course!' Jack didn't need to know that she hadn't any other big projects on right now.

'I'll get my PA to email you.'

Tamara disconnected the phone and screamed at the top of her voice. She'd done it! She had got the job that was going to make Parker-Brown PR a force to be reckoned with.

When Esther arrived a few minutes later, it was all she could do to stop herself from jumping up and down.

'We got the pitch,' she yelled, drawing Esther into her embrace. It felt a little awkward but she couldn't help herself.

'That's fantastic!' Esther's eyes widened and she grinned.

'Jack was so impressed with your ideas,' Tamara added as they sat down in the office. 'He thought it was genius of you to think small to aim big. And even though it wasn't planned, I want to thank you for taking charge when you did.'

'Really? I—'

'I wouldn't have won the pitch if it weren't for you.'

'Well, it doesn't matter how you got it,' Esther exclaimed, 'only that you did.'

Tamara punched the air. She peered at Esther with a childish grin. 'Let's go out for breakfast – my treat. I can't stay indoors. I feel fit to burst!'

They left the flat in a tizzy of excitement, talking nineteen to the dozen.

'I'll get on to my contacts,' Tamara said, taking the steps down on to the pavement. 'We can get started on copy and having a think about the campaign reach, and who exactly to get in touch with. And, because we don't have much time, maybe we can use that to our advantage and create a sense of urgency. It's going to be a huge challenge but we have to make this the must-have book of the summer by word-of-mouth.'

They walked along the street and Tamara's phone went off. It was a message from Jack. After reading it, she put a hand on Esther's arm to slow her.

'Jack has invited us to join him at Ascot for the Royal meeting!'

'Really?' Esther looked perplexed.

'He says he already had a box booked, and, as you'd mentioned it in the pitch, he thought it apt we join him, and get to know the team. Clever girl, Esther Smedley.'

Esther smiled at her. 'Wow. I've never been to Ascot. I doubt I have anything suitable to wear.'

'It's only strict dress rules in some areas.' Tamara clapped her hands in glee. 'We can go shopping. I know some fabulous places. You'll look a million dollars when I've finished with you.' She paused. 'Not that you don't look a million dollars *every* time I see you. You're so stylish. I wish I had your figure. Sorry, I didn't mean to insult you.'

'You couldn't insult me.' Esther waved away the remark. 'Ascot! Amazing!'

Tamara grinned, adrenaline rushing through her as she thought of what was to come. That giddy feeling washed over her once more. This was going to be *so* exciting.

'Wait until my parents find out.' She was already back on her phone. 'But first, I have a friend with a boutique in Ladbroke Grove. He'll have the right dresses for us. It will be my treat to you for helping me win the pitch for *Something's Got to Give* … Mario, darling. It's Tamara Parker-Brown.'

As she spoke to him, Tamara pushed aside her fears that she would have to max out her credit cards again. She should be able to pay them all off soon anyway. Keeping up the image was far more important.

11

Esther had been surprised to hear that Jack was having a box at the Royal meeting. It was something she hadn't bargained for, but it would certainly make things easier for her. It would mean that she might be able to get to know Jack away from the office, possibly spend some time alone with him. She'd have to think about how best to do that.

But that afternoon was all about the outfit. As she and Tamara made their way across London to Ladbroke Grove, she had to contain her annoyance. It pissed her off that Tamara assumed she was poor because she was temping. How judgmental.

But then people like Tamara, born with a silver spoon in her mouth, wouldn't know any better. And did she actually think *she* could style *her*?

She pushed away her irritation and, surprisingly, in no time at all, found out that going shopping with Tamara was both excruciatingly embarrassing and a giggle at the same time.

The boutique scored high marks. From the outside, no one

would miss it. The old, wooden paintwork was a bright but gaudy pink, framing tiny, criss-crossed windows. It had the feel of an antique shop and as Tamara pressed down the handle, Esther laughed when an old-fashioned bell rang out to announce their arrival. She hadn't heard one of those in years.

Inside was even more daring. Under their feet was a red, velvet carpet that would have been seen in any public house during the seventies. Bottle green, upholstered chairs were scattered around the edge, amidst white walls with shelves bulging with designer handbags and shoes. At the back of the room were the clothes.

It shouldn't have looked stylish altogether but somehow, it did.

Mario Tiano, the boutique owner who was in his late sixties, had a distinct eye for detail. Dressed in a red and blue ensemble that would have looked as good on any twenty-year-old model strutting down a catwalk, his grey hair was slicked back in a ponytail beneath a shiny, bald head. Groomed eyebrows and nails set him off as eccentric without the added dramatic nature of everything he did.

'Darling, it's been too long. Mwah.' He greeted Tamara with exaggerated air kisses. 'You look fabulous. Have you lost weight?'

Esther refrained from rolling her eyes as she stayed in the background. It was the oldest trick in the book. Compliment someone on looking thinner, whether they were or not.

'You say the sweetest things, Mario.' Tamara giggled again. 'I am very well, though. This is Esther.'

Esther had stayed in the background, hoping the old man wouldn't feel the need to come too close to her. But just in time, she composed herself.

'Pleased to meet you, Mario.' She smiled and held out her hand.

Mario lifted her fingers to his mouth and grazed her knuckles with his thin lips.

'Delighted to meet you too.' He leisurely gave her the once-over, nodded and turned to Tamara. 'She's a beauty. An English rose. But then, so are you!'

Tamara stifled a giggle as he led them both to the back of the room and rummaged through the rails where the one-off outfits were hanging. He handed them dress after dress as they drank champagne. Esther didn't drink much as she wanted a clear head but she did pretend that the bubbles were having an effect on her.

Tamara looked ridiculous in most of her outfits and it was more than Esther could do at times not to laugh when she came out of the fitting room. She could have been more of a bitch by saying yes to some of the creations that Mario put her in, but even she wasn't that heartless. Still, when Tamara came out in an understated, cream shift dress, with pink kitten-heel shoes, a pale pink cropped jacket and a pillbox hat with lots of lace and frills, she gasped.

'You look amazing,' Esther exclaimed as Tamara twirled around.

'It suits your shape perfectly, darling,' Mario insisted, nodding his head so hard Esther had visions of it rolling off.

'Do you think?' Tamara was still twirling. While she was smitten, Esther popped on the dress she had seen earlier, the one with the price tag that had made her eyes bulge. Money was no object to Tamara so it was only fair that Esther took advantage of that. Tamara's parents were loaded; they must have helped her out with setting up the flat.

Esther shimmied into the dress, a riot of colour and

quite the opposite to Tamara's ice cream ensemble. Tones of red and green both clashed and complemented her hair and skin tone. She slipped on a pair of heels, held her hair up away from her neck, and went back out into the shop.

'What do you think?' she asked, acting all demure, yet knowing she looked incredible. It was amazing how well-tailored clothes could make you feel too.

Mario's mouth dropped open. 'Oh, wow! Darling, you look sensational, doesn't she, Tamara?' He didn't wait for a reply. 'You have *got* to wear that. It's absolutely stunning.'

'It is!' Tamara was smiling, not a hint of envy.

Esther smiled at them both before doing one final circle in front of the mirror. All of a sudden, she was eight years old again. She was with her mum, choosing a dress for Abigail Riley's tenth birthday party. She had been so excited to be invited and wanted to look her very best. Her mum had gone out of her way to find her the nicest dress. She could remember feeling as she did now when she had slipped it on. Excited, beautiful, powerful. How her life had changed. She pushed dark memories away and concentrated on the task in hand.

But then she stopped, glancing at herself one last time. What would her mum think of her now, twenty-four years later? Esther missed her so much at times, but it was easier this way. She couldn't disappoint her if she didn't know where she was. And she wasn't going to be proud of her when she found out her intentions.

'It is beautiful.' She sighed loudly, her shoulders drooping as she walked back to the changing rooms. 'I wanted to play Julia Roberts for a moment and feel like a pretty woman.'

'You need to have more confidence! You *are* a pretty woman. With or without this fantastic dress.' Tamara looked at the tag and didn't even bat an eye at the extortionate price. 'I said this was my treat and I meant it. You got me the contract with Dulston Publishing. That's the reason we are going to Ascot.' She smiled at her. 'You and I are going to have a fabulous time.' She clicked her fingers. 'Mario, we'll take them. Do you have a hat to go with Esther's outfit?'

'I have the very thing,' he squeaked in excitement.

Esther tried not to roll her eyes. It was laughable to see Mario almost fall over his feet to get to the back of the room. Instead she smiled at Tamara.

'I don't know what to say, other than thank you!'

'I think you should say, yes, Tamara, I would like to work with you after my trial period ends.'

Esther grinned. 'Really? You're saying I can stay?'

'Of course!'

'Well, I'm saying thank you again.'

Tamara drew her into her embrace. 'I think I was very lucky to find you, Esther Smedley. You and I are going to be spiffing together.'

Esther laughed inwardly at her strange choice of words, but she managed to hug Tamara back this time. This was all going so much better than she had anticipated. It was fabulous that the two of them were getting on so well after so little time working together. Imagine how gullible she would be after a few months, if Esther had to stick around for that long.

And maybe when Tamara found out how much she'd been tricked, she might not be so trusting in the future.

12

———

Tamara could almost feel sweat dripping from her as she made her way through Leicester Square towards West Street. She was meeting her parents for supper at The Ivy. Having Esther around had been the perfect excuse not to make it for lunch, as she didn't like to leave her there alone long during the day. Still, she was glad to get out into the fresh air, even though it seemed as hot outside as it was indoors. Plus, the outfits she had bought for herself and Esther had wiped her out for the time being, so it was nice to have supper paid for.

Tamara had so much on her mind. *Something's Got to Give* was due to be launched in less than a month. She had created an extensive project plan and, along with Esther, had started to work on bringing it all together. Of course, it would be easy to start off with because everything needed doing as a matter of urgency. She would have to keep an eye on things because one late delivery could mean everything else being pushed aside and getting later and later, meaning failure to deliver.

Tamara was surprised everything had been left so late.

Jack had told her that pre-orders of the book should have been selling-in better off the back of the author's previous title, but as it was a different genre – this was a psychological thriller rather than women's fiction – it hadn't had the cross-over they were hoping for. Pre-order sales were lacklustre, but they all knew they had something special on their hands, hence there now being more money to splash around.

The book had to hit the right audience. Jack had offered 200 copies on the week of publication. He'd mentioned giving them out in Central London but she'd managed to persuade him not to. Tamara's smallest room had become the store cupboard for all the stationery and gifts they'd had branded with the cover. She had wondered whether to do a treasure hunt around some of the places it was set using some of the cheaper items.

Dulston Publishing was the first reputable company Tamara had worked with and the fact that she had won the pitch had gone down surprisingly well with her parents. They had insisted on taking her out to celebrate, although she was certain it was more her father's idea than her mother's.

At the table she was shown to, she greeted her parents with the usual hug for her father and a peck on the cheek for her mother. Elizabeth Parker-Brown wasn't an affectionate person, no matter how much she portrayed that to the outside world.

Tamara had always suspected her mother wasn't truly happy. Despite the many charity functions and business lunches Elizabeth was involved in, she had watched her become even more blasé as the years had passed.

At sixty-four, her father, Miles, was two years older than her mother. Although he was a descendant of old money, he was a ruthless business man and had added a lot more to the family wealth than had been handed down to him. He planned on retiring next year, but Tamara wasn't sure he would. He didn't really seem ready for it. His work had consumed him over the years. And what her mother would do with him around her feet all the time, she couldn't begin to imagine.

She watched him now as he folded out his napkin on his lap. He was a tall man, with a preposterous laugh that was embarrassingly loud but extremely infectious. It made his large nose and squinty eyes wrinkle in an amusing way. Luckily, his positive outlook on life meant that she heard that laugh often. Tamara's brothers had his hair colouring and brown eyes, his receding hairline and a tiny paunch that they all struggled to keep at bay.

Tamara looked very much like her mother. Although Elizabeth's hair was grey, she ensured no one ever saw it. It stayed the dark-brown shade Tamara could always remember it being and the exact same length that skimmed the bottom of her chin.

Tamara had her eyes too, a few shades darker brown than the men in the family with speckles of hazel, and her penchant to put on weight as soon as she looked at food. But that was where the similarity stopped.

Elizabeth told her often that she should have started a family by now. She was constantly asking when Tamara was going to give them grandchildren, as if she didn't have enough with six already. Most of the time, Tamara ignored the jibes. They stung but she wasn't going to settle down with anyone just to please her mother.

'Are you having your usual risotto primavera for starters, Tamara?' Miles asked as he closed his menu and placed it back on the table.

Tamara nodded. She always enjoyed dining at The Ivy. The restaurant was celebrating its centenary year after having a recent refurbishment and was by far her favourite place to eat. It had the feeling of opulence with its shimmering central bar, oak-panelled walls and stained-glass windows, soft lighting, and a collection of contemporary art. It had always felt rich to Tamara, even though it shouldn't as she was far too much of a regular visitor.

Her parents were members and dined there at least once a week and they would often ask her to accompany them, but she would always try to get out of it. She would make up any excuse rather than suffer the disdain of her mother.

'So, my little girl is running a big campaign at last,' said her father.

Tamara smiled at Miles, but as she looked to her mother, her heart sank.

'Are you sure you can handle the pressure, darling?' Elizabeth gave Tamara one of her weary looks. 'It's going to be so much hard work for you, especially in a male dominated industry.'

Tamara frowned. 'Publishing is not led by men, Mother. It's very much controlled by strong and powerful women.'

'Yes, but darling, the women only do the tedious side of things, like editing behind the scenes, I expect—'

'Oh, don't be so patronising.' Tamara couldn't help but raise her voice. A few diners looked her way and she felt a flush to her cheeks. Being brought up with money had done her mother more harm than good. She was such a snob.

'How is the new woman working out?' Miles interjected. 'Ethel, is that her name?'

'Esther,' Tamara corrected him. 'She's doing really well. She has such a flair for the work.'

'Good, because this could be a huge opportunity for you.

When I spoke to Jack he was really pleased that you were going to be working with him.'

Tamara's heart sank at this revelation. 'When did you see Jack?' she enquired.

'Oh, a few days ago now.' He flapped his hand around. 'He plays golf at my club; didn't I tell you?'

'No.' Tamara's lips formed a tight smile. 'You didn't have anything to do with this, did you?'

'Of course he did, darling.' Elizabeth reached across the table for her hand. 'You don't think you got this by talent alone? You haven't any experience, nor any luck, securing large contracts like this before, so your father put in a good word for you.'

'Well, I didn't try and pay him off, if that's what you're insinuating.' Miles had the decency to lower his eyes, but Tamara wasn't sure if his cheeks were reddening because of embarrassment or a little too much wine. 'He said you'd got the job on your own merits anyway.' He raised his empty glass in the air to garner the attention of a passing waiter. 'I think more champagne is called for.'

'I don't believe this.' Tamara glared at them both in turn, trying to hold in the tears she could feel stinging her eyes. 'For once I wanted to do something on my own merit.'

'That will be a first,' Elizabeth replied.

Tamara gasped at her petulant tone. If her mother stopped to think how much she had held her back over the years because of her put-downs and sharp comments such as that one, she might show a little understanding. It was the last straw. She wasn't going to listen to anything else.

'I am going to prove you both wrong.' Tamara threw her napkin down on to the table. 'If you'll excuse me, I have work to catch up on. Sorry, it won't wait.'

'Darling,' Elizabeth shouted after her as she marched

out of the restaurant, 'we're having *A Window to The Ivy* for dessert. I know it's your favourite thing. Darling!'

But Tamara kept on walking. Not even the temptation of chocolate mousse and sponge filled with a velvety cherry centre could entice her to spend another second in her mother's company.

In Leicester Square, she passed a young Chinese woman taking a selfie, her family intent on squashing into the frame behind her. Several groups of teenagers overtook her on the pavement as they rushed to their next destination, their language as colourful as their clothes. A woman handed a young girl an ice cream. Her shrieks of joy could be heard long after she had passed.

Everywhere she looked, people seemed to be having fun yet she was feeling so ... low. How could she be such a disappointment to her parents? This was her time to prove herself, yet, even before she'd tried, her previous failures had been thrown back in her face.

After a few minutes, her footfall slowed and her breathing began to return to normal.

She was going to do this. With Esther's help, she was determined to prove them wrong.

13

It was half past seven when Esther left her flat again that evening. She had only been there long enough to grab a shower, a change of clothes, and a slice of toast. It was still absurdly hot as she sat on the Central line tube. Even with a T-shirt and Capri pants, she was sweltering. Her flat pumps were needed tonight though, no heels for her. A denim jacket hung over her handbag.

She looked around the carriage as it rattled along, trying not to scratch at her wig as it was making her itch in the heat. She'd had the black geometrical bob look for a while now, and even though it wasn't to her taste, she quite liked the persona it created. Every time she wore it, it made her feel like Uma Thurman in *Pulp Fiction*.

Esther was always quick as lightning when the tubes were full. It was easier to catch someone unaware that way, but that was best done during the rush hours. At this time of the day, there were empty seats everywhere.

The summer months made her task much simpler and she exited Covent Garden tube station with a smile as the sun hit her again. It must still have been twenty-two degrees, a clear sky promising more of the same in the morning. Smells of takeaway food wafted towards her as hordes of people ate on the run. Babbles of conversation intermingled with car engines and horns, laughter and the odd burst of music.

She walked across the cobbles next to the market stalls, the night seeming to come alive. In a matter of seconds, she passed by three buskers, a magician and two singers, one with a guitar. People were drinking and having dinner everywhere, their chatter loud.

Esther loved London for that, nothing like where she'd come from at all. But it was at times like this that she could let her past ride over her, and drink in the here and now. Everything was working out the way she had planned. Jack Maitland wouldn't suspect a thing and she could have some fun in the meantime. She just had to decide how far to take things.

The wine bar she chose was full, both inside and outside on the pavement, but she managed to grab a table in the square as someone was leaving.

She got her phone out and pretended to look at something on the screen. A waitress came over and she ordered a glass of sweet white wine. Surreptitiously, she glanced around the tables. A family of four sat to her left. The parents of boys aged around six and three. The youngest one was feeding himself and making such a mess but he was happy enough. The older child was showing his dad something on his iPad.

To her right, three women sat hunched close together enjoying a gossip over a meal and a bottle of prosecco. One had her handbag on the table; the other two rested them in between their feet on the floor.

She moved her chair closer to them. Her toe was almost

inside the handle of one of the bags, her heart pumping its usual erratic beat. As it slid towards her across the paving, she kept her eyes up, still looking around, wondering if anyone could see her.

She looked at her watch as if she was waiting for someone. All the time, her foot was hooked through the handle and the bag was coming to her. It took less than thirty seconds and then it was under her table.

Without further ado, and no thought to the waitress who would come back with a drink to find her gone, Esther bent to put the bag she was about to steal inside her own, picked it up, and jumped into the crowd of people walking past. She made it a rule never to look back but she could guess that the women would still be chatting, oblivious to what had happened.

She raced out of Covent Garden, dived into the next bar she saw and made her way through the crowd to the ladies'.

Inside a cubicle, she checked the contents of the bag and almost laughed out loud. She had struck lucky with this one. There was an iPhone and a mini iPad. They would be locked and maybe traceable with 'Find My' apps, but Colin, her pawnbroker, wouldn't mind that. There were ways of getting around anything now. She switched them both off.

The purse contained one hundred and forty pounds. She pulled out a bottle of scent – Chanel – and sprayed it liberally around her neck and body. She sniffed: it was a nice aroma for a change. Some women had weird taste in perfume.

Quickly, she rummaged through each pocket to see if there was anything else worth taking. There was a case for sunglasses. Michael Kors; that might be worth something second-hand.

When she was certain she had everything with a value,

she removed a large plastic bag, with a high street store logo emblazoned across it, from the pocket of her jacket. She then tucked the stolen one into the carrier bag and placed her own back around her body.

Outside on the street again, she pushed the carrier bag into the nearest bin. It was a shame she couldn't keep the designer bag and flog that too, but she hadn't finished for the night yet. She continued on her way towards her favourite store. She had seen the exact thing she was going to buy.

An hour later, with two wallets added to her haul, Esther returned to her flat. Once the door was closed and bolted, she breathed a sigh of relief. She had been caught shoplifting and pickpocketing many times during her teens, always dreading a hand on her shoulder as she left somewhere.

There was a time when she'd stopped doing it but it hadn't taken her long to get back into the habit again. The trouble was, she was good at it. She only went out every now and then; she wasn't greedy. Besides, she was having too much fun working with Tamara at the moment; although that in itself was a double-edged sword, as she needed money for better clothes.

And energy; she needed to stay alert. Which is why she was glad she had no temptation of amphetamines in her flat right now. The urge to score never left her.

She went into the bathroom, ignoring the smell of the damp that lingered no matter what she did. Dropping to her knees, she pushed on the bath panel. It gave way enough for her to slip her hand inside and retrieve the biscuit tin that was hidden behind it.

The tin contained her money, her passport, and a few other items. It wasn't the safest place to leave her valuables but, after searching around for anywhere else, it had been the only choice. And if anyone came after it when she was in, she would do whatever it took to keep it with her.

She added tonight's takings to the cash that was already in there. Even though she knew how much there would be, she counted it all. There was over three thousand pounds now.

She tucked it away back in the tin and rested her hand on her one saving grace. She pulled it out carefully and laid it on the bed. Inside a blue towel covered in bleach spots was a hand gun. Danny Bristol had given it to her after he'd used it.

Danny had told her to lose it, and when she had refused, he'd left her with a black eye and split lip. But then she'd thought perhaps it might come in useful so, rather than dispose of it, she'd kept it. Danny had found out and had been trying to get it back ever since, hence why she was avoiding him. But he wasn't having it until he gave her the money he owed in return.

Danny had stolen a thousand pounds from Jamie Kerrigan and then put the blame on her. When Jamie had been found dead earlier this year, his dealer had come after her too but luckily, she had evaded him. If she ever saw Danny again, she would get her money back first and then barter over the gun. She still wanted what was hers.

The smell from the bag of chips she had brought back wafted into the room and her stomach growled. She sat down to eat them in front of the small television, catching up with the news. There wasn't much happening, only the usual bad stuff with the occasional glimmer of a happier event.

She glanced at the dress she had bought, hanging from a coat hanger on the door. She hadn't been able to resist new shoes too. Her wardrobe needed refreshing with all the events she'd started to go to. There might even be more opportunities to mingle with people who left their possessions in her reach.

If she chose her targets carefully, in public places, she could make a fortune before she moved on again.

14

Tuesday, 20 June

Although Esther knew that Tamara was nervous about the first meeting with Jack after the mess she had made of the pitch, she was looking forward to it immensely. It wasn't her who had screwed up everything – in fact, she was aware she had saved the day. But that was only for her own interests, and not Tamara's. If Parker-Brown PR hadn't been successful winning the pitch, Esther would have found another way to get close to Jack Maitland, even though she had been repulsed at the feel of him when they shook hands.

At Dulston Publishing, they were shown into the board-room again, this time by Oscar. Jack and Ben were already seated. Esther noticed there were no signs of either Simone or Arabella, which she was sure would go down well with Tamara.

They sat down across from the men, settling into their

chairs with the usual small talk about the continuing heat-wave, before Jack began.

'First of all,' he said, a huge smile on his face, 'I'd once again like to say how we're all really looking forward to working with you. I've started on some of the suggestions that you sent through already, but we're all keen to see what else you have planned for *Something's Got to Give*.'

As Tamara ran through the things they had discussed, Esther studied the three men in turn. You could tell Jack Maitland was a natural leader as he listened intently to Tamara, nodding his head when necessary and giving her his full attention. His fringe kept flopping down in his eyes and he continually moved it out of the way. Esther wondered if he knew how much he did it out of habit, or if he thought it was charismatic, cool, charming. Only she knew the real word for him, and that began with the letter C too.

He caught her observing him and she looked away momentarily. When she glanced again, he was still regarding her. She put on a warm smile and then turned her attention to Oscar.

Oscar was nodding too but he was so exaggerated in everything he did that he looked like one of those nodding dogs you see in the back of people's cars. His folded arms and torso leaning back from the table gave away much more. She wasn't sure why he wasn't open to them as they hadn't ruffled any feathers. But he was the editor of the book. Maybe he felt it was his duty to sell it too. It wasn't: selling and promoting a book were two different things.

It surprised her that Oscar was an editor. His pompous attitude seemed far better suited for sales. But she could see right through him. She could tell by his accent and manner-isms he thought that everything should be handed to him on a plate. He would never lower himself to doing mundane business tasks, not like Tamara.

'I think what you're suggesting makes perfect sense to me,' Jack said, breaking into her thoughts as she was about to study Ben.

But Ben had been watching her.

'So Esther, now that you are back in the room with us, what do you think?' he asked.

'I'm sorry?'

'Well, you've clearly had a late night. You haven't stopped yawning yet.'

Esther snapped her eyes up to his. 'You were discussing whether to target a corporate website or a particular mum blogger, asking which we should aim for first.'

Ben held up his hands in mock surrender. 'I stand corrected. I thought you weren't listening. So what do you think?'

Esther went over the pros and cons of their choices, all the time in the back of her mind fuming at his put-down. Her forehead became clammy, but she was burning inside with rage too. How dare he make a fool of her.

The rest of the meeting followed through without a hitch. Esther came away with a full page of things to do, actions to create, and contacts to get in touch with.

Afterwards, they sat and chatted about Ascot, which was the day after tomorrow. Everyone was looking forward to letting off a bit of steam.

Jack's phone rang and he excused himself from the room. Oscar mentioned a spreadsheet to Tamara and she followed him when he said he would show it to her. It left Esther sitting across from Ben.

Ben spoke first. 'Esther, I'm sorry about earlier. It was my chance at a bit of humour but I was out of line.'

'You were.'

Silence dropped on the room.

'Peace-offering coffee?' He looked over at her, tinges of red visible on each cheek.

'Okay.'

Esther watched as he made his way to the machine in the corner of the room, and waited until one drink was in its china cup and saucer. Then she moved over to him, blocking his way. He turned to her with it and, in one quick move she slapped the palm of her hand underneath the saucer and pushed it up in the air towards him.

A dirty, brown puddle crept over Ben's white shirt. The cup and saucer crashed to the ground, making a thud on the thick carpet tiles. As the hot liquid began to burn his skin, he pulled the material from his chest.

'Argh, you stupid ...' he started, but his words stuck in his mouth when he saw the look on her face. Although he matched her glare, it was his skin that reddened again.

'Oops.' She covered her mouth with her hand. 'I hope you have a clean shirt with you.'

She watched his Adam's apple bob up and down as he swallowed. 'What's wrong with you?'

'Don't *ever* put me down in front of people like that again,' she said.

'I didn't put you down! I was trying to—'

'If you put one fucking hair out of place from now on, I will make you regret it. Do you understand?'

She turned and left him in the room. He didn't even have the courage to mutter anything. Anger simmered inside her but she wouldn't be pushed around, walked over, belittled by anyone ever again, not least by some jumped-up idiot who thought he was God's gift when he obviously wasn't.

Back on the tube home that evening, Esther recalled the conversation, still angry from the altercation. She hoped Ben would take heed of what she'd said to him. Because if he ever belittled her again, she would grab hold of his balls, twisting and squeezing until he begged her to stop, and then she would continue for the sheer pleasure of bringing him to his knees.

No one would put her down like that and get away with it now.

But as the night wore on, she began to realise how much she had overreacted. Ben had tried to make a joke. He hadn't known her long; how was he to know that she would be so touchy? Okay, it had been a stupid attempt at humour, but he hadn't set out to be vindictive.

On the other hand, she had. She'd need to watch that from now on.

15

Tamara placed her hand on the back of her neck before moving her head from side to side. Her lower back was aching so she raised her arms in the air and stretched. She and Esther had been working flat out since they'd had their last meeting with Dulston Publishing.

The clock on the wall said it was nearing 6.00 p.m. It was officially the end of their working week as tomorrow they would be in Ascot and then she was taking Friday off. She'd given Esther the day off too. She was getting bogged down with so many things that she'd felt it necessary. Also, she wasn't sure she'd be able to resist all the champagne tomorrow and didn't want to work with a pounding headache.

'Let's call it a day,' she said, closing the lid of her laptop. 'I don't know about you but I'm bushed.'

Esther looked over. 'I haven't finished the graph that you asked for.'

'It can wait. Besides, we need to be fresh for tomorrow. Are you looking forward to it?'

'Immensely.' Esther shut down her laptop too. 'It's very exciting. I bet you've been to Ascot lots of times.'

'Yes, I have, and obviously Jack grew up there.'

'Oh. I didn't realise.'

'Don't you know who his father is?'

'No, should I?'

'Reggie Maitland?'

Esther frowned.

'He was one of the wealthiest and best-known horse breeders in Ascot.'

'Really?'

'Yes, he's a multi-millionaire. I met him a few times when I was younger. He's a bit of a tyrant though. Apparently, he's got a nasty temper. According to my father, he expects everything done just so, and if it isn't ...'

'Poor Jack,' Esther sympathised.

'Indeed.' Tamara paused. 'Are you doing anything nice this evening?'

Esther shook her head and sighed. 'I have a date with the TV.'

'Do you fancy a glass of something chilled before you leave?'

'I don't see why not.'

'Marvellous. I won't be a tick.'

Tamara rushed into the kitchen. There was always champagne chilling in the fridge, even if it was a cheaper brand than she'd been used to, so she pulled out a bottle and located two flute glasses. She took out a few small bowls and filled them with munchies: mixed fruit and nuts, cheese sticks and a few olives.

Stretching to the back of a cupboard, she retrieved the

multi-pack of crisps that she had always got a stock of. There were two packets left.

With no sense of aplomb, she arranged everything on a tray and took it through to the office. Esther had moved over to the small seating area she used to talk to clients and visitors. It was decorated in blue and white. At the far end, set around a stripped-wood fireplace, was a large, navy corner settee covered with cushions of every shape and size. Behind it, bookcases adorned the wall from ceiling to reclaimed oak floor. A small television was hidden inside a cabinet built into an alcove opposite, and a large coffee table took up the rest of the space.

At the other end of the room, the dining table, which had belonged to her grandparents, took pride of place by the window. You couldn't see that it sat ten people and was made of antique oak because it was covered in an array of notepads, Post-it notes, a small whiteboard, boxes of leaflets and pens, and several proof copies of the book, *Something's Got to Give*, in a pile next to an open laptop.

As Tamara set down the tray, Esther reached over for a crisp.

'I'm starving,' she said, before popping it in her mouth.

'If you have time, I have a fresh pizza. It would only take ten minutes to cook.'

'Oh, please, ignore me. I don't want to put you out.' Esther put a hand to her chest.

'I only have a date with the TV this evening too. It would be great to share it with you.'

'Well, in that case, yes, please. I'd love to.'

Over pizza and champagne, they chatted amicably. Before long it was nearly 8.00 p.m. and they had moved on to a bottle of wine. Even though the drink was making her feel tipsy, Tamara didn't want the evening to stop. She couldn't remember when she'd had a night in, or out for that matter, with a friend. So many of them had slipped away over the past few years.

When they got on to the subject of men and past relationships, Tamara became a little inquisitive.

'So how come you're single, Esther?' she wanted to know.

'Well, so far I've been engaged once, and lived with one man for three years. I thought we would marry and have children eventually but then he left me for another woman, said he didn't want to marry or start a family and neither did she. They're married now – with two kids.'

She grimaced. 'Oh, you poor thing.'

'No, no—' Esther shook her head fervently '—I think I had a lucky escape. What he was trying to say is that he didn't really want to be married and have children with *me*. I'm better off without someone like that.'

'Would you like to have children?'

'Yes, one day. How about you?'

Tamara nodded. A silence dropped on the room as they both thought about the question posed.

'I've been on my own for a year now, and even though it's lonely at times, I like my own company,' Esther added. 'The area I live in could be better but my neighbours are okay. I won't be there for long though. I have my eye on a better place. What about you?'

'Me?'

'How come you haven't been snapped up by some rich bachelor and swept off your feet? You must meet so many eligible men in your line of business.'

'I suppose I do but I'm not actively looking. I was engaged to a man – Michael Foster.' Tamara swallowed, trying hard to suppress memories that were bursting to the front of her mind. 'We'd been together for nine years. We'd made plans to marry, and then, three months before, I found out he'd been having an affair with one of my friends for the past eighteen months.'

Esther gasped and covered her mouth with her hand.

'I was so upset that I wouldn't accept it was over, so I ...' Tamara looked away to hide the discomfort clear on her face. It was a few seconds before she turned back to Esther.

'I kept turning up at the flat – ours at the time, although I'd moved out after I'd found out about his infidelity – and he would say I wasn't welcome. I tried to get my belongings out of it but he said I needed to have someone with me because he didn't want to see me on my own. He didn't trust me.'

'What?' Esther looked outraged.

'He wasn't sure if I would set him up, take things that weren't mine.'

'But that's ridiculous! You wouldn't do that.'

'It was all so petty at the time. He was the one who'd had the affair yet I was the one who had to leave the flat and everything I knew. He turned my friends, and most of my family, against me and in the end, I had no one to turn to. He told a pack of lies about me.'

'That's diabolical!' Esther retorted.

Tamara nodded in agreement. 'I'd never had a serious relationship other than with Michael, and after that I lost my confidence.' She stopped before she said too much, choosing her next words carefully. 'I didn't socialise for a while. It felt good to opt out of society, while I straightened myself out.'

'I can imagine,' Esther soothed.

'But when I was ready to emerge again,' Tamara continued, 'I found everyone had moved on. Michael was still with her so I could no longer be part of that circle and I didn't know many other people.' She paused, not wanting to tell Esther everything. Some of it was too embarrassing.

'That's when I decided to set up my own PR company. I thought I could combine my love of books with something creative. I wasn't sure if it would work or not but at least I had something to concentrate on. My parents helped me out with funding initially so it wasn't too much of a gamble. Now I have a few friends but no close ones, not like before.'

'You have me,' Esther said.

'I do, thankfully!' Tamara grinned. 'Life is good at the moment. I get lonely at times too, but there is lots to look forward to.'

'You don't need a man if you have a good girlfriend to cheer you on.' Esther prodded herself in the chest and giggled. 'And doesn't everyone say that love finds you when you least expect it?'

'I guess. Maybe it will find me soon then, because I am way too busy to think about men right now.'

'Hear, hear.' Esther held up her glass. 'Let's hear it for good girlfriends.'

Tamara raised her glass too. 'Good girlfriends.'

16

_____

Esther had intended going home from work and then out
again on the dip but spending time with Tamara had been
pure gold. It would have taken her weeks to get all that
information about her, lots of which she could use in the
future.

Tamara had shown her weak side, her vulnerability. She
was lonely and Esther needed to play on that. She had to be
the best friend she could.

Yet, being so friendly all the time wasn't easy. It was hard
to be around Tamara all the time and not want to snap at
her. She was so used to having money that she flaunted it,
thinking nothing of spending a fortune on a lunch or dinner
out. The champagne they'd drunk was over twenty pounds a
bottle and it hadn't even been a special occasion.

But Esther needed money, even though she'd wanted an
early night to prepare for the trip to Ascot the following day.
Sometimes she hated pickpocketing innocent individuals,
but other times, like now, she was aware of the money that
was bandied around in the circles she was mixing in and she
had to fit in. She didn't want to keep wearing the same

outfits for work but equally she didn't want to keep dipping into her stash or else she'd never have enough to get away.

She decided to hit the crowds for an hour, see if she could nab a wallet or two. It was a nice evening. People would be enjoying themselves, not paying as much attention. There might be some easy pickings to be had.

She walked along Victoria Street, towards Westminster Abbey, the Houses of Parliament, and Downing Street. There would always be pickings there, as long as she was careful. The tourists were still out in their droves. Most of them were looking at the sights, or taking photos, too preoccupied to watch where her hands would be.

Even the tacky stalls with their paraphernalia declaring 'I LOVE LONDON' emblazoned on them looked better in the summer. Up above in the distance, she could just about see the top of Big Ben on the horizon. It really was a magical place to live, if you kept your wits about you.

Because she hadn't been living in the capital for long, Esther wasn't well-known around the area. And even if she had been, there were plenty of smaller places she could choose from. She didn't work a regular patch, not anymore. It was too risky.

It wasn't long before she had what she needed. It was so much easier during the longer evenings in some respects as people were more relaxed. They didn't have as many places to hide their belongings so would have them on show more. In the same vein, though, Esther didn't have as many places to hide her pickings.

It had been much better when she had been working in a crowd. There were so many distraction techniques to use. If there were two of you, one could divert a victim while the other dipped into a pocket or a bag. Asking someone for directions, usually with the help of a printed map was a great distraction tactic. So too was dropping coins on the floor, a willing passer by stooping down to help while a part-ner-in-crime rifled through their bags.

Esther used to work with some of the other girls she'd known if she was desperate for a fix. If ever she heard a shout behind her, she could pass the stolen goods on to an accomplice so if she was stopped, the bootie was well gone.

Working on her own was more lucrative but twice as dangerous. She would go after easy dips, a jacket over her arm while she popped a hand in a pocket. Or she'd watch for someone on the tube, do the dip just as they were about to board the train and then stay on the platform while the passenger was oblivious to the fact they'd been robbed.

Esther stopped at a stall selling purses and handbags, eyeing up the tourists who were wandering around unsus-pecting of her. She noticed a group coming towards her, schoolgirls of around sixteen years of age. A few words in French wafted her way. She joined in behind them, acting as if she was with them.

The aisles were so crammed with people that no one noticed her hand sliding into a woman's open bag, nimble fingers clasping around a purse. She slid it under her arm for a moment, then slipped the strap of her bag off her shoulder and popped it inside.

Hearing no commotion, she let the girls move on, veered to the right, and into a bar. In the toilets, she counted the money. There was two hundred and twenty-five pounds sterling and seventy-five dollars. Why tourists walked around with that much money, she would never know.

Esther wasn't interested in any credit cards. They would be stopped quickly enough, plus she wanted to work on her own. Selling them on would mean involving others. She would pawn anything decent but she much preferred to work in cash.

After dumping the purse in the toilet cistern, she left the bar. Outside there was still a bright and balmy blue sky, and everywhere was so busy because of it. One more hit and she would be done. She walked around looking for prey.

Despite the heat, a loud burst of laughter made goosebumps erupt over her body. She would know that sound anywhere.

Danny Bristol was sitting at a table outside a bar, in front of her. He was with a few other people she knew. They were laughing at something he was saying.

Esther hadn't got her black wig on to hide behind so she put her head down and turned back, hoping no one would spot her. She quickened her pace, away from the group of people who knew her so well.

After a minute, she slowed down, chancing a look over her shoulder. There seemed to be no one following her but it had been a reminder that her past would catch up with her one day.

Had Danny come into the city for the evening or was he living here now? She wouldn't put it past him to turn up out of the blue looking for her. But with everyone in tow, maybe they had been having a night out. She had got this far without anyone finding her.

Esther decided to leave for home. Going for another hit didn't seem quite as enticing now.

Once back in the safety of her flat, she took out her notebook, added on her takings from that evening and put everything away again. Tonight had been very lucrative and tomorrow she would stop at Colin's to see if he was interested in any of the other items she had stolen recently. If he wasn't, they would go into the nearest bin too.

But an hour later, she was in bed with no signs of sleep. She began to pick at the cut on her leg, making it bleed. Seeing Danny again had freaked her out. If he caught up with her, he would probably give her a good beating. And if he didn't find her, she would always be looking over her shoulder.

The sooner she got out of London the better really. Even though she had something to do here, it was too risky to stay anywhere for long. For now, she needed to give everyone she came into contact with the impression that she was sticking around for good.

That would be enough to keep anyone from finding out what she was really there for.

17

Monday, 13 March

Carley and the major crimes team had been working to solve the murder of Jamie Kerrigan for two weeks but so far had drawn a blank. There wasn't anything captured on CCTV footage nearby that would be of interest to them. There was nothing pointing on the alley itself, and on the street, there had been people seen but no one, except their victim, going into it.

It led them to thinking Kerrigan was meeting someone and his attackers had been waiting for him. Carley had scoured cameras from around the wider area with the CCTV analyst but they hadn't been able to ascertain who had been lying in wait. Neither was the back of the alley covered.

Carley had accompanied Max to question anyone they were aware of who was associated with Kerrigan. But even if anyone knew anything, they were staying tight-lipped. Apparently, no one had been arguing with Kerrigan. No one had a grudge against him. There wasn't a bad word said about him, which was a suspicion in itself. The crew Kerrigan belonged to was known for not speaking out against each other. There was definitely some sort of cover up going on.

Their main suspects were still Danny Bristol and Ewan Smith, but both had given each other alibis. They had been together on the night in question, watching television at Danny's flat. Having been in trouble before, they had been able to pre-empt all the questions they would be asked, so their answers were watertight. And being unable to find the weapon used in the murder meant there were no clues other than its make – a Glock 17 9mm safe-action pistol.

So Carley was surprised as she looked up from her computer to see Max waving her into his office.

'We've received a call from a neighbour of Ewan Smith's. He thinks he might have heard a gunshot last night.'

'And he's only just ringing it in this morning?' Carley checked her watch: it was 11.30 a.m.

Max shrugged. 'Nothing surprises me anymore.'

Carley shrugged on her jacket, picked up her phone and keys and followed Max out of the building.

In recent years, Shoreditch had become popular and fashionable, with accompanying rises in land and property prices. An inner-city district in the east end of London, it was still undergoing transformation, and the area where Ewan Smith lived was as worn as it had ever been.

The estate was a large sprawl of council housing, mainly tower blocks. Pre-war builds had nowhere near enough room to accommodate today's mass of cars. They were parked everywhere, resulting in vehicles struggling to pass.

Carley followed Max as they jogged up the steps towards

the third floor of the tower block. A man in his fifties, with combed-over hair and greasy skin was waiting for them.

'I can't be sure,' he said. 'It may have been his television. But I've knocked and knocked this morning and he hasn't come to the door.'

'Are you positive he's in?' asked Max.

'I heard his door go about eleven last night when he came home. He sometimes gets me a paper in the mornings, or puts a bet on for me.'

'What time did you hear the shot?'

'About fifteen minutes after he came in. Don't look at me like that.' The man raised his hands in the air before dropping them dramatically. 'What happens if I'm wrong? I don't want to get beaten up for poking my nose in. I can't—'

Max held up a hand for him to stop. 'I don't suppose you have a key?'

The man shook his head. Max told him to step back, then he kicked at the door lock but it didn't budge.

'Reinforced?' asked Carley.

'I wouldn't put it past him.'

Max radioed through for a trained officer to bring an enforcer, also known as the big red key. While they waited, they knocked on a few doors to see if the neighbour's story could be corroborated. Two of the eight were answered, and neither of their residents had heard or seen anything.

Once the door was forced open, Max went in first and Carley followed behind, her baton flicked out in readiness.

'Police!' Max shouted. Two officers followed behind him.

'Bathroom's clear. So is the bedroom,' said one of them.

'Kitchen's clear,' replied the other.

Carley and Max went into the living room, their steps tentative. Ewan Smith was on the settee. His head had fallen to their right, revealing a gunshot wound above his ear.

Brain matter was splattered on the wall behind him, clear from the amount that he was dead.

Carley covered her mouth, turning away for a moment.

'How can anyone do that, and at such close range?' She dry-retched.

While she composed herself, they flicked on latex gloves and Max went around to the front of the body.

'There's no weapon so it couldn't have been suicide.' He checked for a pulse and shook his head before radioing the details through to the control.

Carley pointed to a whiskey bottle and a half-full glass. 'Unfinished drink. I wonder if he came back alone and someone was waiting for him or if someone came afterwards and took him by surprise.'

'With no signs of forced entry, I'd say his murderer was invited in.'

She looked around the room. There was nothing out of place. For all intents and purposes, Smith looked like he had fallen asleep in front of the television after a night out.

'Someone could have sneaked up behind him and taken a shot,' Max said.

'The list of people he would have upset in the past is going to be huge for this one.' Carley pointed out the obvious. 'I wouldn't know where to start.'

'I think Danny Bristol will be our first port of call, see what we get from him and go from there. There's nothing we can do here while the forensics team is in. Let's pay him a visit.'

Carley was aware they didn't want to disturb any of the evidence so was glad when Max began opening a few drawers in the kitchen. There was nothing that he could see straightaway, even though there were a few more hiding places. They'd have to wait until the room was swept and searched and see if anything came back.

They each took one more glance around before leaving the flat. There was nothing either of them could do for Ewan Smith now, except find his murderer.

18

Thursday, 22 June

Esther woke early. After spending more time out than she had anticipated the night before, and then having a fitful sleep because of seeing Danny Bristol again, she'd have to preen herself to perfection today. She wanted to make the best impression she could to entice Jack Maitland into her bed.

The bathroom smelled of bergamot pear, heliotrope lilies, and musk sandalwood. The cream had rubbed into her skin so quickly that she felt pampered. She was glad she'd taken the time to steal the purse from a tourist in a department store last week so that she could buy the accompanying shower gel and deodorant spray too. Everything needed to be seamless today.

The beauty products were a special treat. It meant that even in the crummy space, with its mould coming through behind the toilet cistern and in between the cracks of the tiles, she couldn't wait to get showered and into her dress.

As she lathered up, she thought about the day ahead. Esther had certainly lucked out meeting Tamara. Despite first impressions, she hadn't expected her to be so accommodating. Her vulnerability was kind of appealing, if not nauseous at times, but she could handle that.

Spending time with Tamara and learning all about her past had been a bonus. Tamara was trusting her much quicker than she had envisioned. But then again, that wouldn't be hard. Her acting was superb at the moment. There had only been that one incident with Ben that could have given the game away.

She dressed carefully that morning. Even though she would hate every minute of it, she was going to make sure she spent as much of the day as possible with Jack. At least he seemed personable.

It had been a bonus to get an invite to Royal Ascot, and she was even getting paid for taking the next two days off. Tamara had insisted; she wasn't going to complain.

She popped on her hat, and smiled at her reflection through the dirty wardrobe mirror with the crack across the bottom. The colours in the dress brought out the green in her eyes, and even though her hair was dyed auburn, she loved its shade.

Clothes really did make the person. Esther looked very hoity-toity, she mused, which was just as well because she was way above her class. She ran her hand down the dress to smooth it, reached for the pashmina shawl that Tamara had been determined to buy her too, and popped it over her arm.

With one final check in the mirror, she pouted, blew herself a kiss, grabbed her bag, and headed outside.

The weather was glorious as she bounced down the steps on the balls of her feet. Storms were forecast with some much-needed rain, but she hoped they would hold out for today. She didn't want anything to dampen her spirits.

It was a ten-minute walk to West Brompton station where she needed to catch the Overground train across the river to Clapham Junction. She was meeting Tamara there in an hour. It was only two stops but she wanted to get there in plenty of time.

Esther knew she looked good so she raised her shoulders higher as she walked. Her heels tapped rhythmically on the pavement, bringing more attention to her. It made her feel powerful.

Heads turned as she walked along Trebovir Road. It was embarrassing but liberating at the same time. Everyone could see she was going somewhere special. They didn't think *she* was special, which was a shame. But for now, all eyes were on her.

'Spare a few coins for a meal,' a voice came from the pavement. She looked down, seeing a man in disarray, dirt smeared on his face, his hair matted. By the side of him, a Jack Russell terrier was curled up asleep.

Her heels tapped on the pavement like bullets from a revolver as she marched past him but then she stopped. She closed her eyes momentarily thinking back to a time when she'd had to beg on the streets to survive. Rummaging around in her bag, she took out her purse and drew out a five-pound note. She went back to the man and thrust it in his hands.

'Thanks, miss!' His eyebrows raised in surprise.

'Get yourself something good with it, mind,' she said before turning on her heels.

Once she was seated on the train, she sent a text message to Tamara.

On my way. I know I'm early but I couldn't sleep. I'm so excited. See you soon.

A message came back almost immediately.

I'm on my way too! See you there.

She smiled to herself.

The day was getting off to a good start, even though she was nervous about returning to Ascot. She tucked her emotions away, safe in the knowledge that no one would interfere with them. No one would want to.

'Going somewhere nice, love?' a lady sitting across the aisle from her asked.

'Ascot Racecourse,' Esther replied, a little taken aback. She was used to being ignored round and about in London. People walked with their heads down or eyes fixed straight ahead to avoid any kind of contact. It must be the outfit, she assumed.

'How divine. You have the perfect day for it. I hope the weather lasts.' The woman beamed at her. 'And I hope you enjoy yourself. You look radiant.'

'Thanks.' Esther smiled back, hoping as she did that the woman wouldn't want to engage in a full-blown conversation. She didn't want to encourage her but neither did she want to be rude. Her parents had brought her up to respect her elders.

Luckily, the woman settled back down to the magazine she had been reading. Esther studied her for a moment. Layers of brightly coloured clothes for when it became too hot, the pearl necklace around her aged neck was probably a family heirloom and her face was made up with a skilful hand. Silver-grey hair curled in a set. It made her think of her mum, how she might look now. Although she wasn't so old, she would obviously look very different than the last time she had seen her when she was seventeen.

Esther should have complimented the woman back, but it was too late now. Instead she relaxed in her seat, turning her head towards the window. Although she quite liked the 'being nice to everyone' attitude she portrayed, she would be off in a minute anyway, so it was hardly worth the effort.

19

Tamara waved to Esther as she disembarked the train and pushed her way across the platform through the crowds. She held on to her hat as it clashed with the brim of another woman and then ducked underneath her.

'You look wonderful,' she exclaimed, greeting Esther with an air kiss. 'That dress suits you more on second viewing.'

'Thank you.' Esther almost squealed. 'I'm so excited.'

'Me too. Come on, we need platform two.'

The next train to Ascot was due in ten minutes and they joined the throngs of elaborately dressed passengers as they waited for it to arrive. Tamara hadn't had a day off in a long time. Building up the business had been her priority for the past twelve months. So she very much felt like a child, shivers of excitement rippling through her.

There was no sign of Jack Maitland, nor any of the team from Dulston Publishing as the train pulled in. They got on board, and she pointed to a seat with a table. 'Quick, grab that!'

Esther shimmied along the seat to settle next to the

window. 'What's Royal Ascot like?' She looked at Tamara, shyness in her expression.

'I haven't been for several years now,' Tamara replied. 'Although it was a family tradition until I was in my late teens. My parents sometimes go but they're giving it a miss this year.' She looked at Esther. 'Did you live in Shoreditch all your life?'

'Yes.'

'What was it like?'

Esther shrugged and Tamara could tell she had made her feel uncomfortable.

'Nothing to talk about,' Esther finally replied. 'I'm an only child. I lived there with my parents and left when I was twenty-one.'

Tamara waited for her to say more but Esther didn't elaborate. It struck her that she might be embarrassed. Everyone around her seemed to be wealthy. Did she feel the odd one out?

'I know I'm lucky to be brought up with money,' she said, 'but sometimes it isn't a blessing. There are certain things expected of you.'

'Such as?' Esther was all attentive now the conversation had moved away from her. Tamara wondered whether to confide in her. It felt slightly indulgent saying that her wealthy upbringing was sometimes more of a hindrance than a help. She paused, and then decided to go for it.

'According to my family, by now I should be married with a husband that I dote on and who I run around after. I should have at least two children, who should be in private schools. I definitely shouldn't be running my own business.' She raised her shoulders up and then down in defeat.

Esther pulled a face. 'That's a little old-fashioned, isn't it?'

'That's my parents, for you.' She nodded. 'My father is old school but a gentleman for most of the time. My mother is a nightmare. She's a stickler for tradition. "No woman in the Parker-Brown family has ever gone out to work," she keeps on telling me. And I keep on telling her that I'm not going out to work – I *own* the bloody company – but she won't have it.'

'Do you have brothers and sisters?'

'Two older brothers and a younger sister.' She sighed. 'I know I'm a disappointment to my parents. They brought me up well. I was educated at Marydale Grammar School for Girls and then I read English at Oxford. Law had been my parents' choice but I had been adamant. Once I'd finished my studies, I went to live in Spain teaching English to middle-grade children.'

'Good for you.' Esther seemed impressed.

'My parents weren't happy about it – my mother because I was working at all and my father because I hadn't followed in his footsteps. It wasn't enough that both my brothers were lawyers too. But after twelve months, I was homesick and came back to London anyway.'

'What does your sister do?'

'Cordelia? Oh, she's never worked after having her first child at twenty-two. I didn't want to follow tradition, so I went to work for my brother, Jonathan.'

'And then you started Parker-Brown PR,' Esther said.

Tamara nodded. 'Of course, my parents had been totally against it, but working in publishing PR is a good career choice for me and, well, I'm making a living from it slowly.'

'So we'll have to make sure this campaign for *Something's Got to Give* is the best and biggest by far,' Esther remarked, 'so that your mum can eat her words when you are so successful that *everyone* wants to hire you.'

Tamara wished that she could bottle Esther's confidence. Her own brothers and sister never had any problems. While they got on with their lives, knowing the exact path to follow, Tamara had meandered down a long and winding road with lots of diversions.

But she was better now. She was much better, actually. Maybe when she next visited the doctor's surgery he would reduce the dosage of her tablets.

She grinned, delighted in dreaming about what Esther had suggested. Imagine if the campaign was a success. Tamara could end up with a lot more business. The ideas they'd come up with so far had been innovative, but they did have the best secret weapon possible. The book. If this was seen enough, it was a sure-fire winner; not like some of the bestsellers she had read that really hadn't lived up to the hype. It was such an interesting concept, and so brutal.

Esther had been looking out of the window on to the platform, but she turned back to her with a wicked grin.

'Since we won the pitch for *Something's Got to Give*, and found out we were invited to Ascot, I've been waiting for this moment.' Her eyes lit up like a child's.

Tamara frowned when she remained quiet. 'What?'

'You and me.' Esther pointed to each of them in turn. 'We're "Girls on The Train!" Like the Paula Hawkins's bestseller. Get it?'

'We're hardly girls,' she said, nudging her, 'but yes!'

As their laughter rang through the carriage, it struck Tamara that she hadn't laughed so much in a long time. Esther was certainly having a positive effect on her.

20

Esther felt guilty about Tamara. She was being set up and she didn't deserve it. But people like her made Esther sick. Brought up in a family with no money worries, she bet all she would have been concerned about as a child was which colour ribbon to put in her hair and whether it matched her fancy dress and shoes. She doubted that Tamara had suffered ridicule and bullying to the extent she had.

She could bet Tamara hadn't wanted to stay away from her fancy school for fear of being called a slag and a slut constantly, being ostracised, getting the occasional thump or kick in the back as girls gathered around her. Esther would bet she would never have failed her exams because she was so stressed over the death of her father, thinking she was to blame.

Yet hearing her talking about her family, it seemed that Tamara hadn't had a good time lately either. Even having money didn't make people happy, it seemed. Although it must help, as privileges wouldn't have to be earned. Food and clothing, as well as a bed to sleep in would be the norm. It was just love that was missing.

Esther liked Tamara. She was fun to be around, and she knew she had changed Tamara's life for the better already, even in the short time that they had known each other.

She turned her head to her right as something caught her eye. Jack Maitland and four men came rushing across the platform, jumping onto the train with seconds to spare. They were all dressed in stylish suits, which didn't go well with the red and white flimsy carrier bags they were holding. She watched as they came into the carriage and walked down the aisle, loud and laughing. Oscar was holding his chest, cheeks red at the exertion.

Through Tamara, she'd learned that Jack was married with twin boys, aged eight. His wife, Natalie, worked in Harrods as a buyer and was often out of the country. Their children had a nanny but were palmed off on grandparents too.

Esther realised that Jack was above her class but he didn't really know that, and, even though he repelled her, she still had to seduce him.

He caught her looking at him. Making his way politely down the aisle, he stopped in front of them.

'Ladies,' he said with a smile, 'you both look delightful.'

Behind him, Oscar nodded. 'Absolutely stonking,' he guffawed.

Esther did her best not to roll her eyes. She smiled as wide as she could, knowing they wouldn't see how much she hated being with them.

Jack introduced the other men in their party. If she remembered rightly from the website, Richard, Giles, and Brett worked on the production side of the business.

'There don't seem to be any spaces left for us to sit altogether,' Jack pointed out. 'May we join you?'

'Of course,' Tamara said.

Esther smiled widely again. Both men slid into the seats opposite them. Richard, Brett, and Giles sat down a few seats in front.

Esther glanced around. 'No Ben?' she asked.

'He's got the runs,' Jack explained. 'Came on last night, apparently.'

'Poor Ben.' Tamara doled out the sympathy. 'That's terrible at the best of times but awful on a day like this that only comes around once a year. It's sad that he'll miss it.'

'He might catch a later train and join us if he's feeling better,' Jack added.

'Oh, let's hope so.'

Esther said nothing. She doubted he would turn up later. He was probably still too embarrassed about their recent spat. She must have made him uncomfortable. Good, he deserved it after his stupid attempt to belittle her, although he needed to man up if he let a small thing like that get to him. She tried to hide her smirk.

'I'm so glad you could both make it today,' Jack said, sitting opposite her.

Esther could see his eyes twinkling already, and wondered if he had dabbled in a pick-me-up. She couldn't see Jack doing that kind of thing, if she was honest, but you never knew with these rich sorts. Esther made it one of her missions to find out before the day was finished.

'Wouldn't miss it, Jack,' Tamara purred.

Esther loved Tamara's posh accent. How she wished she had learned to speak better before now. At least her fake accent didn't give away exactly where she came from. That would have been embarrassing. She had an edge to her voice, not a rich tone in sight, but she was sure no one would guess where she originated.

Oscar pulled out a bottle of Bollinger. 'Let's get this show on the road,' he yelled.

'Hurrah,' she replied, watching Tamara's smile widen.

Jack popped the cork, and, without too much overspill, poured champagne into the plastic glasses. Oscar handed them around to their group and they raised them up in the air afterwards.

'A toast, I reckon,' Jack said. 'To Dulston Publishing and Parker-Brown PR working well together. And to *Something's Got to Give* becoming publishing's next big thing.'

'The next big thing!'

Their voices rang out around the carriage, much to the annoyance of the couple who were sitting across the aisle from them. Clearly being in the middle of all these toffs wasn't something they were comfortable with either.

'There's no doubt it will be a bestseller,' Tamara remarked. 'Some of the best marketing campaigns have covered abysmal books with no soul or character, and they have still sold in their thousands. We have the most fantastic novel too. It's going to rock the book world.'

Jack raised his glass in the air. 'I'll drink to that.' He turned back to Esther. 'What do you think?'

Esther leaned forward, all the time her gaze never leaving his. 'I think it will do really well.' She smiled. 'I'm positive everything possible is being done to ensure its success.'

'It's in very good hands.'

When Jack winked at her, the air between them almost crackled with electricity. Esther noticed that charming twinkle again, hoping it was directed at her.

Finally, she broke the spell by looking out of the window. She didn't want to give anything away, not yet. Tamara might put a stop to it and that would never do.

21

Tamara wished she was as confident as Esther as she surreptitiously watched her chatting across the table to Jack. He was showing her a map of Ascot Racecourse, pointing out where the box he had booked was located.

She smiled at no one in particular. It was amazing how easy it was for Esther to talk to people. Oscar had turned to face Richard and was chatting animatedly to him, his feet out in the aisle.

She sat there feeling a little flustered that no one was talking to her, waiting for someone to notice. She didn't want to interrupt Jack and Esther, but thought she should have been seated across from him if anyone. It didn't seem right that he was showing Esther the detailed map of the grounds.

She supposed she could have joined in, but she wanted them to bring her into the conversation. She didn't want to come across too needy, not today of all days.

'There's a new area this year, the Village Enclosure. It looks like it will be a lot of fun, with alfresco dining and cocktail bars. Live bands and DJs even. We have passes to enter.' Jack tapped on the paper. 'We also have passes for the Grandstand. We'd have to wear morning dress for the Royal Enclosure—'

'Including top hats?' Esther queried.

'Yes.' Jack nodded. 'I'm not into that much of a malarkey so we won't be allowed in there. But there's lots to do elsewhere. The day starts at two when the queen rides past for the royal procession. Then the races begin. There are six in all, the last one at five thirty-five.'

'Sounds exciting,' she heard Esther say, hanging on to Jack's every word.

'Once the racing has concluded, it's live entertainment. Or you can sing around the bandstand, which is another tradition, and a fantastic end to the day, especially with the weather as it is. Then everything wraps up at nine, that's if anyone is still standing. It's a long day of drinking and eating.'

Oscar turned back to her then to refill their glasses.

'Remind me how long you two have worked together before you started on the pitch for us?' Oscar asked, once he had completed his duties.

'Only for a few weeks,' Tamara replied. 'I hired Esther on a temporary basis. She's been amazing for the business though, as you know.' She raised her drink in the air and smiled at Esther as she looked over upon hearing her name. 'She has such a great eye for PR campaigns and is an excellent copywriter.'

'Stop it.' Esther waved a hand in front of her face. 'You're embarrassing me.'

'Sounds like you need to add her to your staff.' Oscar nodded knowingly. 'Especially if the campaign for *Something's Got to Give* is a triumph. Jack was very impressed.' He put an arm around the man's shoulders. 'Weren't you, Jack?'

Jack nodded, his fringe falling in his eyes. He swept it away again before speaking.

'If this campaign is a success, then I'm sure this might be the start of a long and prosperous partnership. I think you'll need more staff, then, or a partner maybe.'

Tamara laughed, a bit intimidated by his openness. She liked Esther, but not enough to make her a partner. She was unwilling to trust anyone for that, even if it meant keeping the business small.

This venture with Dulston Publishing could be the start of bigger and better things. It could prove her parents wrong, and even make her mother sit up and listen. But Esther would never be her equal, no matter what. She wasn't of the same class as her, the same breeding.

Esther had been educated at state school. She hadn't even been to university. She was fine as an assistant, but it was Tamara who would run the business. Maybe she could keep her on side for a while, fool her into thinking she was more than she was. There was no harm in that.

She watched as Esther lapped up the attention, her fingers fiddling with her hair, winding down a tendril that had strayed from her updo. Who could blame her? Brains and beauty were a great combination and Esther had them both.

Tamara had brains, though. People always underestimated her because of her soft streak but she was well aware that Esther could be the one to take her business to higher places. She might come up with the ideas and the campaigns but it would be *her* name, Parker-Brown PR, that would be on everyone's lips.

She gasped inwardly. Gosh, she sounded as stuck-up as her mother!

'One step at a time.' She turned to her employee with a

smile.

Esther raised her drink and clinked the plastic glass with hers, giggling at the silly noise it made.

The tannoy burst into life and the operator gave a minute's warning that they would be arriving at Ascot.

Relief flooded through Tamara. She needed to check on her make-up as she had a feeling, with the heat of the day, she would be looking like a ripened tomato.

She wafted a hand in front of her face. How on earth the men were feeling with their jackets and waistcoats on top of their shirts she didn't know. She was practically glowing and not in a good way.

'Ah, Ascot,' Jack said with a sigh. 'I used to live here when I was younger.'

'Yes, Tamara mentioned earlier,' Esther responded.

Tamara turned to her, a puzzled expression on her face. Esther's tone had a touch of cynicism and iciness about it. But Esther cleared her throat and smiled.

'It's a beautiful place,' Jack continued. 'I was incredibly fortunate to grow up with so much land around me, and of course there were the horses. But I didn't get to see my parents much. My father was deeply disappointed when I didn't want to follow his career.' He went quiet as he gazed out of the window for a moment. Then he turned back to them, his smile returning.

'Do they still live here?' Tamara asked. 'Your parents?'

Jack shook his head. 'They moved to London in twenty-twelve. Much closer, yet I still don't see them any more often. Families, huh?'

As passengers began to get up from their seats and gather together their belongings, they followed suit. Tamara held in a sigh. It seemed she wasn't the only one who had trouble being everything their parents wanted them to be.

22

Esther shimmied to the end of her seat and stood up, running a hand down the front of her dress to straighten it out again. Thank goodness it hadn't creased as much as Tamara's, which now had more pleats than a Roman blind around her middle.

She stood in line along with everyone else, feeling the excitement, as they waited for their carriage to come to a stop. As they were ready to disembark, she felt Jack's hand on the small of her back.

'You smell as gorgeous as you look,' he whispered into her hair.

Esther could feel his breath on her neck. She smelt his aftershave, a mixture of black orchids and plums if she wasn't mistaken. Her cheeks flushed when she glanced at him. Was he flirting with her? And he a married man? Tut, tut. She smiled but chose to say nothing, hearing him chuckle as they moved nearer to the exit.

Once they were all on the concourse, Jack clapped his hands to get everyone's attention. 'Let's do this!' he cried, pointing in the direction of the taxi rank. 'Let's go spend some money.'

Inside Ascot Racecourse, Esther's nerves ratcheted up as familiar scents invaded her senses, and scenes around her reminded her of a world she was no longer a part of. She tried to control her breathing, hoping not to get too stressed by the huge throng of people they joined as they made their way to their box. It might seem strange but, unless she was out on the steal, she hated such close proximity to so many people. The sense of isolation engulfed her more. She was certainly a nobody in this crowd.

Jack had been right. The dress she was wearing did seem more apt for a wedding. The men were mostly wearing suits, and the women were far better dressed than she had anticipated. She cursed under her breath. How could she have thought she looked acceptable this morning? Some of their hats alone must have cost more than the dress Tamara had bought for her. And these women oozed class too, whereas she was only pretending.

Maybe it hadn't been such a good idea to come here after all. Too many memories were forcing themselves to the front of her mind, suffocating her, reminders in every direction she looked. And the horses. How she missed the horses.

'Man up, Esther,' she muttered under her breath and lifted her shoulders in the hope it would bring back the confidence she had felt deserting her.

She tried, *really* tried, but she couldn't get lost in the excitement that was buzzing in the air. It all seemed such rigmarole. Men walking around like penguins and women like porcelain dolls. It wasn't her scene at all. A feeling of light-headedness began to envelop her as people pushed and cajoled her.

Luckily, once they had been shown to the box, Esther

could relax a little. The room Jack had chosen was in prime position. It would comfortably hold about twenty people, standing room only, but today had been laid out for lunch. Three round tables stood in the centre. The wall to their right was lined with waist-high cabinets, with a black marble worktop full of drinks and glasses. Coffee cups and hot water dispensers stood at the ready, and trays of pastries. She saw Richard take one. As he caught her eye, he looked at her sheepishly.

'Travel sick,' he explained, wiping crumbs from his mouth. 'Need a little sugar.'

Esther nodded, knowing exactly how he felt. She was nauseous too but it was with nerves and trepidation, hate and revenge churning her up in knots.

Beyond them all was a glass partition overlooking the racecourse, with a door leading on to a small terrace. She moved towards it to look out. Below them, thousands of people were sitting in their seats, walking around or stopping to chat. She was so glad she was up here, out of the way, and that there was somewhere to place their bets quite close by. She wouldn't have to leave the box if she didn't want to.

Jack came to stand beside her, holding two glasses of champagne. He passed one to her.

'I've heard from a good source that they have over three thousand staff on hand this week,' he told her.

Esther raised her eyebrows in jest, remembering those figures as part of their pitch. 'I wonder where I've heard that before.'

'I guess there might be more now the Village Enclosure has been opened.'

'Do your parents ever visit?' she asked.

'They came down earlier in the week, for the first two

days. I booked the box for today so that I could avoid them. It's easier.'

'Ah.'

Tamara had gone to the bathroom but was now walking towards them. Oscar appeared by her side and said something to her. Her head went back and she guffawed. Esther held in her distaste. She didn't like Oscar. He was opinionated, loud and brash, but at least Tamara would have her hands full with him so that she could spend time with Jack.

She looked around the room at the people in her group. Did she stand out as the poor relation? Jack, still standing by her side, was clearly a millionaire. The box was small but she'd checked out the rates on the website. Prices started at ten thousand, eight hundred pounds, rising to fourteen thousand, seven hundred pounds. Just like Tamara, he must have had money passed down to him as the publishing house he owned wasn't that big. Yet, to treat his staff was remarkably thoughtful, and a testament to his hard work that he had cash to splash.

The racing started, and two hours in Esther's annoyance began to show. Getting a little frustrated as she lost every race she tried for, she helped Jack to choose a few horses to place bets on. But then she struck gold and backed a winner. A Long Way to Go netted over three hundred pounds.

When Jack had collected the winnings, he handed a wad of cash to her.

'I can't take this.' She gave it back to him.

He looked hurt. 'Why ever not?'

'Because you paid for the bet, so the money is yours.'

'But you won it.'

'A lucky guess after all the losers.' She laughed. She wasn't taking his money.

'Please,' he insisted, putting it in the palm of her hand

and then curling her fingers around it tightly. 'If you think I'm after anything in return, then you're mistaken. You won this fair and square, like you won the pitch for *Something's Got to Give*.'

Like you won my heart. Esther wouldn't have been surprised if he had come out with a corny line such as that. Jack was a smooth talker but he was a creep. Even though this was what she wanted, he was giving her the come-on, despite being married.

In the end, she decided to take the money but she wasn't going to thank him. She put it away in her purse and picked up her glass. It was almost empty so he reached for it, his hand lingering over hers as he looked into her eyes.

'A refill?' he asked, his voice playful.

Esther nodded.

Jack moved to the bar behind, and she gazed out over the racecourse as everyone got ready for the next race. It felt good to be up here in her ivory tower, away from strangers – although it had crossed her mind more than once or twice that the dipping would be rife for a good pickpocket.

Tamara sidled over, her eyes bright and shiny. 'Are you enjoying yourself?' she asked.

'Yes. You?'

'Very much so. That Oscar is a wild one.'

Esther saw Jack with his arm around Oscar's neck. 'Well, I would,' she teased.

'You would?' It was Tamara's turn to frown.

She shrugged. 'You know. With Jack, if he wanted to.'

Tamara continued to frown and then her eyes widened when she grasped Esther's meaning.

'But he's married!'

'I meant hypothetically speaking, of course.'

Tamara's mouth dropped open for a moment and then she laughed. 'You're so naughty,' she said.

Esther laughed along with her. It felt good. Perhaps the champagne, or the ambience of the day, was finally getting under her skin.

The trouble was, she wasn't sure if that was a good thing or not.

23

Esther left the room and made her way along the long corridor, almost bouncing on the plush carpet. It was relatively quiet there, and a blessing after standing on the balcony with the crowd below. A man rushed past her on a mission to use the bathroom. Two women chattered about someone named James being too common and brash. A couple in their mid-twenties were muttering under their breath, trying not to show they were in full argument mode, which was quite funny to watch.

Paintings and framed photographs lined the walls either side, making a mini gallery as she walked. Winners and riders of years gone by, plaques with names engraved for each year. She was too tipsy to read any of the small print. Unexpectedly, her eyes fell upon an illustration that made her stop dead.

It was a charcoal drawing on a pale cream background. A pair of men's brown riding boots, a hat on the ground next to them and a crop leaning against them. It was the simplest of images, and fitted the venue and decor beautifully, but it brought memories that Esther had long buried rushing to the forefront of her mind.

A sharp pain whipped across the back of my legs. Even through the thickness of my jodhpurs, I felt its sting. I stumbled forward, my hands on the stable floor covered in straw and manure.

Another lash crashed across my back. And then another one, followed by two more in quick succession.

'Stop!' Tears stuck in the breath I was struggling to catch.

'Shut up.' It was a male voice.

Before I could scramble away, he seized hold of my hair and yanked my head back. I tried to scream but a hand then pushed me face down into the straw.

I thrashed around, but the weight on my back meant I couldn't breathe. And then he turned me round to face him, straddling me. I heard the crack of his hand on my face before the pain tore through me.

The room began to spin. Esther held on to the wall.

'Hey!' A hand grasped her elbow and she felt Jack's warmth against her clammy skin.

'Are you okay?' he asked.

She nodded, unable to speak.

'Do you need some air? I can take you outside if so?'

'I'm fine, if a tad embarrassed. I think I had a little too much champagne.' For a brief moment, she wanted to be in his arms, shielded instead of sickened. Then she quickly stepped away.

'Come and sit down for a moment,' he said.

He guided her to one of many settees that were dotted along the corridor. They sat down together; her legs still felt shaky. Her hands shook too, the fear taking hold of her with that one powerful image. She knew she wouldn't sleep that night, or if she did her dreams would be plagued with memories that would turn into nightmares.

As more racegoers milled around in the corridor, Jack didn't push her to speak. He just sat next to her, keeping her company while her breathing and colour returned to normal.

After a few minutes, Esther treated him to a faint smile. 'I'm sorry about that. Thanks for sitting with me.'

Jack held up a hand. 'You don't need to apologise. It's hot, we've been drinking and getting excited. It's a bad combination sometimes.' He paused for a moment as a couple walked past. 'We're continuing the party back at my house afterwards if you'd like to join us?'

'Oh, I don't think your wife would want us intruding.' She looked him straight in the eye.

'She's out of town until tomorrow evening. It's a sleep-over at my place tonight. She knows how rowdy we can get so we have an arrangement. She and our boys go to stay with her parents in Kent and she goes shopping and out for a meal with old friends. I'm not sure which of us spends the most money, if I'm honest.'

Esther gave him another half-smile. She didn't want to hear about his wife, only her whereabouts.

'How are you feeling now?' Jack touched her arm gently.

'Much better, thanks.'

He stood up and held out his hand. She grasped it and he pulled her upright. He held on to it as they stood there together.

His mouth opened and for a moment she thought he was going to say something. But he closed it again.

'I'll see you back in the box,' he said eventually and then left her standing.

Esther watched him until he had disappeared from her view.

Alone in the bathroom, she went into the last cubicle in the row. With one hand over her mouth as she gagged, she lifted the lid in time to vomit in the toilet. She retched until it hurt her chest and then, exhausted, she flopped to the side, propping herself up against the wall.

This day had mostly been agony. She hated coming to places like this, with all this money and upper-class twattery. She wasn't like the Parker-Browns or the Maitlands of this world. She never would be.

If only she had some speed to remove the frustration she could feel building up.

She pulled out a blister pack from inside her purse and spied only two diazepam tablets left. She had already taken one earlier to get her through the day. Having another could tip her over.

Screw it.

Esther snapped one out and swallowed it before she could stop herself. She had a few more hours to go yet to keep up appearances.

Outside the cubicle, she surveyed herself in the mirror above the sinks as she washed her hands. For a moment, she was alone in the room. If she had felt better, she would admire its chrome decor, treat herself to a splurge of the decadent hand cream and spray on the perfume left out in the dressing area. She loved the little touches that made everything special. It was one of the things she would never get used to mixing in these circles, but one she enjoyed.

The colour had come back to her face but she refreshed her make-up to add a little more. It was a time for a dark lipstick, daring, a little vulgar but oh so powerful.

Fooling everyone today was only the start of everything.

24

It was half past ten by the time the train arrived back in London. Tamara woke up, her head resting on Oscar's shoulder, his head on hers. Across the table, Jack and Esther were looking at her. Esther had a hand on her arm.

'Next stop is ours,' she told her.

'We can share two cabs to my house,' Jack offered. 'Do you both still want to come back?'

Esther nodded discreetly at her. All Tamara wanted was to go home and collapse on her bed but Esther had been good to her, and she knew she wanted to hang around with the men a little longer. She wished she had her stamina. Esther didn't seem drunk at all.

She lifted her head, felt it pounding and grimaced. 'Do you have any painkillers?'

'Yes, you'll need to take them with water, though. Wait until we get to Jack's.' Esther stood up and came around the table. Putting a hand underneath her arm, she pulled. 'Come on, let's get you some fresh air.'

Esther was right. Tamara was much better when she got off the train. The champagne had made her feel sick but because she hadn't drunk anything for a while, she began to perk up again.

They climbed into two cabs and sped off. Everyone was invigorated now they'd had time to relax and get a second wind. They had to pull a paralytic Richard from the window as he shouted to passers-by. The driver told them to calm down twice and Tamara prayed Richard wouldn't throw up.

Jack lived in Holland Park. The cabs pulled up in front of large wooden gates with a two-metre wall either side. Tamara could just about see the roof of his home as she stepped out onto the pavement. Her feet and back were aching with the standing around they had done all day and she really wanted her bed. She would stay for as long as it took to be polite and then she would make her excuses and leave.

Esther was laughing at something Jack was saying as he typed in a code on a keypad. The gates opened up to a gravel driveway and they crunched along on it for a few metres until the house was in full view.

It was a rectangle building of epic proportions. Oak double doors stood proud in the middle of four, large windows downstairs and a pillared porch had a veranda upstairs with French doors leading into a room. The oak-framed garage to the side could easily store three cars.

Jack had obviously done well for himself in publishing. It was exactly what she saw herself living in when she was married with children, she mused, as she followed behind him and Esther. It would suit her lifestyle as much as his.

Jack let himself into the house and switched off an alarm before opening the doors wide for them all to clamber through. It was a good thing there weren't any adjoining properties. Tamara was sure they would have woken everyone up. As it was, it was close to midnight and some of

Jack's neighbours were bound to be unimpressed. Thankfully, she wasn't working tomorrow.

Esther came towards her. 'This place is amazing, isn't it?' she whispered.

Tamara looked around the large hall with marble tiles on the floor, and a staircase in the middle leading to a galleried landing. The walls were covered in delicate cream striped wallpaper, a bank of photos of two boys covering one of them almost from skirting board to ceiling.

There were double doors to their left and they followed Jack into a sitting room that was the size of her whole flat. The couple had impeccable taste. Everything was grey and white with a dash of sunflower yellow here and there to break up its clinical feel. Despite itself, it felt warm and homely.

'Sit yourselves down, ladies, and I'll get more drinks.'

'I'll help,' Esther offered.

While they left her to perch on the leather settee, she ran a hand over the soft feel of it. How could they have chosen white with young children around?

Oscar came bouncing into the room after having disappeared to the bathroom. He sat down next to her. Her stomach rolled over as he rested a hand on her thigh. He'd told her several times that day that he was free and single. Not young, he had laughed, but definitely young at heart.

'I've had a great day.' He turned to face her. 'Not least because of the races but because I've had fun with you.'

Tamara blushed, delighted at his wide grin. 'I've had fun too,' she told him.

He took her hand and pulled her to her feet. 'Come on, I'll show you around. It's an amazing place.'

She didn't have much choice as he was already walking out of the room and towards the kitchen. Everyone else was in there and she could see why. The walls were covered in a row of white gloss cupboards from floor to ceiling. Florescent pink lighting on each base plinth gave the room a glow of an 80's disco. A large island held a sink within its black marble top and was lit up at the bottom too. But as eye-catching as the kitchen was, it was the bank of windows that opened up on to a large, landscaped garden that drew her eyes.

Outside, beyond most of the group who were sitting around a large wooden table, was a manicured garden. A vast array of shrubs and flowers were in pots or buried along the border around the fencing. In between, everything was illuminated by coloured lanterns. It all lent itself to a magical feel. Tamara guessed the children loved it.

Esther was sitting next to Jack, Giles, and Brett at the other side.

'Where's Richard?' Tamara wondered aloud.

'Gone to sleep the day off.' Jack pointed upstairs. 'There are six bedrooms. You're welcome to stay over if you like?'

'That depends on whose bed she will be sleeping in.' Oscar roared with laughter. 'Come on, I'll show you the rest of the house.'

Again, he pulled Tamara by the hand, this time up the stairs and on to the galleried landing. He opened one door to see Richard asleep, fully clothed, lying on his stomach.

'Can't take his ale.' He laughed again.

The next door opened into a young boy's room. A single bed in the shape of a racing car was on the far wall, toys piled high in several clear boxes beside a row of wardrobes.

'I'm not sure which twin sleeps in here, but this room is Jack and Natalie's.' Oscar pointed to a door and marched past it, stopping at the next. 'And this is a spare room.' He turned to Tamara, swaying slightly, his speech slurred. 'You can stay in here if you like.'

'Thanks. I'll let Esther know, and we can share.' Tamara stayed on the threshold but he pulled her inside and closed the door behind them.

'Or we can get to know each other better.'

Oscar's lips found hers as his body crushed up against her. Tamara found herself responding to his touch and in seconds she was kissing him back with vigour she could never recall having before. His lips moved to her neck, delicately brushing over her skin, making her moan in pleasure.

She realised that she was glad he wasn't married.

25

The whiskey Esther was drinking had lulled her into a false sense of security. She'd kicked her shoes off under the table. Brett and Giles were in the kitchen making coffee for everyone.

She was trying to keep her temper in check after glancing around Jack's house with envy. It was something she had always dreamed off – a loving husband, children, and a family home. Would she ever get that? Surely it wasn't too late for her.

The whiskey was warm as it went down, the night turning a little chilly. She shivered as a breeze floated over her bare shoulders.

'So tell me, Jack, how well do you get on with your wife?' she asked.

'I guess things could be better.' He ran a finger up and down her forearm, making her shiver even more. 'It's a good job we have the boys or the house would be so quiet.'

'Do you think you'll always be together?' Esther wanted to sound him out, even though she wasn't looking forward to her mission. She needed to keep him talking because if he didn't remove his hand she might slap it away and that would never do.

'I'd miss my boys if we separated but I wouldn't stay together for them. We all deserve a little love and happiness.'

'Have you ever been tempted to stray?' They stared at each other. She could see Jack's eyes shining with lust and knew if there were only the two of them he would have leaned across and kissed her. She needed to prepare herself for that moment, to make sure she didn't repel him.

'Not until now.' He paused. 'Sometimes you seem so familiar, as if I've met you before, and yet—'

A scream came from inside the house. For a moment, Esther froze as she looked at Jack. Then she got to her feet. 'Tamara!'

Jack was close behind as she ran through the kitchen and raced up the stairs, taking them two at a time. Another scream pierced the air, but this time it didn't sound so severe. Esther kept on searching. It was coming from her right.

She opened three doors, shouted Tamara's name, until she found them both. Oscar was on top of Tamara on the bed, undoing his belt with one hand, the other in the middle of Tamara's chest, pinning her down.

Tamara's hair was all over the place and her dress had been pushed to the top of her thighs. She had one shoe on, the other was nowhere to be seen.

'What the hell is going on?' Esther pulled Oscar away from Tamara.

Oscar turned to her with a frown as he staggered about, trying to steady himself. 'We were getting to know each other ... in the biblical sense.'

Esther leapt at Oscar and punched him in the face. 'You bastard! You should have stopped when she said no.'

'Esther!' Jack took hold of her forearm as she raised a fist to strike Oscar again. 'Stop. He wasn't doing anything wrong!'

'My mouth.' Oscar's hand was covered in blood as he drew it away from his mouth. 'You've split my lip.'

'I'll do more than that if you come anywhere near her again.' Esther relaxed her body in Jack's arms, hoping that he would think she was calming down. She turned back to look at Tamara who was sitting on the bed. Her eyes were wide but not with fear. It was more with horror, and she was looking at her, as if Tamara was scared that she would strike her next.

'You were screaming,' she protested. 'I thought he was attacking you.'

'He was tickling me,' Tamara said. 'It was a bit of fun.'

Oscar's hands went up in the air. 'I wasn't doing anything she didn't want me to.'

'I'm sorry. I thought you were ...' Everyone was looking at Esther. 'I thought he was ...' She turned and ran from the room.

Jack reached to stop her but she brushed his hand away.

She flew down the stairs and stopped in the hallway, turning around in a full circle, unsure what to do. How had she read the situation so wrong? She could have ruined everything. Jack might not even want to speak to her now. She had assaulted a member of his staff.

Stupid Esther.

She raced into the kitchen and retrieved her belongings, wrapping her pashmina shawl around her bare shoulders as she began to shiver.

'Esther, what's going on?' Tamara appeared in the doorway.

'I'm so sorry.' She turned to her before slipping on her shoes. 'I thought he was attacking you.'

Tamara shook her head. 'It's not me you should be apologising to. I can't believe you did that. What on earth made you hit him?'

'I heard you scream and I thought you were in trouble. I was only looking out for you.'

'I'm fine. I can look after myself, especially with Oscar. He's a pussy cat.'

'But I thought—'

'You didn't think! You just lashed out.' Tamara pinched the bridge of her nose before looking at her again. 'Look, it's late. We've all been drinking. I think I should call a cab.'

They stood in silence, neither knowing what to say. Esther wasn't sure how angry Tamara was. She had certainly sobered up pretty quickly.

Both women looked up as Jack came into the room.

'Jack, I'm so sorry,' Esther began, but he held up his hand for her to stop.

'He's fine. He's sleeping it off.' His face was unreadable too as he went past them and out into the garden to join Giles and Brett. They stayed in the kitchen, waiting for the cab in silence.

Finally, Esther was relieved to hear a vehicle pulling up outside. Tamara went to let Jack know they were leaving and then marched past her out into the driveway.

'I can't believe what you did,' she hissed as soon as the cab had moved away from the kerb. 'You're lucky to come away without an assault charge.'

Esther hung her head down for a moment. Having had

time to think about what to say, she took a deep breath before beginning.

'There was someone I knew – Amy Farmer. She was my best friend. We'd known each other since primary school. She was raped when she was sixteen.'

Tamara turned to her with a look of shock, so she continued.

'We lived two streets apart so we split up on the main road. He could have come after me but instead he went her way. I found out the next day.'

'That's terrible. Did they catch the man who did it?'

'No. Amy changed completely from that moment on. No one, not even me, could get her to realise it wasn't her fault. We'd been as thick as thieves until that day. We told each other everything and yet no amount of talking about it did any good.' Esther chanced a glance at Tamara as they stopped at traffic lights. 'She killed herself when she was eighteen. She couldn't take the shame.'

'You poor thing.' Tamara's tone seemed lighter now. 'And you thought Oscar was attacking me when I screamed?'

'So did Jack!'

'Oh, Esther, I'm so sorry. We were fooling around.'

'I'm so embarrassed.' She looked away momentarily. 'But Amy was like a sister to me.'

'It doesn't matter.' Tamara shook her head. 'I can understand why you reacted the way you did, but I hope it doesn't mean we lose the contract after all our hard work.'

'I'm sorry,' she repeated.

It was Tamara's turn to look out of the window. 'We'll have to keep our fingers crossed that Jack doesn't feel fit to remove us from his payroll.'

Esther said goodnight to Tamara as they arrived at her flat, and then she got the cab to drop her off in Earl's Court

Road. The night air was warm but her skin was hot anyway. She marched along, all the time trying to keep her fury locked away.

That fucking Oscar. He could have ruined everything. Why did he have to do that to Tamara?

It had brought memories flooding back as she had seen him pawing her. And now she had lost her temper in front of everyone.

She turned off the main road, walked past a bin and lashed out at it, giving it a swift palm slap. She banged at it again and again, groaning loudly.

A light went on at a window on the opposite side of the street. Esther hurried away. Tears streamed down her face as her anger inflated. What was wrong with her?

She needed to be liked by them. She *had* to be or else everything would fall apart around her.

She had invested so much in this. She couldn't let herself down now. Not after the hard work she had put in trying to like them all, fooling Jack.

Shit, she hadn't thought they might lose the contract. Tamara might fire her now. She would have to get in quick with apologies to everyone. It was imperative to keep Tamara on side. She was the key to everything at the moment.

Esther would have to prove her trustworthiness again. She would have to throw herself into the campaign for *Something's Got to Give,* and hope that the incident would blow over.

And pray that Tamara didn't find out that Amy Farmer was never a friend of hers. It was the first name that had popped into her head after the incident.

Amy Farmer was her probation officer.

26

Monday, 26 June

Tamara fastened the straps on her shoes just as the cab pulled up outside her flat. She quickly applied another layer of lipstick, checked her reflection in the hall mirror and was out in thirty seconds.

The driver had the side window open and a blast of warm air tried its best to cool the interior. It had been another scorching day. The weather had been the only topic of conversation lately. Everyone wanted it to break, although everyone wanted it to continue. It would be great if she was lying on a beach on a Greek island, she mused, but not in a stuffy city.

Her stomach flipped over in excitement as the cab made its way through the traffic towards Borough Market. She was meeting Oscar that evening, her treat to say sorry after Esther had assaulted him last Thursday. She was taking him to Roast. She'd dined there many times and when she'd mentioned it to him, he'd said it was one of his favourite places.

Even though they weren't on a date, Tamara still wondered what would happen after dinner. Not that she expected them to go straight back to his place and sleep together. She meant more in the sense of could this be the beginning of a new relationship.

She couldn't help but wonder what would have happened if Esther hadn't interrupted them. Would it have been a drunken one-night stand, or would it have led to something more fulfilling, more long term? She hoped he thought the same.

Borough Market, situated south of Southwark Cathedral, was one of Tamara's favourite places too. With its glazed roof and green, metal girders, it almost felt as if they were outdoors. Before it had opened to the general public, it had been a wholesale market, providing produce to greengrocers alongside Covent Garden. Not only had it been featured in several iconic movies, her favourite being *Bridget Jones's Diary*, but the range of speciality foods was second to none.

The aroma would always hit Tamara first, people freely walking round with tasters – cheese, baked bread, and meats galore. Then the noise of the hustle and bustle. When she was younger, Tamara had enjoyed nothing more than walking around the aisles herself, tasting all the different European products.

Roast was on the first floor and overlooked the market stalls. Oscar was already seated when she got out of the lift and was shown to her table. He stood up as she walked towards him.

'Darling, Tamara.' He kissed her on the cheek before

hugging her warmly. The host pulled out a chair and placed a napkin on her lap when she was comfortable. He introduced their waitress for the evening and then left them to decide what to eat.

'I hope you don't mind but I took the liberty of ordering a bottle of champagne,' Oscar said.

'No, that's fine.' Tamara nodded as he went to pour her a glass, trying not to panic about the cost. But it was all part and parcel of the publishing world. Hardly a day went by when she wasn't invited to some swanky restaurant or bar to launch a new book, hear an author talk or celebrate at an event. There were only so many canapés she could stomach though, and eating dinner in the week was a luxury at the moment.

'I want to stress how deeply sorry I am again, Oscar,' she said again, launching into her apology once they had chosen their food. 'Esther is sorry too. I do know she is beyond inconsolable.'

Oscar brushed away her comment and took another sip from his glass. 'Please, it's all in the past. Jack explained what had happened to her friend. It was one of those things.'

Tamara smiled at him warmly. She could still see the remains of the scab where his lip had split and was yet to heal fully. It had been a terrible end to a wonderful day but luckily everything had gone smoothly afterwards. She had rung to speak to Jack the next day and sent a box of organic cupcakes.

As their meals were brought over, they settled down into the evening. The food was always delicious at Roast and she tucked into her meal of red mullet with olive braised vegetables and chargrilled artichokes. Oscar had sirloin steak on the bone from the grill with chimichurri and chips. When she saw him stuffing it into his mouth as if he hadn't eaten in a week, she rather wished she hadn't. He was a messy eater.

They chatted amicably about the launch of the book, before they moved on to the topic of the weather. But there didn't seem to be any chemistry between them. Oscar's laugh seemed quite false at times, hers too.

Tamara realised she didn't like him too much when she was sober, and actually thought, in retrospect, that Esther had done her a favour. He was far too boastful for her liking. The only thing they had in common seemed to be work.

She removed her napkin and pressed it to her lips. Ah well, she wasn't going to find love with him then. As she was about to ask for the bill, she noticed a couple being shown to their table.

Tamara smiled when she saw who it was. It was an old friend of hers, Sophie Wilburt. She and Sophie had gone to the same school and remained close friends for a number of years. She waved but when the woman caught her eye, she quickly looked away. Tamara put her hand down quickly, hoping Oscar hadn't noticed. But he was too busy studying the dessert menu.

Tears brimmed in her eyes. Sophie had been a good friend until Tamara's relationship with Michael had ended. Tamara never thought she'd be snubbed by her. Not after all this time too.

'I think we'll call it a night.' Oscar laid the dessert menu on the table. 'I'm not one for coffee for coffee's sake, and I have an early start in the morning. Would you like to share a cab home?'

Tamara shook her head vehemently but then realised

that Oscar was only looking to give her a lift. Her cheeks reddened, but at least she was relieved he didn't want to take things further, and the night hadn't entirely been wasted. Bridges hadn't been burned but firmly built again. Now all she needed to do was concentrate on getting the book launched.

27

Tuesday, 27 June

Esther had called into House of Fraser on Victoria Street before heading home. She was going out again that evening. She fancied hitting the hotel bars and picking up some unsuspecting man who was away on business. If she was lucky, she might get a good bout of sex. If she was unlucky, she'd get away with his wallet and whatever else she could sell on.

She was still smiling to herself, thinking about her earlier conversation with Tamara. She'd been telling Esther that dinner with Oscar hadn't turned out so great. In a way, she had been happy about that. She didn't want Tamara to end up with anyone like him. All he thought about was himself.

As she walked to the tube station, she heard her name being shouted. She turned her head. Jack stood across the road, waving to get her attention.

She waited for him to reach her, moving to one side so

as not to stop the flow of pedestrians. This could go one of two ways, she surmised, after the fool she'd made of herself on their return from Ascot. Although she had apologised profusely over and over about hitting out at Oscar, she still recalled the night with embarrassment. It could have meant the end of everything. Was he now catching up with her away from the office to warn her about her behaviour?

To her relief, Jack was smiling when he drew level with her.

'I've been to a meeting,' he said. 'I was on my way home when I spotted you. Do you fancy a quick drink?' He pulled his shirt away from his torso. 'That is, if you want to spend any time with someone who is hot, and possibly very smelly.'

Esther's laugh was false but he didn't seem to realise. Slowly and surely, she was reeling him in. She nodded enthusiastically.

'That would be nice.'

They walked to the Albert, each catching up with what the other was doing work wise. She stayed outside while he went in to get drinks. The pavement seemed to be as full as the bar, and even if it was noisier, it was definitely cooler.

He joined her moments later and they stood together. Unsure what to say next, they smiled at each other. To give him his dues, Jack was great eye candy and really good company, with a dry sense of humour that she loved, but still, every time he touched her, she had to stop herself from slapping away his hand.

Now he was asking her why she was single. She wanted to say why don't you mind your own business, but instead, she pushed away her anger and concentrated on the task in hand, which was lying through her teeth.

'I've been on my own now for six months after a long relationship went sour. It finished at my insistence, though.'

'What happened?'

Jack leaned across the table for her hand but she managed to pick up her glass at the same time. Again, she began to talk about her made-up life.

'We were going nowhere but I don't think either of us wanted to break up.' She smiled at him shyly. 'The sex was non-existent; we hardly spent any time together, like passing ships in the night. I'd do my own thing more than want to be with him. He'd be off out with friends.'

A car horn peeped as a driver cut another up and she jumped. She began again, on a roll now.

'Occasionally we got together, maybe a holiday here and there but we were both ready to get back to routine and normality as quickly as possible. I think in the end we became more like flatmates and even that wasn't enough. Eventually I left him and lodged with a friend.'

'Ouch.'

She shrugged. 'Much better than staying together for the wrong reasons, don't you think?'

'I guess.' Jack took another sip of his drink.

'Tell me about your children,' she said.

Jack's wide smile made her so angry. He had what she would never have. She'd always wanted a family of her own but she doubted any man would stay with her long enough.

'They are two great boys. To be honest, I wish I was around more for them during the week and I'm always busy most weekends even when I am at home. But I suppose it means they can have the best of everything.'

'Are things any better with Natalie?' Esther fingered the stem of her wine glass, as she tried to get him talking about his personal life again. She hadn't learned as much as she'd hoped after the trip to Ascot, because of the scuffle with Oscar interrupting everything. 'I don't mean to pry, but ...'

Jack sighed. 'It's complicated.'

Esther waited for him to open up more but he looked ahead wistfully. Maybe he felt as much of a failure as she did in her life. Good, she smirked.

They chatted for a few more minutes and then Jack downed the rest of his drink. 'I need to get back, sadly ... I've really enjoyed your company.'

'We could do this again?' Esther suggested, staring directly at him. 'I've enjoyed it too.'

He leaned forward and kissed her on each cheek. 'I'd like that.' He smiled.

She stared into his eyes. She knew that look he was giving her had meaning.

Once on the tube home, Esther wiped at her cheeks where Jack had put his lips. Why did he have so much and yet clearly thought he could have more? He wanted his wife and she was sure he wanted her as well. Of course, she would have him but, despite that, why couldn't he be satisfied with what he had?

It was past 8.00 p.m. when she exited the tube station and made the last few minutes' walk home. She couldn't be bothered going out again now.

She turned into Trebovir Road, and stopped. There was a man sitting on the steps. She recognised the stoop of his shoulders first. Then the sweep of his dirty-blond hair, the tuft of a beard. Large hands were clasped together in front of him as he smoked a cigarette.

It was Danny Bristol.

She wondered whether to double back, but even as he turned his head, caught her eye, and stood up, she realised there was no point in running. He was a persistent bastard.

If she didn't speak to him now, he would come back until she did. He might even break in to her flat and wait for her. She couldn't have him doing that, especially knowing what he would be looking for. If he found it, he would take her money too.

With heavy feet but shoulders held high, she made the last few steps between them. Maybe the anger she felt towards Jack would serve its purpose after all.

As Danny jumped down the steps to street level, Esther took a deep breath. It was time to sort this out.

28

'Hello, Tiger,' Danny greeted Esther. 'Long time no see.'

Esther managed a faint smile. 'How did you find me?' she asked.

'I have my ways.' Danny's grin was in no way friendly. 'It's not hard to keep tabs on you, even with a wig on. I prefer your hair blonde though. That red looks cheap and the black is so *severe*.'

Esther said nothing. He was trying to unnerve her, intimidate her but she wasn't the weakling she had been a few years ago. Getting what she wanted from him had been part of the bigger plan too.

'I saw you in the city,' he continued. 'I followed you to Westminster, watched you for a couple of days. I thought you lived there but then I realised you must work there.' He sneered at her. 'Quite the little wage earner now, aren't you? I wonder what your new boss would think if she knew the real you, hmm, Tiger?'

Danny had always called her that. She'd met him when she was seventeen and he was twenty-one. They'd been in the same pub and a fight had broken out. She'd tried to stop a man from attacking her friend. Danny had pulled her away as she'd jumped on the man's back. She'd ended up giving him a feisty kick in the balls and doing a runner.

She'd avoided the pub for a while because of his threats but when she'd bumped into him two weeks later, he'd been all over her. They'd started dating and only when it was too late to leave did she realise he'd reeled her in. He'd told her they had a connection, that he wanted to be with her. But he wasn't really interested in her, only what she could do for him.

The relationship had been damaging. It was on-off, brutal, and reinforced everything she thought of herself: she was a bad one, she didn't deserve to be loved, and she wasn't going to get the happy ever after that she craved.

Danny should have been her saviour but instead he'd got her hooked on drugs. She'd started dealing for him, and eventually selling herself to pay off the debts she racked up with him. Back then, she'd been so wasted, she hadn't realised any of this, but now she was clean, she saw him for what he was: a manipulating leech.

She stepped around him, almost flinching as she waited for his hand to reach out and grab her. 'Are you coming in?'

He turned and followed her into the hallway. She closed the front door behind them, took him through to her flat and into the living room. Watched as he eyed the place up.

'Not bad,' he stated.

She laughed. 'It's a shit hole.'

'Better than some places I've stayed. Surprised you can afford it on your own though.' He glared at her. 'You do live here alone, don't you?'

Esther nodded. She went through to the kitchen. There was a half-open bottle of wine in the fridge.

'Don't you have any lager?' Danny asked. 'Or whiskey?'

She shook her head. 'I could make you a coffee instead?'

He grabbed a handful of her hair and pulled her backwards towards him. 'I don't want a fucking coffee,' he seethed, spittle flying over her face. 'But I do want what you have of mine.'

'Ow, let me go!' Esther squealed, but Danny's grip tightened.

'Where is it?'

'Don't Danny,' she pleaded, fearing losing a fistful of hair if he didn't loosen his fingers.

He brought his face down next to hers. 'Where is it?' he demanded.

'I spent it,' she told him. 'I had to. I needed things.'

'I mean the gun.'

'I don't have that either.' His fingers tightened and she yelped. 'I sold it on.'

'Who to?'

'Some guy in a pub. He gave me a hundred quid for it.'

'You sold my fucking gun?'

His fist rose in the air and she lowered her chin into her chest. She couldn't let him mark her face.

'I'm sorry! The gun was hot and I got rid of it for you. You do believe me, don't you?'

'I'll never believe anything you say. But the old crowd misses you.' He sneered.

She didn't want to think about the others. She wished she could wipe out her past but it was burned into her memories. She had been nothing when she was with them. She was worth more than that now.

'I know you still have it.' Danny broke into her thoughts. 'I always know when you're lying.'

It was then that Esther clicked in. He would never harm her because then she couldn't tell him where the gun was.

Of course, he might ransack the place and find it in time but if someone heard him and called the police, he wouldn't want to draw attention to himself. Because the gun was evidence against him. It linked him to at least two murders. She was going to take it to the police once she was on her way out of London.

'Why don't we have that drink?' she said.

Releasing his grip, Danny pushed Esther forwards. She managed to stay on her feet, but her hip connected with the corner of the worktop, making her grimace. Pain shot through her, yet she didn't cry out. She wouldn't give him the satisfaction.

She rubbed at her head before she searched out a bottle of vodka. All the while, Danny's eyes flicked around the flat. Esther could see him searching out potential hiding places. She wondered why he wasn't trashing the place right now.

She had to get rid of him, make sure he never came back.

This man had ruined her life. *He* was the one who had hooked her on drugs. *He'd* made her sleep with his friends to pay off his debts. *He* was the one who had beaten her if she ever crossed him.

He was the one who had said he loved her. Yet, for every punch, slap, bite, or kick, Esther had vowed to get revenge one day.

While he wasn't looking, she slipped her hand behind the bread bin and located the knife. There were several of them strategically placed around the flat for this very occasion. She tucked it into the waistband of her trousers before he came back.

She handed him a glass. 'Cheers.'

Esther kept her hand on the bottle. She had to look for every opportunity to get Danny out of her flat. It wouldn't do to hit him with it. He was harder than that, could retaliate and hurt her. But she did know what she could use instead.

'I need the bog.' Danny stood up. 'Is it through there?'

She nodded. It was possible he'd rip the bath panel off as soon as he stepped foot in the room. But he wasn't leaving with the gun, or any of her money. Behind the settee was another weapon. At the last minute, she changed her mind about the knife and reached for that instead.

'Oh, and Dan?'

His hand rested on the doorknob as he turned to her.

She drew back her arm and with all her force, hit him in the face with a baseball bat. Blood splattered across the room from his mouth and he dropped to his knees with a groan.

It was the element of surprise that she needed as she raised her arms up again.

29

Esther sat on the floor with her back to the wall, staring at Danny. By the time her anger was spent, his face was a bloody mess and he wasn't moving. She'd prodded his foot several times to no avail. But she couldn't get herself to move towards him, because she would be disappointed if he was alive.

She was glad that she'd taken the bat to his head; that he had suffered as much pain as he'd inflicted on her over the years. She wouldn't be sorry one little bit if he was dead. Well, apart from having to dispose of his body without being caught.

But then, as panic set in about how much trouble she'd be in, she crept across to him. His face was swelling already, bruising forming underneath all the blood. His hair was matted in the stuff. She reached for his wrist and felt for a pulse. There was nothing.

'Dan.' She nudged him in the chest. When there was no response, she squeezed his arm. She pressed her fingers to his neck, ignoring the unpleasant feeling of his blood on the tips. Still there was no pulse.

He couldn't possibly survive the amount of times she had hit him.

She had killed him.

There was no hysteria. She couldn't quite understand her feelings but it seemed as if a weight had been lifted from her. Gone were the times where she would have to look over her shoulder, dread the thought of what he would have done to her now that he'd found her. He would have made her work for him again.

She kneeled beside him. First, she checked his pockets. Finding his wallet, she checked through it, taking out the notes. She placed the leather pouch by her side, aiming to get rid of that tomorrow. She searched through the inside of his jacket, stopping when her hand felt something squishy. She pulled out a large clear bag. Her eyes widened when she saw what it contained.

Amphetamines. Speed, all in tiny bags measured out and ready for distribution.

Shit. She ran a hand through her hair as the urge to take a bag and snort it up her nose right now became so strong that she shuddered. Quickly, she put it with the wallet, vowing to get rid of that in the morning too.

For the next half hour, she got to work cleaning her flat, hoping to erase all trace that Danny had been there. Then she set to work on him. First, she covered his head with a plastic bag to stop the blood from leaking again – really, she couldn't stand to see the sight of what she had done – and then she dragged him to the front door. She removed his shoes in case they might make a noise along the floor. By this time, it was midnight; far too early to make a move.

She waited until 2.00 a.m. before opening her front door and creeping outside. The light in the hallway came on automatically, and she cursed. She wouldn't be able to break the bulb. She would have to be quick.

Most people in her block would be asleep by now, and at least she didn't have any stairs to bump him down. If anyone did come home, or hear her and come to investigate, she would have to say he had knocked on the front door and begged for help and that she was going to ring the police. That was if she could get the bag off his head quick enough.

She would have to be extremely quiet.

She unbolted the back door and crept out, closing it quietly behind her. At the bottom of the garden were the remains of an old sectional garage. The roof leaked and it had weeds growing inside it, but it was full of building materials, and rubbish collected over years. Esther had searched it out as soon as she'd arrived, and it was clear that no one went in there.

Inside was a large, plastic bunker full of compost. It took twenty minutes to remove enough of it to make a hole to put Danny's body inside. Getting him to somewhere else would have been much trickier.

She wasn't sure if he would start to smell, hidden inside the compost, but by that time she would be long gone.

It had taken her what felt like an age to get Danny out of her flat, along the hallway, and through the back door. Once outside, she felt a bit better but knew she still had to be quiet. Sweat poured from her at the exertion. Rigor mortis hadn't quite set in as she'd pushed his body into the compost and covered him over.

Afterwards she rested for a minute. No lights had come on in any of the flats or surrounding buildings so she'd gone inside. She quickly cleaned the hallway as best as she could afterwards. No one would notice a few extra stains on the threadbare carpet.

Once back inside her flat, she took a shower to rid herself of all the dirt and blood. It was nearing 4.00 a.m. and, even though she was exhausted, she wasn't going to get any sleep now. Maybe she could …

The white powder in the bags was calling her. She picked one out, placed it on the palm of her hand, staring at it. She wanted it so badly but she was scared of the consequences.

Yet after what she'd just done, she needed something. A little bit wouldn't hurt to take off the edge.

30

Thursday, 6 July

The night before the launch of *Something's Got to Give* held mixed emotions for Esther.

First, she had enjoyed being friendlier with Jack over the past two weeks after the debacle with Oscar.

Second, she had been exhausted after pulling some really late nights to get everything ready in time for publication day. She and Tamara had worked flat out.

She had surprised herself by quite enjoying it but she had been sleeping badly, the images of Danny still as vivid in her mind as if the attack had happened yesterday. The amphetamines had helped her to forget but she had taken more than she would have liked. Her ex turning up on her doorstep had served as a sharp reminder about how gullible she used to be.

At first she had taken what she'd done to him in her stride, but once the anger had gone, the panic set in. She'd been so freaked that she'd taken more of the speed, which had had a calming effect.

But then she'd had a bit of a panic when her neighbour from above had asked if she'd heard anything the night she had killed Danny. She'd told him she was a sound sleeper; had asked if anything was missing or if he'd noticed anything untoward afterwards, and when he'd said no, she'd prayed that would be the last of it. He didn't seem the snooping type and, besides, it didn't look as if anyone had gone into the garage after her, once she'd come out. She'd checked on several occasions since, to make sure. In time, she hoped he would forget hearing anything, unless he was prompted, of course, and she'd be long gone by then.

Still, seeing Danny had been satisfying. In the end, it had been messy, but at least she knew it was over now. There was no point dwelling on the past.

Over the next few days, as the launch had drawn nearer, word had begun to spread about *Something's Got to Give*. The key bloggers they had targeted started sharing their reviews, social media lit up with the hashtag #DidSheDoIt and pre-order sales went through the roof on all the digital platforms.

On the night of publication, the book was sitting at number five in the UK Amazon charts, and print sales were heading for a spot on the *Sunday Times* bestseller list. Everyone was buzzing about its initial success.

Esther was eager to see Jack's house again, and was even more intrigued about meeting some of his family and friends. Especially his wife.

She had arranged to meet Tamara at Holland Park tube station, and was only a few minutes late.

'Hi!' Tamara waved at her as she came up the steps from the tube and out onto the pavement.

Tamara was dressed to impress in some navy and white number that had probably cost a small fortune. Her hair was blow-dried, make-up fresh too. She looked really nice, to be fair. Since they'd met, Tamara had taken more interest in herself; obviously, Esther noted, she was a good influence.

'I thought I'd be the one who was late.' Esther held up the gift bag she was carrying. 'Had to stop for the champers.'

'Ooh, great, thanks. You look lovely!'

'You too.' Even now she wasn't used to Tamara complimenting her all the time. 'Is that dress new?'

Tamara nodded. 'Got it at the weekend.' They began to walk. 'Can you remember the last time we were here and you split Oscar's lip?' Her laughter came out as a guffaw and she all but snorted.

Esther pretended to be embarrassed. 'Don't remind me. I'm still so humiliated about it.'

'From what I've seen of him afterwards, I'm glad I didn't sleep with him. He's so pompous.' She turned to her. 'Where did you learn to hit like that? I never did ask you at the time.'

'I'm the only girl in a long line of male cousins. I was such a tomboy when I was younger and I learned to handle myself.'

'Sounds like fun.' Tamara laughed. 'I used to play rough and tumble with my brothers but mainly I played with my sister. My favourite toy was my Barbie doll.'

'Action Man for me.' She laughed too. She hadn't even seen one of those, never mind played with one.

The gates were open when they arrived at Jack's house. Blue and white balloons hung from each post and there were streamers thrown across the many ornamental bushes.

'Everything matches my dress,' Tamara giggled.

Esther forced a smile and some canned laughter. She

was more concerned about getting inside and checking out Jack's wife.

Low music and voices swelled as they crunched across the gravel towards the house. Bunting was strung above the front doors, which were open too. A large-scale photo of Simone holding her book with a huge, soppy grin stood proud on an easel.

The night was warm as they entered the house, giving everything a tropical feel. They each took a glass of champagne from the waitress in the hallway before moving into the lounge.

Simone was surrounded by people, Jack and Arabella on the periphery. Her smile lit up the room as she saw them and waved. She looked so happy, even Esther enjoyed seeing it. Simone seemed far from that frightened little mouse they first saw at the pitch. There was a large stack of books at her side, ready for her to sign. She seemed in her element at last.

Esther wished she could be that carefree one day. Maybe she could write a book, or have some sort of goal to aspire to. She had never set out to do anything in her life. Simone would be leaving a legacy for her family, her children, whereas what would she be leaving behind? Chaos? She giggled to herself, coughing to hide it.

'Ah, here they are.' Jack's arm came out as they walked towards him. He was wearing expensive jeans and a white designer shirt, open at the collar. A waft of his aftershave caught her nose and she breathed in the smell of him.

'Ladies and gentlemen,' Jack added, 'may I introduce you to the best PR company I have had the pleasure of working with. This is Tamara Parker-Brown of Parker-Brown PR, and her lovely assistant, Esther Smedley.'

Esther's smile was waning now, unable to believe Jack

had called her that. She was way more than the hired help and well he knew. But it didn't matter because everyone wanted to talk to Tamara. Esther might as well have been invisible.

She stood by Tamara's side but not one person said anything to her. They were all over Tamara and Simone. Simone, she could understand as it was her book launch and publication day, but Tamara?

How could she not bring her into the conversation? On balance, she had been the one who had instigated all of this so she shouldn't be ignored.

A few minutes later, with no one attempting to speak to her, she walked through into the kitchen before she lost her temper. Like the first night they'd been there, the bank of windows in the kitchen had been pulled back to welcome the garden into the house. Esther was so glad she'd been able to enjoy the hot summer. She'd hated being cooped up last year.

'Don't hit me.'

She heard a familiar voice and turned to see Oscar shielding his face. He said the same thing every time he saw her; the joke was getting old now but she still smiled.

It almost slipped from her face when she saw that Ben was standing by his side. He had heeded her warning to keep his distance since she had thrown coffee all over him. It had surprised her when he'd kept quiet about the incident, even more so since she had hit out at Oscar that night. Yet he didn't fool her at all. Ben was a good actor, the same as she was a brilliant actress. She could always recognise a bully.

She'd seen traits of herself in him, of Danny Bristol too. Always thinking he was going to get the upper hand. She wondered how Ben was at home, and how he treated his wife and children. Did he rule the house or was that a mask he hid behind too?

True colours always emerged. She should know. She tried so hard to keep her dark side hidden, yet it sometimes popped up unexpectedly.

'Oscar!' She put a hand on his arm, the closest he was getting to her. 'Everything seems to be going well.'

Oscar nodded. 'All down to you. I don't know why you let Tamara take all the credit.'

'Who me? Well, I am *just* her assistant.' Her voice came out harsher than she had intended but Oscar laughed.

Ben downed his drink and excused himself. Esther watched him until he had left the room.

'Well, I doubt you'll be short of work again because, without you, she wouldn't have done all this.' Oscar was still talking. He clinked his glass to hers and then downed the remaining liquid in one go. 'Would you like another?'

She nodded, if only to get him to leave.

Laughter rang in the air again. She looked to where it was coming from. Through the open doors to the sitting room, she could see Jack. Next to him was a man who looked very much like an older version of him. The woman by his side had Jack's eyes and nose. She said something to Natalie and they looked in her direction before laughing.

Overcome by loathing, Esther reached out a hand to steady herself on the kitchen worktop. She stood for a minute, breathless and overcome with nausea.

Jack spotted her as he came into the kitchen.

'Not again,' he laughed. 'What is it with you and champagne?'

His eyes were twinkling, his mouth in a smile so she could see there was no malice. But there were several people milling around so Esther couldn't express what she'd thought about his earlier introduction.

Jack came and stood next to her. 'You look amazing in that dress,' he whispered. 'One of these nights, I'm going to see what's underneath it.'

Esther snorted with laughter. Oh, he really did know how to lay on the charm.

'In your dreams,' she whispered back.

'Yes please.' He grinned and then reached past her for another bottle.

Esther followed him with her eyes, a lazy grin forming. He was still hers for the taking.

31

Feeling like a spare part, Esther decided to go back to join Tamara. She was talking to the couple she'd spotted earlier, with Jack's wife.

'Esther, let me introduce you to a few people.' Tamara linked an arm through hers. As all eyes turned her way, that familiar state of panic invaded her senses. She could feel her skin reddening but she managed to stay calm this time.

'These are Jack's parents, Reginald and Gabrielle. And this—' Tamara pointed to the woman beside them '—is Jack's wife, Natalie.'

Natalie Maitland wasn't quite what Esther had expected after the conversations she'd had with Jack. Of course, she'd seen photographs of her dotted around the house, but she'd assumed as his love had faded for her that she must have let herself go. But the image standing before them was every bit of someone who took great care of her appearance.

Even in kitten heels she was as tall as Jack, her pale lilac dress showing off toned arms and legs. She flicked away long, blonde hair, revealing blue eyes. French manicured nails had a line of rose gold separating the white tip from the shimmering pink. Her smile was welcoming but Esther could tell it was false as she held out her hand.

'I've heard so much about you.' Natalie looked her up and down, obvious to everyone that she was checking her out.

'Only good things, I hope.' Esther could see the woman's smile was false. 'I'm really pleased to be working with Jack and his team. There's so much I can learn from them too.'

'Indeed. Jack speaks highly of you.' Natalie turned away from her and addressed Tamara. 'I'm sure he'll be working with you in the future. He has some marvellous books coming out.'

Esther stood like a lemon again as she was rudely dismissed.

She wasn't into this socialising lark. She found it very hard to make small talk, even when on her perkiest behaviour. So much crap about this and that just to make people feel special.

A shadow crossed in front of her and she looked up to see Jack's father.

'And who are you?' he asked.

Esther took a deep breath. 'I'm Esther Smedley. I work with Tamara as—'

'Her assistant, Dad.' Jack came to her side. 'I told you that earlier.'

Esther stiffened. How could he put her down again?

'You look familiar.' Jack's mother peered at her.

'I don't know why,' she replied.

'Have we met before?'

Esther shook her head, feeling heat building on her cheeks. She turned to Tamara but she was busy chatting to Natalie, laughing about something.

'Maybe you've waited on me at one of the many charity

events I go to?' Gabrielle nodded as if answering her own question. 'Are you positive you weren't a waitress at the V&A, for the Women's Institute summer party?'

Esther nodded slowly. 'I'm positive.'

'I could have sworn you were handing out drinks there … my mistake.'

'No, definitely not me.' Esther needed to move away before she said something she regretted. 'Will you excuse me for a moment?'

She went outside. If she wasn't careful, she was going to blow her top again. How dare those women insinuate that she was working class fodder.

There were so many guests in the garden area that it was hard not to stare at people. Suave couples, groups of women gossiping, groups of men no doubt trying to outdo one another. But everyone seemed to be smiling, laughing and joking, enjoying the ambience.

She dug her nails into the palms of her hands. Why couldn't she have a good time? She didn't fit in, no matter what she did. No matter how hard she tried.

She heard a noise and turned her head. Jack was walking towards her, a goofy smile on his face.

'Piss off,' she told him.

If he was taken aback by her language, he didn't show it.

'I'm sorry about that,' he said. 'I made a hash of things. I didn't want to bring you to anyone's attention.'

'So, you tell everyone I'm just an assistant – twice? You humiliated me in front of everyone, your parents, and your *wife*. And she's a nice piece of work, isn't she? Trying to put me in my place. What's her problem?'

'She doesn't have a problem. I do.' Jack stepped closer. 'If I spoke highly of you, people might see that I have feelings for you and I don't want anyone to know.'

The last rays of the evening sun hid his features as it showed him in silhouette. But Esther could tell he was being sincere.

'It was my fault,' he added. 'I should have introduced you properly.'

'Yes, you should.'

He held his hands up in surrender. 'Consider me chastised.'

He was smiling now, as if everything was all right because he had apologised. Esther reined in her temper.

'Jack!' Natalie appeared in the kitchen, beckoning to him. 'You're wanted for speeches.'

'Better run back to wifey.' Esther raised her eyebrows in mock jest. 'And I suppose I'd better go and do my assistant duties.'

'You're not going to let me forget this, are you?' They walked together towards the house.

'It will take a lot of persuasion,' she whispered.

Tamara was waiting by the door. 'Let's get some photos to share with the press.'

Esther nodded. It was the last thing she wanted to do, but she turned on the charm as she went back inside and joined everyone in celebratory poses.

Everything went without a hitch. It was all smiles and applause, and happy people congratulating Simone. Arabella said a few words about her client and her latest book. Then it was Jack's turn to do the same.

'Finally, I'd like to raise a glass to the team behind Parker-Brown PR. To Tamara Parker-Brown, whose tenacity and vision undoubtedly helped *Something's Got to Give* to be seen in all the right places, and Esther Smedley, the best wingman one could ever wish for.'

Everyone raised their glasses. Esther stared at Jack as he

caught her looking, eyes smiling, an expression that he was hoping to be forgiven. She knew his game but for now, it was too much. She lowered her eyes.

The minute the congratulations were over, she put down her glass and slipped out of the room, intending to leave unnoticed. This world was phonier than she was. So many people had annoyed her that evening.

'Esther!' Tamara shouted after her as she disappeared into the hallway. 'Where are you going?'

'I'm tired.' Esther didn't even turn to face her. 'I'll see you tomorrow.'

'Wait!' Tamara touched her arm. 'Is something wrong?'

She paused, trying to find the words to speak through her anger. 'I was made a fool of earlier.'

'I don't follow.'

'Well, you wouldn't because you've never been called an *assistant* and then supposedly recognised because everyone thinks you're only good enough to be a waitress.'

'It was only mistaken identity.' Tamara shook her head. 'I'm sure she didn't mean anything by it.'

A couple walked past. 'Goodnight. Hope to see you again soon, Tamara.'

'Absolutely.' Tamara beamed. 'I'll be in touch.'

Esther shook her head. *Had* she become invisible? Her fingers balled up into a fist and she fought to keep her hand down by her side, to stop it from smashing into Tamara's face like it had done with Oscar. It didn't matter who she hit out at. It just had to be someone.

She tried to calm her breathing, force the hatred and anger down. It needed to be contained before she did something else she would regret.

A waiter came past holding a tray, several full glasses of

champagne alongside a few empty ones. Esther realised she had two choices about how the night could end.

She picked up two glasses and nodded to Tamara. 'Come and sit with me in the garden.'

She had to calm down before she blew her cover. It was getting harder by the day to contain herself. If she wasn't careful, she was going to spoil everything.

Because even if she had been a waitress at one of the charity events that Gabrielle Maitland attended, it wasn't where she had first seen her.

32

Friday, 7 July

It was past 1.00 a.m. when Tamara finally staggered through her front door. High on endorphins as well as fizz, she felt elated that the launch had gone down phenomenally well.

Most of the guests, as well as Simone and Arabella, had left about eleven-thirty, but the party had continued into the garden. Esther had disappeared around midnight and quite frankly Tamara had been pleased. One minute she was laughing and giggling; the next she was so maudlin. She didn't understand her at times. She was so likeable but there was something about her that she couldn't quite put her finger on.

She wondered if Esther was as lonely as she was, and all the attention they'd been getting from Jack and his team might have taken its toll. She'd noticed Esther and Jack chatting in the garden, heads close together as if they were planning something, but when she'd asked her about it, Esther had shrugged and said she couldn't remember. It seemed odd, but then again, with the champagne swimming around in Tamara's veins at the moment, she doubted she'd remember much in the morning.

She slipped off her heels and threw herself on to the settee, laughing out loud. She was too wired up to sleep, wishing she could lie in tomorrow morning, but there was so much to do. Tamara had met many potential clients and she wanted to follow through with them while the leads were hot.

She'd counted nine business cards that had been thrust into her hands that evening. One man asked if she would run the social media platforms for his business. Obviously, she'd told him she was inundated with work. She'd giggled to herself when he then said he would pay whatever it took.

She pulled herself up from the settee and went into the kitchen. She took a bottle of water from the fridge and gulped back as much as she could. The iciness took her breath away and she coughed. But at least that might stop the headache being so bad in the morning.

Even when she went to bed, she couldn't sleep. The evening was on replay through her mind, her ears ringing with the sound of music and conversation.

Things were finally turning a corner for her, the episode with Michael becoming a distant memory. She couldn't be happier.

But she had to admit, now that the #DidSheDoIt campaign was gathering momentum, it was actually down to Esther.

No, she thought, she should give herself some credit. Esther might have started everything but it was because of her hard work and vision that they had succeeded.

Tamara had noticed in the short time they'd worked together that, although she was very focussed on some things, Esther lost interest in others rather quickly. Esther was always after the next shiny object, whereas she would prefer to sit back and work with what she had, rather than step on to the bandwagon of ideas. Sometimes doing that kind of thing was a waste of time and effort. She was happy to try new things, but she didn't have a lot of time to waste.

She smiled as she stretched out like a cat in the bed. Someone had actually called her driven that evening. She'd had to stop from laughing in his face. It was only when she was coming home in the taxi that she thought about it, and she *was* driven. She had found out the hard way how to become a success in business by making mistakes, learning from them, and carrying on. Other people might have given up a long time ago, admitted defeat. But no, she'd kept on going.

And she'd succeeded. *Something's Got to Give* would be the making of her as well as Simone Byatt.

Things were definitely on the way up for her. She deserved her success because she'd proved that she was strong.

Whether that was down to her, or Esther giving her the confidence and belief she needed, it didn't matter. For now, she would tuck away her niggles and doubts and celebrate her success.

33

Esther's journey into work seemed to go on forever. Standing in a packed tube with a head full of banging drums and a mouth like a cesspit wasn't her idea of fun. She'd thought of staying in bed, saying she was sick, but she also needed to know what she'd said and done. She could only remember the evening up until 10.00 p.m. when she had taken a little amphetamine to give her a lift.

She hoped she hadn't embarrassed herself, but come on, assistant? She was so much more than that. She'd been well educated, enjoying school immensely and even though the incident had stopped her going on to further education and university, she'd relished the opportunity to learn later in life.

She heard her phone ring as she was coming up from the tube at Victoria and scrambled to get it out of her bag in time. Jack's name flashed up on the screen.

'I'm so sorry about last night,' he spoke before she could. 'I tried to find you again but Tamara told me that you'd left. I really didn't mean to upset you.'

'You didn't. I was tired. It's been a busy week.' Esther

wasn't going to let him know he had got to her. At the same time, she sighed with relief. She must have behaved fairly decent or else he wouldn't be sounding her out now. He didn't have to ring her; he could have gone through Tamara if he was disappointed in her behaviour.

She heard him take a deep breath. 'Natalie is away with the boys next weekend and I wondered if you'd like to spend Saturday with me, at the house?'

Her smile widened. 'I'd love to, but I'm sure Natalie wouldn't like it if I was there with you alone.'

'I can switch the cameras off while you're here. Hang on a moment.' She heard him mumbling to someone. 'I have to go. We'll talk later?'

'Oh, yes, I think we will.'

His laughter rang in her ears as she disconnected the call. The knot in her stomach untied itself and completely dissipated. She had Jack exactly where she wanted him. All her game playing had worked.

No one knew she had met Jack way before she had started to work with Tamara on the pitch for *Something's Got to Give.* Esther had planned on seducing him over time but the day out at Ascot had been a bonus. Even going back to his house and the unfortunate scene with Tamara and Oscar could have been a disaster, but luckily it had all worked out, and everything had been forgotten.

You see, Esther wasn't the loving type once you got to know her – *really* know her. Not the Esther she showed to everyone, but the person underneath. The one she kept well hidden.

And even though Tamara suspected her of trying to bag a rich man, she didn't know the half of it. She was after revenge. The Maitland family was going to rue the day they

heard of Esther Smedley, and Jack had come one step closer
to getting her what she needed.

She almost skipped into work, blowing a kiss to Raj as
he was pottering around in the hallway. It more or less felt
as if she was falling in love with Jack when in actual fact she
was high on getting even.

Tamara was on the phone when she let her in. While
she continued her conversation, Esther made their usual
drinks and sat down across from her. Tamara's hands were
waving about as she talked. When she disconnected the call,
she smiled at her.

'I have so many offers of work coming in.'

'That's great news.' She smiled. 'I hope that means you'll
need staff too.'

'Possibly.'

'Well, if you need a partner, you know I'm your woman.'

The look on Tamara's face wasn't the reaction Esther was
after. Her smile had disappeared, quickly replaced by a
frown. Did she doubt her? Why wouldn't Tamara want to
employ her permanently? Hadn't she done enough to prove
herself? Wasn't she worthy of a job with her?

Esther's throwaway comment had backfired. Even
though she wasn't going to stick around for much longer,
her good mood evaporated in seconds.

The look on Esther's face shocked Tamara. When Esther
had said she wanted to partner up with her, she wasn't sure
if she was joking or being deadly serious. Either way, she
must have shown her horror as Esther quickly put her head
down and got back to work.

Tamara tried to make eye contact with her for the next

half hour or so to give her a smile, gauge how she was feeling, but she never looked up. Not once.

'Do you have the latest graph with the Amazon rankings and the Neilson figures?' she asked for want of something to say.

'I can get them for you,' Esther said, still avoiding eye contact.

'Great, I'll make coffee while you do.'

When she came back into the room with the drinks, Tamara gave in. She couldn't sit through the silence and awkward atmosphere any longer. It unsettled her, made her feel inferior.

'Esther, have I upset you in some way?' she asked.

'No.' This time Esther did look at her and her smile was as bright as ever. It didn't seem to reach her eyes though.

'That's funny because you've been really quiet since you made your remark about being my partner.'

Esther waved off the remark. 'That was a joke.'

'Good, because I'm really sorry but it can't happen. I enjoy working with you but I can't hire anyone else permanently. If any of this work does actually come my way, I would definitely still continue to employ you on a temporary basis.'

'It really was a joke,' Esther insisted. 'All I ask is that you give me a good reference when you no longer require my services. I like temping and getting to work with different people anyway. Learning keeps me on my toes.'

It was Tamara's turn to wave away the comment. 'I have no intention of letting you go yet.'

'Understood.' Esther held out her hand. 'Is that my coffee?'

Tamara gave her the mug. Again, Esther disappeared behind the laptop, avoiding her eye. She sighed inwardly.

Having staff to look after was more difficult at times than she'd envisioned.

The room dropped into another awkward silence. Tamara disliked them and usually went to fill them first, but this time she didn't. It lasted over an hour before Esther spoke to her and everything returned to normal.

When she had left for the day, Tamara sat back and thought about what had gone on. Having Esther around all the time made her mood swings more noticeable. One minute she was up and the next she would be downcast.

She tried not to laugh out loud as she realised that she was about to quote the book title they were working on in her mind.

But it was apt because something had to give if their working relationship was to continue.

34

Danny Bristol lived two streets away from Ewan Smith, in an identical block of twelve flats, four to each floor. Before they had left Smith's flat, a CSI had mentioned there were several sets of prints coming up already. A knock on a few of the doors of the remaining flats had unveiled that there had been a party a few nights ago. Music had been blasting until 2.00 a.m., despite protests from some.

Danny Bristol lived in flat 309 with his sister, Lindsay Copperly. Max knocked on the door and a scrawny-looking woman with a screaming toddler hoisted on to her hip opened it. She rolled her eyes at them, even before she had seen their warrant cards.

'Will you shut up for one minute,' she roared to someone behind her who was competing with the noise level. Then she gave out an exasperated sigh. 'He's not here,' she snapped. 'I haven't seen him since yesterday.'

'Can we come in for a moment?'

'You don't believe me?' Lindsay held open the door. 'Be my guest, check wherever you like.'

They followed Lindsay inside. Carley checked the two bedrooms first and held her breath as she stepped into the bathroom. But at least the kids looked clean, and the living room was tidy, despite the stale smell of body odour.

'Do you know where he was last night?' Max asked. 'Or where he will be now?'

Lindsay shook her head, hoisting the crying child up further on to her hip. Carley held in a grimace as snot from the little boy's nose ran into his mouth. Lindsay caught her looking, pulled a tissue from the sleeve of her jumper and wiped it clean.

'I don't know where he is and I don't really care,' she said. 'He took my social money last night. It's supposed to last a week and he left me with a tenner. What the hell can I buy with that? It won't even cover my fags.'

Carley let out an irritated sigh. 'Did he say where he was going last night?'

'Out with his mates.'

'Do you know where?'

The sounds of *Peppa Pig* exploded into the room. Lindsay grabbed for the television remote that her eldest child had switched on to full. 'Will you leave that thing alone,' she yelled before turning to them again. 'Look, I told you I haven't seen him since yesterday morning. If you see him before me, tell him that he's a dead man walking. I'm sick of him and his thieving.'

They left minutes later, fully satisfied that he wasn't in the property.

'Do you believe her?' Carley asked once they were heading down the steps to the ground again.

Max shrugged. 'I think I do. So if he didn't stop here and he isn't at Ewan Smith's place, where the hell is he?'

'Sleeping off a hangover, no doubt.' Carley had arrested Danny for drunk and disorderly on many occasions.

'Can you check the CCTV footage around Smith's flat if there is any, see if we can pick anything up?' Max said. 'Start from his street and work your way out. Someone will have seen him leaving his flat and at what time. Or maybe even walking home, grabbing a bite to eat. We need to know who he was with last night.'

'Seems funny, Sarge, doesn't it?' Carley queried. They were at ground level now and broke out into the open air. 'First Kerrigan and now Smith. It's as if the gang is imploding.'

'Or someone is making it seem that way.'

'Re: Kerrigan, we have prints on record from numerous people in the room. We've ruled out some of them, but most were in a group of squatters in an old church hall in Shoreditch. They've been moved on from there since it was demolished earlier this year. Shall I keep trying to locate them?'

Max paused for a moment, before nodding. 'Yes, keep looking. It seems strange that two of the three in the same group of friends have been wiped out. But I'm not ruling out that any of them had a hand in Ewan's death. Not until we've spoken to them all. Put a call on the system to locate Bristol. We'll soon nab him.'

Carley nodded as they got to the pool car. 'They've all got records a mile long.'

'Keep digging.' Max started the engine. 'Keep on top of forensics and let me know when they've come back.'

35

Monday, 10 July

It was past 9.00 p.m. when Esther got home that evening. The rest of the weekend had been hectic after the book launch, and she had worked above and beyond her hours of contract. She felt exhausted but it kept her mind occupied. Also, Jack had been texting her throughout the day, so much that she'd been forced to put her phone on silent and reply only when Tamara was out of the room.

They'd met for a drink after work. Things were going fine between them now, and she reckoned she'd be able to move along a step quite soon, get the incriminating evidence she required.

On her way into the house, she collected the mail from her box and let herself into her flat. Flicking a light on and closing the door with her foot, she opened the first letter. Her shoulders dropped. The direct debit for her electricity bill had been rejected again.

She sighed, wondering if she should ask Tamara for a

loan as she wasn't due to be paid for another week. She wasn't going to use her own money and it was partly Tamara's fault anyway. Now that Esther was going out most evenings to launches or dinners as she integrated herself into the crowd, she had to have even more clothes. She had to wear expensive outfits to blend in with her new crowd, didn't she?

The next letter wasn't any better.

'Shit!' Esther sat down at the tiny kitchen table and read it all through before groaning loudly. It was an eviction notice giving her twenty-eight days to clear the property. She screwed up the letter and threw it to the floor. Then she poured herself a neat whiskey and downed it in one. She wanted it to calm her, so that she didn't have to take anything.

Why did this have to occur now, especially after what had happened with Danny, buried in the garage? She needed more time, a month, two at the most. It was imperative that she kept the roof over her head until then. There was no way she could go back on the streets, and she couldn't carry her money around with her. It was too dangerous.

She reached for her phone and, thinking positive vibes, rang the number on the letter.

'Mr Ripley, how are you? It's Esther Smedley,' her voice rang out. 'I was—'

'You got my letter, I presume?'

'Yes, I'm terribly sorry for the mix-up. I've started a new job and had to work a month in hand. My wages should have gone in on time but I can't see them. I'll be chasing this up first thing in the morning. I'm so embarrassed.'

'It's too late. This is the second month you've missed. I have tenants lined up who *will* pay on time.'

'But surely you can give me a few weeks? I've paid up until now.'

'And what happens if you don't pay then?'

'I'll get it sorted first thing in the morning.'

'I've heard it all before.'

'I won't let you down,' she said.

There was a pause on the line. 'If the money is in my account by the end of this week, then fine. If not, you're out on your ear in twenty-eight days.'

'It will be there.' Esther sounded confident but inside she was fuming. She had lived in so many squats in her late teens and early twenties that had been better than this and rent-free. He wasn't having a penny extra from her for living in this dump. She'd given him more than he deserved already.

She had kept up with her rent for three months purposely when she'd moved in, but it seemed it wasn't long enough to garner trust. She now knew that her landlord would throw her out in an instant rather than end up out of pocket. She'd never liked him; he was a sleaze ball. Renting out this kind of hovel, his sort always was.

She disconnected the phone, dropped on to the settee, arms folded and glared at the wall in front of her. Just as she thought everything was going well, something always came up. Twenty-eight days wasn't enough.

That night she tossed and turned in her bed trying to think of a way around everything. The heat was oppressive, making her unable to sleep, feeling frustrated when she couldn't.

But by the time morning came around, Esther was clear what she had to do. Maybe it wasn't too late to put it all into place before she was evicted. She needed to double her efforts to get more money, not the odd wallet here and there, but the real wad she was after.

Her shoulders drooped. She didn't really want to push things but it looked as if she would have to bring things forward.

It would have to be this Saturday when she would be with Jack.

36

Tuesday, 11 July

Tamara was glad to be home when she finally got out of the cab that evening. She sighed into the quiet as she closed the front door behind her and kicked off her shoes. With having Esther there during the week now, sometimes it never felt as if she had a moment to herself.

Even though it was half past ten, and she'd already had two glasses of champagne, she decided to open a bottle of wine. Pouring a large glass, she reckoned a long bath and a book would finish the night perfectly. Anything other than *Something's Got to Give*.

Tamara had been pleasantly surprised to see how much Simone's novel had taken off since the launch. Of course, she'd had a helping hand in its success by getting word out about it, but it was Simone's skill as an author that had kept the book in the public eye.

They had been celebrating that evening after a mention on a TV book club had sent the book straight to the top of the Kindle charts. Over the past few months, she'd taken to checking book charts on a more regular basis, seeing what was going up and down, what was sticking and what had been around for a long time. So to find it at number one was extremely satisfying. Everyone involved had done a great job, pulling together to make the campaign a success.

She ran a bath, and checked the emails that had come in over the past hour. There was one from Jack, copying in Esther, congratulating Tamara on getting the publisher their first number one. Tamara's smile was wide. Everything had gone so much better than she ever could have anticipated.

Jack had sent her a separate email too. She paused in the hallway as she read it. He wanted her to work on another campaign. It was a smaller project but he felt assured that she was confident, and he would be happy to chat it through with her and Esther. She liked that about Jack. He was always good at giving compliments. He went out of his way to make everyone feel special, without being too false.

Esther had been weird again that evening though. Tamara didn't know what had got into her. She'd been quite snappy today and, if she thought back, it had started before the launch of *Something's Got to Give*. She noticed Esther hardly drunk at some events and at others she piled down the fizz, as if trying to get a high.

Esther's ideas were great, there was no doubt about that, and being in demand was good too. But as much as Tamara enjoyed working with her, she wasn't sure about how she carried herself outside the office when she was on business for her – and in publishing that could be quite a lot of hours.

Was it worth inviting her to work on another project, she wondered, as she removed her clothes in the bathroom? She'd have to think about it.

Tamara lowered herself into the water with an appreciative sigh. Still she couldn't help but smile. Maybe things would calm down now that the book had been launched successfully. She'd already lined up one or two projects to look at. How exciting that she had so many to choose from.

Life was definitely good right now.

37

Saturday, 15 July

Esther slipped on her latest new dress and pushed her feet into the highest pair of heels that she owned. She checked her reflection in the cracked wardrobe mirror and held up her hair, wondering whether to tie it up with a few strands falling or leave it loose completely. In the end, she went with loose.

After a liberal spray of perfume, she searched out what she needed and left the flat. So much depended on this meeting with Jack today. It was the pinnacle of everything she had been working towards and even though she was apprehensive, she had to go through with it.

Could she do it without showing her disgust? You'd think she'd be used to it, the many men she'd slept with before now. But this mission, although really important, went against the grain, even for her. Still, if today went well, it would soon be over.

She'd tried not to drink too much the night before,

wanting to keep a clear head. The amphetamines she'd been taking would give her the courage to go through with what was necessary. Of course, she could stop taking it at any time but she needed a little more to block the nerves today. This meeting was about getting Jack to give himself to her.

The gates were open when she arrived at his house. She rang the bell and hopped up and down on the balls of her feet as she waited for him to answer.

Jack threw open the door and took a long and appraising look at her before welcoming her inside. He reached for her hand, kissing her fingers gently.

'You make me smile so much,' he told her.

'Glad to hear it,' Esther replied. 'So what's the plan for today?'

'Well, the weather is being kind to us again so I thought we could make the most of it. Maybe a barbecue later, if we haven't drunk too much.'

'Sounds perfect.'

'Come on.' He marched her through to the kitchen.

As Jack opened the fridge and took out a bottle of white wine, Esther ran a hand over an antique sideboard. Anger rushed through her as she noted the studio portrait of Jack, Natalie, and their two boys when they were babies. They were all happy families and smiles.

He doesn't deserve to be happy.

Wine poured, she followed Jack out into the garden. They sat down on a lounger each. The sun beamed down from another cloudless sky, tempting her to lie back and just be happy.

She stretched out her legs and threw her arms over her head. If she closed her eyes, she could imagine she was on a tropical beach, the sea lapping close by.

'They reckon it might touch thirty degrees this afternoon,' she said, before taking a sip of her wine.

'You look hot enough now.' Jack's eyes flicked over her figure with appreciation.

No one had looked at her like that in a long time, she realised, apart from when she was on her way to the races. She supposed this could be good or bad, whatever she chose to make it.

She only had to do this once so she decided that today would all be about fun. Let tomorrow be when things started to get nasty. For now, she was going to go with the flow. She'd had far worse men in her time.

Soon they had finished one bottle of wine and were halfway through another. At the bottom of the garden, it was secluded away from prying eyes and ears, yet it still caught the sun. They weren't overlooked at all. For the first time in a while, she wished she'd had this kind of stability, with a husband and two children. Part of a family.

'Penny for your thoughts?'

'Hmm?' She turned to him, aware he'd been watching her. Jack had music running through his iPad so she was saved by the tune. 'I'm listening to the song. It brings back happy memories.'

'What do you like to listen to?'

'All kinds of things really. I'm not into any classical stuff, mind.'

Jack laughed. 'Neither am I. What makes you think I would be?'

'Your lifestyle.'

'My lifestyle?'

She closed her eyes and lay back again. 'Well, you're clearly a millionaire.' She bit her lip, cursing herself for being so blunt.

'So I have to listen to classical music? I'm more of a classic man, myself. I like Bowie, Queen, Phil Collins, Genesis.'

'You're an old rocker.' She laughed, realising he hadn't been offended.

'No need to tease me.' He paused. 'You know, I very nearly didn't hire you and Tamara.'

'Oh?'

'We were struggling to shift copies of the book, but we thought we could still turn it around. All the good PR companies were unavailable so we decided to interview a group of smaller ones, in order to steal a few good ideas and then run with them ourselves.'

'You sneak.' Esther laughed.

'That's business! But your pitch was so good that we decided to give you a shot.'

'You wanted us.'

'I wanted you.' Jack leaned over and ran a finger up and down her arm. Goosebumps broke out over her skin, despite the heat, and everything became serious.

'Esther, can I ask you something?'

'Hmm?'

There was a pause before he spoke again. 'Do you want to sleep with me?' His voice was full of emotion, husky with lust, yet had a shake to it.

Esther kept her eyes closed. 'Do you want me to?' she asked.

'Of course, but I'm married.'

'Why didn't you tell me that in the first instance?' She sat up with a grin on her face, but his smile had dropped. 'I was joking,' she told him. 'Look, this isn't right but it *feels* right, you know?'

Jack looked away for a moment, before returning his

gaze. 'I'm nervous and I do feel guilty so maybe if we take things slowly, if it's meant to be then it will.'

'Okay.' Esther pulled him to her, a tiny kiss and a nibble of his lip as he looked into her eyes. He might want it to happen slowly but she was still going to encourage him at every opportunity.

It had to be today.

She kissed him again.

38

Everything was going great until Jack pulled away.

'What's the matter?' Esther asked, shielding her eyes from the sun.

'I can't do this.' He sat upright, dropping his shoulders dramatically. 'I'm sorry. I really want to and you know I think so much of you, but I can't.'

'Yes, you can.' Esther put a hand behind his neck again, trying to draw him back into her embrace. But he pushed her away and stood up.

'I've been such a fool.' He ran a hand through his hair and then turned back to her with a pained expression. 'I shouldn't play with your feelings like this, but this doesn't seem right.'

'You haven't actually tried anything to see if it feels right or not,' Esther huffed.

He shook his head. 'I – I love my wife and even if the passion has gone, I can't be unfaithful.'

Esther looked away before he could see the resentment in her eyes. She didn't want to hear this after he had turned her down. Rejected *her*. How cruel could he be, telling her this to ease *his* conscience?

He reached for her but she snatched her hand away.

'You men,' she seethed. 'You're all the same.'

Jack frowned. 'What do you mean by that?'

She got to her feet as quickly as she could. Barefoot on the grass, she swayed, only then recognising how tipsy she was. She prodded a finger into his chest. 'Do you know something? I really hate you right now.'

Jack nodded. 'You have every right to. I've been a complete bastard.'

'You've only fucking kissed me,' she screamed.

'Hey, calm down.'

'What is it with you? First you put me down in front of your family and Tamara and then you reject me. Am I not good enough to FUCK? Is that it?'

'Be quiet.' Jack took her arm and ushered her into the house. He pulled the doors closed while she stood there fuming.

Esther's fist pummelled at her thigh. She couldn't let him stand there and not finish what she'd set out to do. Everything depended on this. She really wanted her blade right now, to give her instant pain, take away the hurt. How could he do this to her?

'I'm really sorry,' Jack repeated. 'I'll order you a cab and get you home. I don't want to humiliate you anymore.'

'This is just nerves.' She tried one more time to pull Jack into her arms, pressing her body to his. 'Maybe this will relax you.'

He resisted for a few seconds as she kissed him. She thought she had him back but then he pushed her away, roughly this time.

'No! Don't take advantage of me because I'm drunk.'

'Me take advantage of you?' she roared. 'I think it's the other way around.'

'Oh, don't come all innocent with me. You know I'm married.'

'Well, that didn't enter your mind when you asked if I wanted to sleep with you. I thought you were okay with it.'

'I was. But when it came down to it, I couldn't do it.'

'You don't want to, more like.' Esther turned away from him and leaned on the worktop. She stared into the garden in which she'd been happily spending time. Everything had been going fine until he bottled it.

She felt his hand on her shoulder but she shrugged it away.

'This isn't all my fault,' he said.

It was that line that did it. Since the day her innocence had been taken away, she had never been good enough. And now here *he* was, Jack charming Maitland, trying to talk his way out of the mess he'd got himself into by blaming *her*. *He* had led her on. *He* had shown her affection and then drew it away at the last crucial minute. *He* had decided she wasn't enough.

Esther spotted a marble paperweight in the shape of an apple. She wrapped her fingers tightly around it and with a high-pitched scream brought it down on the side of his head.

'You bastard!'

Jack didn't even have time to clutch his wound before he stumbled backwards and dropped to the floor. His head made a sickly crack as it connected with the marble tiles. His eyes glazed over in an instant, thick blood pouring from a cut at the back of his head. He flinched a little before going completely still.

Esther put down the ornament. 'Jack?' she said, but he

didn't move. She nudged his leg with her toes. 'Stop messing around. I'm sorry. Hey, Jack!'

The puddle of blood oozed from the back of his head at an alarming rate. She quickly opened cupboard after cupboard, drawer after drawer, until she located a tea towel to mop it up. Then she stooped down next to him.

'Jack?' She touched his face, but there was no response. Standing up again, she ran her hands through her hair. She grabbed fistfuls and pulled.

She went out into the garden, first sitting at the table, then standing up to pace the lawn. Finally, she sat down on a bench. Shallow breaths hurt her chest. She counted from one to five, then from five to one and repeated it, hoping to calm herself enough to think straight.

Jack was dead and she had killed him.

No one would believe it was an accident. The police would be called, and they would find out everything. Why couldn't she control her temper long enough to get revenge? She shouldn't have even been at the house and now she had hit him with a blunt object and there was evidence of her all over him.

She stood up again and went back inside the house. Trying not to look at Jack, she rushed around, moving and gathering what she needed, placing everything in a carrier bag. Then she went out of the back door and down the side of the house, on to the street.

There were people around but she couldn't stop and think about whether they would recognise her later, once they found out that Jack was dead. She walked briskly enough not to bring attention to herself, keeping her head down but not acting in any way suspicious.

Twenty minutes later she was back, another plan

formed. Jack hadn't moved so he was definitely dead. But she knew what she had to do. She couldn't leave him lying on the kitchen floor or she would be charged with murder.

She reached for her phone.

'Tamara, it's Esther. I'm with Jack. He's fallen down the stairs and hit his head on the floor in the hallway.'

'Oh no, is he badly hurt? Where are you?'

'I'm at his house.'

'What are you doing there?'

'It's a bit delicate. I shouldn't really be here at all. But Jack has a cut to his head and I think he might need to go to the hospital.'

'Have you rung for an ambulance?'

'No, he's a little concussed, I think. I just need you to take us to A&E. Will you?'

'I don't know why—'

'I don't want Natalie to find out I was here.'

'What aren't you telling me?' There was a pause down the line. 'Is there something going on between you and Jack?'

'I – we've been seeing each other.'

'Oh, Esther!'

'I – I can explain everything when I see you. Please. I need your help.'

'Are you sure you don't want me to call an ambulance?'

'We can't. It will bring everything to the attention of the neighbours. If we take him to the hospital in your car, no one will see us.'

'But—'

'Please, Tamara! I don't want her to find out.'

'All right. I can be there in twenty minutes.'

Esther disconnected the phone and tapped it repeatedly

on her chin. Perfect. As she thought what was the best way to move Jack without the blood going everywhere, she thanked her lucky stars that she hadn't slept with him. Now all she had to do was convince Tamara that it had been an accident.

39

Tamara wasn't sure what to think as she drove to Jack's house. She couldn't believe that Jack and Esther had been having an affair. Well, perhaps the signs were there but she didn't *want* to believe it.

She wasn't sure how she felt about it either. It wasn't really professional from either side, especially as they were working together.

She wondered when it had started. It certainly couldn't have been going on long – two or three weeks at the most. Either way she hoped it would stop after this. It could make things very awkward if they were found out.

As she pulled up at traffic lights, she thought back to Esther's irrational behaviour the week before. She wondered if Jack had upset her at the book launch party. Had she been seeing him before that and it had made her feel awkward?

The gates were open when she arrived at Jack's house. Tamara drove into the drive and parked up next to his Audi. Before she had killed the engine, Esther came rushing out of the house.

She burst into tears as Tamara got out of the car. 'It's worse than I thought,' she cried. 'He's collapsed and I can't get him to wake up.'

Tamara rushed after her as she went back into the house. 'But you've called for an ambulance now?'

'No. I told you, I can't.'

'Why ever not?'

'Because I'm not supposed to be here.'

'But if Jack is injured, then the consequences of your actions don't really come into the equation. Are you—'

The front door was open. Tamara caught her breath when she saw Jack lying at the bottom of the stairs. Then she ran inside, dropping to her knees. She touched her hand to his forehead; saw the blood at the back of his head. There was a gash at the side of his head too, the blood congealed slightly.

'He's dead, isn't he?' Esther said.

'I – I don't know.' Tamara took out her phone and dialled for the emergency services.

Esther dropped down beside her. 'Please don't call anyone yet.'

'I have to! You told me he was concussed. He looks like he's – he looks ... Ambulance, please.'

Esther sat quiet while Tamara gave details to the operator. She pressed a hand to Jack's face, talking to him, telling him everything would be all right.

'They're on their way,' Tamara said as she disconnected the call. 'Tell me what happened again.'

'I was out in the garden,' Esther told her. 'We'd been there for a couple of hours, had a bite to eat and got through a fair bit of wine. Jack had come indoors to use the bathroom.'

'But there's a cloakroom downstairs.' Tamara pointed to it, having used it when she was here before.

Esther nodded. 'He must have popped upstairs for something. I don't really know. I was sunbathing and it was about ten minutes before I wondered where he was. I came in from the garden, and when he wasn't in the kitchen, I went into the hallway and I – I found him there.'

'Was he conscious?'

Esther shook her head.

'You told me he was concussed.'

'I panicked, okay. I don't want his family to find out I was seeing him. It would ruin everything they had together. I don't want to be *that* woman.'

'But that's not going to wash with the police when they get here.'

'The police?'

'It's a sudden death. They're bound to be called.'

Sirens sounded in the distance. Tamara stood up, and walked towards the door. But Esther pulled her back.

'You could say you were here too.'

Tamara's eyes widened in disbelief as Esther continued.

'If we were both here, it would look like we were having a meeting and we could say he fell down the stairs while we were out in the garden.'

'You said he *did* fall down the stairs.'

'He did! I mean that it will stop anyone from finding out we were – we were having an affair. Can you imagine what this will do to his family? Whereas if you were here too, it would be a legitimate thing to be happening.'

'On a Saturday?' Tamara wasn't convinced.

'Yes! You could say that you were thinking of this new idea for the campaign and that you were so excited about it that you rang Jack and he said to come over and—'

'You want me to say that you weren't here at all?' Tamara sensed the panic building up in Esther now. But that was a ridiculous notion.

'No, if we were both here it would seem less ... intimate.' Esther's shoulders dropped. 'I know what we did was wrong, but I – I love him.'

'You barely know each other!'

'It just happened! But no one need ever know about it, if you say you were here too. You could say you were working later than planned. You got here about two, we were in the garden. Jack went inside and we came in and found him there.'

Tamara shook her head. 'I can't lie to the police.'

'Please!' Esther begged, tears pouring down her face.

There was movement behind them as two paramedics came rushing in.

'What happened?' said one of them as he dropped to Jack's side.

'We were having lunch in the garden and Jack nipped inside,' Esther replied. 'When he didn't come back, we came in and found him there, didn't we, Tamara?'

The paramedics were too busy attending to Jack to notice that Esther was nodding her head vehemently behind them. Her eyes were pleading.

Tamara paused for a moment. She'd always thought that Jack had been a family man. It had shocked her to learn something was going on between him and Esther. But that was none of her business.

She didn't want to be the one who broke a family's hopes and dreams now Jack was dead.

'Yes,' she decided. 'Yes, that's right. We found him here.'

40

Carley had been the first officer on scene at Jack Maitland's house. She spotted Max as he parked the pool car in a tiny space next to hers and walked towards him, meeting him at the gates.

Every sudden death was treated as if it were a crime scene. When she'd questioned Max about this, he'd told her she would want the best if it were a member of her own family who had died, under suspicious circumstances or not. The words had never left her.

'We got a call at quarter past two,' she told him as he donned the appropriate protective gear of suit, shoe covers and gloves. 'Thirty-seven-year-old Jack Maitland. Fallen down the stairs and cracked his head on marble tiles. He died in the hallway. On close inspection he's taken a bump to the temple too. It could have been as a result of the fall but we'll have to wait for the forensics.

'I've managed to contact his wife. There was an address book in the kitchen drawer with a list of emergency numbers in the front. There's also a mobile phone in the kitchen but it's locked. Mrs Maitland was away with their children for the weekend in Kent. She had gone to visit her parents and was due back tomorrow evening but is now on her way home. She's heading over to her sister's and is going to ring us when she arrives.' Carley moved to one side to let a forensic officer pass them, taking the time to consult her notebook. 'Maitland was with Tamara Parker-Brown and Esther Smedley at the time. They were working in the garden. You've seen the novel that everyone is talking about – *Something's Got to Give*?'

'Can't really miss it,' Max muttered. 'It's everywhere.'

'Well, he's the publisher of that and they're the PR team. Parker-Brown owns the company and Smedley works for her.' She looked around. 'Makes a difference coming into such a palatial home. Our usual inhabitants live in far less glamorous places.'

The body was lying on its side at the bottom of the stairs, eyes wide and staring at nothing.

'Looks like he took a heavy fall,' Max said aloud.

'He did.' Terry, who was kneeling over the torso, stood up to his level.

'Anything you can tell me?'

Terry pointed to the man's temple where a bruise had already formed, blood congealed around a half-inch split to the skin. 'I can't be sure if that caused him to fall so heavily on the marble tiles at ground level. It's possible he tripped at the top of the stairs, hit his head halfway down which rendered him unconscious. Either way, he took one hell of a bump at ground level. I'm guessing death was immediate.'

Carley looked around the hallway. The family photos on the wall showed their man with a woman and two identical schoolboys. She sighed inwardly. It was always the children she felt the sorriest for. Losing a parent at any age can be terrible but to be robbed of one when you might not yet be in double figures was a tragedy. She hoped they had shared many happy memories before today.

Carley moved into the kitchen, checking out everything on the worktops. The forensics team would take a couple of days to get it all to them, see if there were any anomalies. She pointed to three glasses, and two wine bottles on the worktop.

'There's one empty bottle and one half full.'

'Where are the women?'

'They've been taken to the station in separate cars.'

Max opened the door of the large American fridge. He pulled out a small bottle, half full of soda water and then put it back. 'There doesn't seem anything out of place,' he noticed.

As Carley continued to look around, Max completed his walk downstairs and around the garden. After a quick look upstairs, he came back to her.

'I'll get the team to do a better search while the house is empty,' he said. 'In the meantime, I'll wait for Terry's report to come through.'

'You'll be lucky to get anything back soon,' Terry shouted through to them. 'I'm flat out as it is with the attempted double murder.'

Carley sighed. One member of a gang had shot another the previous week and this had been the revenge for it.

It always took a while for evidence to be processed. No matter what the crime, everything had its pecking order, and its budget allowance.

'Can you lead on collating all this as it comes in?' Max said to her. 'Cross reference it, and see if it needs to be esca-lated or if it is as cut and dry as it seems to be?'

'Will do.'

41

The last time Esther was in a police station, she'd been held inside a cell until it was time for her to appear in court. Even then, she had gone straight on remand until she'd been charged. Now, she was shown into a small room with a beige two-seater settee, armchair, and a pine coffee table. She'd been there for half an hour and wondered if they were talking to Tamara or still at Jack's house.

She sat at the edge of the settee, her hands in her lap, all the while her eyes scanning the room. She knew there might be people watching her so she was keeping up the pretence of being upset. Then she relaxed. There were no cameras, only a panic button. And as far as she knew, she was only being interviewed. Neither her nor Tamara were under arrest. If she kept her cool, she could be out of there in no time.

Her eyes filled with tears, but she wasn't upset about what she had done. She hadn't meant to kill Jack, but she had got so *angry* at the situation. Jack had not been willing to sleep with her because of being loyal to his wife, even after all the hard work she'd put in flirting and keeping up the pretence that she'd been attracted to him. It had put paid to her plans.

She'd actually been surprised when Tamara had lied for her. Esther didn't think she'd be the sort to fabricate a story, especially where the police were concerned. She hoped she wouldn't crumble under pressure when they spoke to her.

The door opened and the female officer, who had arrived at the scene shortly after the paramedics, came into the room.

'Hello, Esther. I'm DC Evans. You remember I was at Mr Maitland's house?'

Esther nodded, wondering if she thought she was either stupid or in shock. Of course, she remembered the detective. She'd seen her less than an hour ago.

She studied her face. At a guess, she was around late-twenties, her skin fresh and blemish free. She wore a bit of make-up, and her blonde hair was tied back away from her face. She'd seemed friendly enough earlier but that didn't mean Esther would like her. She didn't trust the police.

But she had to make the woman think she had her total confidence. She sat forward attentively, sniffing and wiping at her eyes as she squeezed out a tear.

'I must tell you that you are not under arrest but you are under caution as one of two people to last see Jack Maitland alive. This is a routine interview.' Her smile was warm. 'Can you tell me what happened from the minute you got to Jack Maitland's house to the time that he died, please?'

'Jack wanted to see Tamara and me, to run through a few suggestions that he'd thought of for the PR campaign we are all working on,' Esther began. 'Jack's wife had taken their children to visit his in-laws, so he suggested we meet there for an hour. Everything has gone a bit hectic since the launch of a book we are all working on so he had been snowed under during the week.'

'What time did you arrive at his house?'

'I got there around half past twelve but Tamara was delayed. I rang her to see where she was around one-thirty; Jack and I had already started on the wine by then.'

'So there was just you and Jack until what time?'

'Just before 2.00 p.m.'

'Do you know why Tamara was delayed?'

Esther waited for her to finish writing before continuing. 'She said she had been catching up on some work and it had taken her longer than anticipated. When Tamara joined us, we chatted for a few minutes and then Jack excused himself. When he got up, I remember he stumbled a bit. We'd drank a lot of wine while we'd been waiting for Tamara.' Esther made her eyes well up with tears. 'I wish we hadn't now.'

Carley's smile was sympathetic. 'So Jack went into the house?'

'Yes. Tamara and I sat talking. At first, we didn't think anything of him not appearing after a few minutes but then it became obvious that he wasn't going to come back into the garden.

'We went inside. I dropped the glasses on to the worktop while Tamara went to see where he was. It was then that she shouted me through as she had found him at the bottom of the stairs. We rang for an ambulance but it was too late.'

'Did you realise he had died?'

Esther nodded slowly. 'We didn't want to admit it to each other, but yes.'

'But you didn't see him fall?'

'No.'

'You didn't hear anything?'

'There was music on in the garden and we were sitting quite a way from the house.' Esther sat up straighter, panic on her face. 'Do you think we could have saved him if we'd heard him fall? Please don't say it was our fault he died.'

'We can't be certain of anything at the moment. We're gathering together the facts. Do you know Mrs Maitland?'

'I met her briefly last Thursday. The book launch was at Jack's house. She seemed nice but I only spoke to her for a few minutes. It was a very busy evening.'

The detective finished writing and slid a small, black notepad and pen across to her. 'Can you read through this, and sign it if you agree with it? If I've missed anything or written something wrong, please say.'

Esther quickly skimmed through it all, and signed it. Everything was fine by her. She just had to wait and see what Tamara had said now.

And then get back to the flat. She had to make sure everything was hidden in case the police came looking.

42

Tamara checked her watch and wondered how long she'd have to be there before someone came to see her. Maybe there wasn't anyone to interview either of them yet, or maybe Esther was being seen first. She hoped it wouldn't be long.

She couldn't believe that Jack was dead. He had so much to live for – a beautiful house, family, a fabulous business, and career. He was well respected in his field and he was going to be sorely missed.

Selfishly she thought about their working relationship and if it would transfer to the new owner of Dulston Publishing. She wasn't sure she could work, for example, for Oscar.

Perhaps the staff members would do a joint buyout. Maybe Natalie wouldn't want to sell, preferring to leave it for her children as their legacy. She could easily get someone in to run it.

She sighed, annoyed with herself. Even if no one was really indispensable work-wise, they were all missed personally. Those poor boys.

Twenty minutes later, the female detective she'd met earlier came in. She sat down opposite her and flipped open a notepad. Her smile was reassuring when she looked up. DC Carley Evans introduced herself again and ran through the formalities before she began.

Tamara moved her hands to her lap as they began to shake. A rush of déjà vu came over her but she buried it quickly.

'Can you run me through your day, and then as you got to Jack Maitland's home please? What time you arrived, what you were doing before, what you did, why you were there etc.'

'I was supposed to turn up to the house around one but I had been finishing up some work.'

'So you left for Mr Maitland's home at ...?'

'Half past one. It's a twenty-minute drive from my flat in Westminster. I arrived at Jack's house just before two. Jack poured me a small glass of wine with soda water and we sat out in the garden.'

'You were celebrating your recent marketing campaign being a success, I believe?'

Tamara nodded. 'The book launch went down really well.'

'You're telling me! I'm seeing it everywhere at the moment.' Carley smiled. 'So all three of you were sitting in the garden?'

'Yes. We chatted for a few minutes and then Jack excused himself. I stayed with Esther outside until we wondered where he'd got to. I needed the bathroom and Esther went to refill our drinks, so we both went in to the house.'

'I'm surprised you didn't hear him fall. He took quite a tumble down those stairs.'

'There was music playing in the garden or I'm sure we

would have.' Tamara watched as the detective wrote down what she said. Then she looked up at her again.

'So what happened then?'

'I – I went into the hallway.'

'You didn't go upstairs?'

Tamara shook her head vehemently. 'I found him at the bottom of the stairs.' She shuddered at the image that came to mind, of Jack lying on his side with a blank expression, blood coming from the back of his head.

'What did you do then?'

'I shouted through to Esther and told her to call an ambulance.'

'And she did that straight away?'

'No. She was a bit hysterical when she saw him so I rang instead.'

'Did you know he was dead?'

'I wasn't certain but we couldn't rouse him awake,' Tamara explained. 'I couldn't find a pulse but then I'm not medically trained so I might have missed it. Then the paramedics arrived.'

Tamara let Carley catch up with her again.

Carley scanned the notes, slid the pad across the desk and handed her the pen. 'Now, you're quite sure that this is an accurate statement of what happened this afternoon?'

Tamara paled. Did she know she was lying?

'Yes, I'm sure,' she told her.

'So you were there when Jack Maitland died?'

'Yes, but I didn't see him die.'

Carley made Tamara feel uncomfortable with her stare. Did she know?

'You've lied to the police before, haven't you, Ms Parker-Brown?'

Tamara gulped. She knew.

43

Esther sat on the low wall across from the police station, keeping an eye on the entrance. It was past six-thirty, and London was gearing up for a Saturday evening. Everyone seemed in high spirits. People were going home with shopping for barbecues, and some were dressed up ready to go out.

She had to see Tamara. She wouldn't be able to settle until she'd heard what she had said to the police. One slip up and everything could be over.

He deserved what he got.

Esther shook her head to rid herself of the images in her mind. She wasn't sure Jack had warranted being killed but she wasn't going to dwell on that. All she could think about was keeping what really happened from everyone.

It was an accident.

Yes, that's right, she told herself. It was an accident. Jack tripped and fell down the stairs.

Her head was banging, her mouth dry, signs she was on a come down from the amphetamines. She'd only got a few bags of speed left now and would have to hide them once she got back to her flat, in case the police decided to visit.

If she had some with her now, she would take a hit but then again, maybe it was best that she hadn't, given the circumstances.

It was over thirty minutes later that Tamara emerged. Her face painted that picture of a thousand words as she rushed down the street. She had clearly been crying, her shoulders drooped.

'Tamara!' Esther shouted.

Tamara turned but, when she saw Esther, she kept on walking. Esther waited for traffic to pass before running across the road. She caught up with her and placed a hand on Tamara's shoulder.

Tamara flinched. 'Please leave me alone.'

'I only want to see how you are.'

'How do you think I am?'

'I know. It's such a shock, isn't it?'

They were nearing the corner of the road, walking past The Dog and Duck. People milled around outside and they moved through them on the pavement.

'I need a drink,' Tamara said and went inside.

Esther followed her. After they were served, they sat down at a table.

Tamara played with the corner of the beer mat before she looked up at her, eyes brimming with tears.

'I didn't tell you everything about Michael. Because of him, I – I have a criminal record.'

'What?' Esther's eyes widened in disbelief.

Tamara took a deep breath before beginning. 'Michael invited me round for a meal one night, about a month after our relationship had ended. We spent about an hour together. I thought everything was fine when I left, but I was arrested several hours later. He had keyed his own car, and cut up his clothes. He told the police that I had pushed my way in, trashed the flat, and assaulted him. He even had a bruise on his face, which he admitted to me long afterwards had hurt like hell as he'd hit himself with a saucepan.'

'The bastard!' Esther leaned forward attentively.

Tamara nodded. 'Michael was so convincing. I was charged with harassment and fined for assaulting him and for damaging property. And then ...' Tamara paused as if struggling to find the right words. 'I became ill and ended up in hospital for a few months.'

Esther covered her mouth with her hand, as if in shock. But inside she was secretly delighted. This was perfect. It could take the scent off her completely if anything pointed to her.

'You poor thing,' she said, as she dropped her hand and rested it on Tamara's.

'That's why I set up my own company. I have a criminal record – despite having the family name behind me, no one wanted to know me then.'

Esther frowned. 'I don't understand what that has to do with today.'

'I didn't want them to find out about my past but they already knew. I should have known they would check their records, but until they did I wasn't going to say anything. Now they think I'm a liar.'

'Why?'

'Because I haven't told the truth in the past. You know how the police can twist things.'

'There's nothing to twist.'

Tamara nodded.

'But they believed you, right?' Esther held her breath.

'I think so.' Tamara pushed aside her glass, not having

touched a drop, and stood up. 'I need to collect my car from Jack's house. They said I could. Can I give you a lift home afterwards?'

'No, thanks. I need some fresh air.'

'Are you going to be okay?'

Esther nodded. 'You?'

'I think so. I feel a bit shocked that he's dead.'

'Me too.'

After Tamara had left, Esther stayed in the pub. She bought herself a double vodka and sat back to enjoy it. She wasn't too worried about anything yet. All she had to do was stay calm.

Besides, she was too busy trying to work out how this new information about Tamara would come in handy.

44

Tamara couldn't rest once she was home. The afternoon's events kept running on a loop in her mind. She deeply regretted lying, especially now that her past record had been brought up. How did she even think that it wouldn't be?

She put her head in her hands and wept, because she was as bad as Esther when it came to lying. She hadn't told the truth about what had really happened with Michael.

Even though she would never forget any detail of what had occurred, she tried not to think about it too much. Sometimes it would rear its ugly head and she'd be down about things for a day or two, especially if things in general weren't going too well. As far as she'd been concerned it was over and done with and she didn't want to remember any of it.

But today had caused a lot of the pain and humiliation to resurface. She dragged a cushion from the settee and hugged it to her chest for comfort. Talking about it with Esther that afternoon had intensified it all over again. The truth was far too embarrassing to tell her because it hadn't been Michael who had done all the things she'd mentioned. It had been her.

She had keyed Michael's car, got into his flat and cut up his clothes. She had punched him in the face when he'd tried to calm her down. He hadn't retaliated at all, except to call the police. That's when she'd been arrested and charged with assault and criminal damage.

Things had gradually worsened then and she'd spiralled completely out of control. She wasn't interested in eating. She began to drink a lot more than usual, often waking up still drunk from the night before. Back then she'd been working for her brother at his firm. She'd had a senior position as an office manager but the responsibility that came with it had been too much.

When she kept ringing in sick, even after far more chances than any normal employer would have given her, she was let go. It had been humiliating but at the time she couldn't have cared less.

Michael wasn't responding to her pleas for help, despite the numerous times she would call him, day or night. When he changed his number, she resorted to emails.

Eventually, he'd rung her parents to see if they could stop her, and they had made an impromptu visit. It had been evening; she'd been in her dressing gown all day, drinking and crying. The flat was a mess; she was in a worse state. She needed help.

Her parents had the money to look after her the only way they knew how. They persuaded her to be admitted to a psychiatric hospital. Tamara couldn't look after herself, so someone needed to keep an eye on her until she was well again.

She'd hated them at the time, but they'd insisted it was

for her own good. She often wondered why her brothers or sister didn't step in to help. It still hurt that they hadn't.

The hospital had been a hideous place. From the moment she arrived, she'd been prescribed strong anti-depressants and for the first two months she'd become a complete zombie. Once she'd taken the heavier dose, the medication was changed to something lighter, and gradually things began to improve. By the time she was due to be released, she was feeling very much like her old self, glad to have the chance to start afresh.

At times, she struggled to understand why she'd reacted the way that she had. Because ever since, she had survived without Michael and she had come out on top. But still it was horrible to look back on. A mental breakdown was not something she was proud of.

So, when DC Evans had brought it up that afternoon, Tamara knew she shouldn't have lied about Jack too. She knew they would find out eventually.

Yet it was a little lie, one of no significance really. She hadn't been there when Jack died but she had arrived shortly afterwards so it was only bending the truth.

And if it meant she kept Jack's reputation intact, then surely there was no harm in it.

She hoped Esther wasn't too traumatised by everything. Tamara had tried ringing her but she hadn't answered. She wondered how she was feeling, hoping she wasn't blaming herself. If Esther hadn't met him that afternoon then Jack might still be alive. That must be going through her mind right now, all the what ifs, buts, and maybes that people tortured themselves about after losing a loved one in an accident.

One thing was clear: Esther should never have started an affair with Jack. It was stupid and irresponsible. Yet because of her breakdown over Michael, in a way she could understand why she hadn't wanted to bring any grief to Natalie Maitland, especially now that Jack had died. There would have been a lot more questions to answer, and it would save Natalie the pain of finding out the truth.

It was going to be hard working on the campaign now. They would have to keep everything going as normal. It wouldn't be fair on Simone and her agent if they let things slip, not now the book was doing so well. They needed to keep things going so they could let Jack's legacy live on, even if he wasn't there to shine.

Her eyes filled with tears at the thought of Natalie and the children. Those poor boys were so young to lose their father. What a waste of life, to trip and hit your head.

45

Esther sat in her flat as she waited for the night to draw in. It was imperative that she left soon, before the police put two and two together. She stared straight ahead, thinking of everything that had happened, how much trouble she was in and how much she faced to lose if she was found out.

It was all out of sync now. Jack dying was never part of her plan and that, plus the recent trouble with Danny and her looming eviction ... well, she must have been more out of control than she'd realised after bingeing on the amphetamines.

She'd thought she was okay without her meds too, letting her tablets lapse after she'd come out of prison. Maybe it would be better to get another dose before she left London. She'd ring the nearest doctor's surgery first thing on Monday morning, see if she could register. Perhaps it wasn't too late to keep her wits about her.

Jack's face was engrained into her memory and every time she closed her eyes, the image of him would appear. His face looking at her, with dead eyes and a blank expression. She knew it would fade in time. It had done before, but it was horrible when it was so real.

At half past ten, she left the flat and turned on to Earl's Court Road. Dressed in dark clothing, she wore a baseball cap, even though her hair was tucked inside her black wig. There were cameras everywhere on the streets. It was hard to get away with anything these days. So instead she had to think savvy, try and mislead the police.

Twenty minutes later, she passed the end of Jack's street. It all seemed quiet and there were no marked police cars present. Esther took this to be a good sign. If the police had suspected foul play, surely they would be investigating around the area more? Still, she hurried past.

Jack's house was close to the children's play area. There were a few people about on the street, but it wasn't extremely busy. No one would be taking any notice of her.

When she approached the gates, they were locked. She'd anticipated this so she shimmied up and over them, jumping down on the other side with a thud. She looked around her, hoping the bang of her feet hadn't brought her to anyone's attention. But there was nothing.

There was a streetlight in front but, other than that, into the park it darkened. She stared into the shadows before beginning to run. Eerie shapes crept up on her. She ran until she came to the bush she'd been to earlier.

She stopped, scanning around to make sure that she hadn't missed anyone who might see her. When she was positive she was alone, she dropped to her knees.

She reached under the hedge until her hand found the black plastic bag that she had placed there earlier, before she'd rang Tamara. Her fingers clasped around it and she pulled it out. Inside she'd wrapped the marble paperweight in the tea towels that she had used to wipe Jack's blood from the tiles.

Looking around again, she pushed the bag inside her hoodie and zipped it up. She jogged back to the fence and was away out on the street in no time. Now all she needed to do was get rid of it further afield. She wasn't about to take it home with incriminating evidence inside it. If the police found that, they might search her flat more thoroughly and she couldn't let them do that until she had left. Finding the amphetamines would be the least of her worries. They would find Danny's body too.

On the walk back, she kept her head down, afraid that she was going to feel a hand on her collar, or a police car would pull up to the kerb at high speed and she would be arrested. She couldn't use her Oyster card, even if the journey had been longer. She knew if the police checked it, they could see where she had been. She didn't want to leave any trace of anything.

As she'd been walking earlier, she'd noticed a house being renovated along one of the side streets. Outside it on the road was a huge yellow skip. Even though by now it was completely dark, again she made sure no one was around, and then pushed the bag inside, hiding it underneath a pile of broken plasterboards and a load of rubbish bags.

Assured it was well hidden, she rushed away. It could be found, if anyone went through the skip, but she had to take that chance.

Esther sighed with relief when she was back in the safety of her flat. How she hated that awful place, but tonight she was extremely glad of it. Exhausted, she climbed into bed. She reached for the bag of white powder that was on the bedside table, licked the tip of her finger, coated it with the substance and rubbed it around the inside of her gums.

It was all she could do not to get out a razor and start self-harming. The pressure to do it had intensified. The only other way she could blot out everything would be to drink herself into oblivion.

But despite wanting to drink, Esther had to stay sober. She needed to be prepared in case the police found out everything too soon.

46

Sunday, 16 July

After a restless sleep, Esther had dozed throughout the day, and woken with a start. She sat up in bed, pyjamas sticking to her, drenched in sweat. Her eyes were watery too. For a moment, she wondered what had made her wake. The recurring nightmare she had whenever she was stressed returning vividly, perhaps?

But then when she recalled the events of the day before, she realised she was in a living hell. She located her phone and checked online to see what was being said about Jack.

They had named him that morning on the local radio news bulletin. There was no mention of suspicious circumstances but they were continuing to look into the cause of his death so not everything had been ruled out.

She assumed they meant routine things. Maybe they would believe her and Tamara. Perhaps the evidence wouldn't point to anything more than a fall.

She logged on to Facebook, to the Dulston Publishing

page, where Oscar had left a post in tribute and a photo of them all with Jack in the middle. She could see herself on there, standing next to Tamara. Both of them were smiling. Would anyone guess that her profile was false? It was one of the reasons she never used social media too liberally. Everyone could look into your business.

Jack had a personal page, with the privacy set as public. There was a message on there from Natalie, with a photo of the two of them and their boys.

Messages of condolence were pouring in now. Esther had known Jack was popular but not how much. She could see people typing as news filtered through. Message after message to say how sorry they were, how shocked, how they would miss him, and what a waste of life. She almost snorted – what did they know about anything? They didn't know hurt like she did.

All of a sudden, Esther thought of her parents. She missed her mum as much as she missed her dad, but she'd stayed away because she didn't want to be an embarrassment to anyone. As much as it pained her not to see her, not to go back and visit, it was the best thing for both of them.

She could still remember when she had left home. She'd been seventeen, and, after another huge row with her mum, she didn't want to stay there any longer.

People knew too much; she couldn't move on from what had happened because everyone kept reminding her. A glance from a woman in the supermarket, the shake of a head from another when she was in the doctor's surgery, a glare from a man while she waited for the bus. It was as if she had liar stamped on her forehead.

But it was the argument with her mum that had been the final straw. She had seen the hatred, the disgust in her eyes at what had happened. Even if she believed her, she didn't like what her daughter had turned into since. She didn't like the late nights, the drinking, the crowd she was mixing with now.

Esther had been late in that night too, and her mum had waited up for her. She'd cried because she wanted her daughter to be safe, to look after herself. Esther could remember screaming at her, right up close. She'd stormed off to bed seconds later but in the morning, before her mum was up, she had packed a holdall full of clothes and left.

She closed the lid of her laptop, almost throwing it at the wall. If she hadn't been so stupid, getting high as well as drunk and then losing her temper, she wouldn't be in this predicament now. Why had she lashed out at Jack so quickly?

But she knew the answer to that. Because it wasn't the first time she had lost her temper and gone too far. She thought back to the worst time of her life. Three years ago, she was sofa surfing, still trying to find her place in society, still failing miserably.

Danny Bristol was someone who didn't like to be crossed but he was no good for her. He had supplied her with drugs, made her dependent and then forced her to work for him; earn the money back he said she owed. It had been humiliating when she thought about it now, but at the time she wanted her next fix and would have done anything to get it.

One night, he'd beaten her after she refused to go out to work for him. He was supposed to be her boyfriend, but he'd turned into her pimp. At the time, she'd thought about getting away, but equally knew that she could never escape his clutches. Danny was an evil bastard. He wouldn't think twice about wasting her if she ever lost her usefulness.

She'd gone out to a club, hoping to dip a few pockets, but instead she'd been chatted up at the bar. His name was

Mitchell Farrier and he was a banker in the city. One drink had led to several and she'd found herself attracted enough to go back to his apartment with him. When they'd started to get frisky, she'd been up for it. But he'd gone too far, she'd felt pressured and hit out ...

Going to prison had been a wake-up call, but it had been a harsh lesson to learn.

It was inside that Esther had become set on retribution. Having time on her own meant she could plan revenge on the men who had let her down. And as soon as she had been released, she'd been on to it. Going back to Shoreditch had been the first thing she'd done. Moving to Earl's Court had been the second.

Killing Jack Maitland had not been part of her plan though, and it had screwed everything up royally.

47

Tamara had spent the morning with her parents at their home. It was strange but Jack's death had her wanting to see them, as if to reiterate that they were still alive. Grief was a funny thing. Even her mother stopped with the put-me-down comments for a change. They had been as shocked as she was about him dying.

Once home, she wondered if she should call Esther or go and visit. Esther had had a terrible shock and although she seemed as if she wanted to be alone, Tamara was eager to learn as much as she could after the events of yesterday.

Then again, would she have been grateful if anyone had comforted her during her breakdown? She wasn't sure. But she had grown very fond of Esther over the past few months. At least she now understood why she'd been on edge. Maybe she needed a friend, a shoulder to cry on.

She sent several messages and when none received replies, she located Esther's address from her files.

In Trebovir Road, she squeezed her car into a space. She walked along the pavement and stopped outside a house. Glancing at the piece of paper in her hand, she took the five steps to the black door of a four-storey townhouse, several doorbells in a row to her right.

She pressed number one. There was no answer, so she pressed again. She was about to try one of the other bells to see if anyone could help her, when a voice came out of the tinny speaker.

'Yes?'

'Esther, it's me, Tamara.'

'I don't want to see anyone.'

'I need to speak to you, and I need to see you're okay.'

'I'm fine.'

'Esther, please. I'm not leaving until I see you.'

The entry system buzzed and the door opened, allowing her access to the building. The door to number one was ajar. Even so, she knocked gently before entering.

'Esther?' She stepped into a narrow, dimly lit vestibule.

'In here.'

Esther was lying on the sofa, covered in a duvet. There was an empty vodka bottle on the table next to a tall glass, and it was obvious from the smell in the room that she had been drinking heavily.

The curtains were drawn so Tamara moved to the window and opened them, letting in light.

'Don't do that.'

As Esther shielded her eyes, Tamara ignored her protests and glanced around the room again, trying not to wrinkle her nose at the smell. She hadn't expected her to be in such a poor establishment. It seemed to be so dated and cramped.

'Have you been like this since we left the police station?' she asked after deciding to stand up rather than sit down.

Esther nodded.

'Why didn't you answer my messages? I would have come to see you sooner.'

'I didn't want to intrude.'

'You don't intrude. Esther, you're my friend.'

'I'm not a good friend. You'll find that out soon.'

'Pardon?'

'Nothing.'

Tamara sighed. From the few words Esther had slurred, she could see she was still drunk.

'Did you get any sleep last night?'

'I can't remember.'

'I'll make some coffee. You're going to have yours black.'

She went into the tiny kitchen at the back of the flat. The small table was crammed with cups, plates, and lager cans. She wondered if these had accumulated since yesterday or if this was the way Esther lived. It was quite shocking to think it might be the latter.

Unable to find any milk in the fridge, she located a clean mug and instant coffee, and flicked on the kettle. She wouldn't have one herself.

Once the drink was made, Tamara took it in and handed it to Esther. She moved aside a pile of clothes from the armchair before sitting down.

'I won't ask how you've been,' she said, smiling kindly. 'But you know I am always here for you.'

'I don't want to talk.'

'Okay. I still can't believe he's dead though.'

Tamara saw Esther stiffen.

'I've had an email from Oscar. There's going to be a get-together tomorrow, a memorial, at half past eleven. I thought we could go together.'

'I'm not going.'

'It's entirely up to you but I think you should. You might regret it later, when things are different.'

Esther didn't speak, just looked ahead. Silence fell on the room again and Tamara realised she had done the wrong thing by coming around. She'd thought Esther might need some help getting to grips with things, perhaps blaming herself, but she was non-compliant. She felt as if she'd intruded on her grief, rather than helped her to come to terms with it.

'Esther?' Tamara tried one more time.

'Will you fuck off and leave me alone!' Esther screamed. 'You know nothing!'

Tamara reeled at her tone and stood up abruptly. 'Okay, I'm going, but I'm on the end of my phone at any time if you need me.'

Esther nodded.

Tamara left her to it. But the more she thought about things as they ran around in her head that evening, she couldn't shake off the feeling that something wasn't adding up. Esther had been grief stricken, of course, but her eyes had been glazed over too. It seemed much more than the drink she had taken.

She supposed it was none of her business how she got through this but she wondered why she was drinking so heavily. Was it only to block everything out? If she thought back to how Esther's behaviour had changed over the past month, had she been taking something then too? And if so, was it because she had started the affair with Jack and was unable to cope with sharing him? It seemed weird but something had changed.

She wasn't sure she trusted Esther. She wasn't sure she was telling the truth.

And Tamara had lied for her.

Had she given her an alibi for something more serious? Had Jack fallen? She shuddered as an image of Esther pushing him down the stairs came to her.

No, Esther couldn't be responsible for Jack's death. Could she?

48

I tried to scream but a hand covered my mouth. My eyes showed fear, my face wet with tears as his other hand found the front of my jacket.

'No. Stop!'

He then pushed it up inside my jumper, squeezing roughly first one breast and then the other.

'Like that, do you?' he sneered. 'Do you like it rough?'

I shook my head. I couldn't move with the weight of him. He had me pinned down.

His hand moved lower, between my legs. I tried to push it away but he slapped me.

'Stay still!'

'No.' My voice came out barely more than a whisper, but I kept fighting. He slapped me again, wrenching my neck to one side.

When he pulled at the waistband of my jodhpurs, part of me wanted to scream again, but I didn't dare. He was too strong for me. I didn't know what to do.

His breath smelled of cigars, his lips all over mine, sloppy. I moved my head away and he grabbed my chin.

'Don't want to kiss you anyway, you little whore.'

Tears poured down my face. I knew what he was about to do was going to hurt. He didn't care about anything but himself.

'No, stop,' I pleaded. But he continued.

And then I saw someone.

Esther woke up, the bottle of whiskey she'd been working her way through almost slipping from her hands. She'd started on the heavier stuff once Tamara had left. She wanted to blot out what had happened for a while longer.

Seeing Tamara earlier had been embarrassing but she shouldn't have turned up out of the blue like that. How dare she come to her home address.

Really, Esther knew she'd been stupid letting her in. She shouldn't have answered the intercom, pretended she was out. Then she wouldn't feel like she did now. As if it was her fault that Jack had died, even though she hadn't meant to kill him.

But it was herself she was most angry with. Would she always be violent around men after what happened to her? Always out of control or would it stop once she had got her revenge?

She'd tried to block out the incident so many times but things kept coming back at her, reminding her of the trauma. She'd wake up dreaming about a man attacking her, punch out into the dark shadows in her bedroom.

She'd close her eyes to stop herself crying when memories came flooding back. And now, after what had happened with Danny, everything was heightened again. It was his fault. He made her do it.

Would she ever find someone who would truly love her, be with her because he wanted to, rather than out of pity or because she had been selling herself? Be with her even after she had told him about her troubled past, so that there were no more secrets. No lies either.

She put the bottle to her mouth again and drank a large mouthful, the liquid spilling from her lips in her haste. She gasped as it burned at her throat. Tears spilled down her face: of pity, not remorse trying not to think of yesterday afternoon.

If that marble ornament hadn't been to hand, she would have slapped Jack. He would have reacted to stop her, they would have argued, and none of this would have happened. It had been nothing more than an accident.

But she couldn't let Jack's death ruin things for her. She had to decide what to do next and when.

And then she sat upright. Maybe there was a way to take the heat from her. She thought about it for a while until another plan began to formulate. She would go to the memorial tomorrow, but first she would meet up with Tamara. She had some things to discuss with her.

She pulled herself from the settee and went through to the bathroom. Kneeling down, she removed the tin from behind the bath panel and took out her insurance policy.

Danny's gun.

Wherever she went, whatever she did, that was coming with her. She didn't need it to set him up any longer but it could come in useful as a bargaining tool.

Because she still needed revenge on one person, and she was still going to go through with that. She couldn't let all this be for nothing. She needed to change her plan, and quick.

She sent Tamara a text.

I'm so sorry for overreacting. Will you meet me in the morning at the coffee shop around the corner from where I live, on Earl's Court Road at 9.30? I would like to go to Jack's memorial. We can travel on from there together. x

A message came back seconds later.

Yes of course. x

Esther laughed. Good old gullible Tamara.

49

Monday 17 July

Esther pushed on the door and stepped into the coffee shop. The large and bright establishment was full to bursting and, the more she thought about it, probably not the right place for this meeting. It seemed noisier inside than it had been out on the street.

She joined the queue of people waiting to be served behind the mum with a tiny baby in a sling and a toddler in a pushchair, two elderly women chatting about the weather, and a woman holding up a mirror while applying mascara to curled lashes.

Esther stared at each in turn, wondering if any of them were content. In the frame of mind she was in right now, it was best to concentrate on others. Everyone would be happier than her considering how her life had gone horribly wrong again during the past few weeks. Sometimes she wondered whether it was worth continuing with it. Would anyone even care if *she* had died rather than him?

She shuffled forward in the queue as the elderly women in front moved down the counter to wait for their drinks. The sounds of the morning rush did nothing to soothe her nerves. Neither did the man behind the till when he threw her a warm smile. Perhaps she should have chosen somewhere she wasn't known.

'Hi, Esther,' the barista said in a thick Irish accent, his dark, wavy hair held back underneath a baseball cap. 'Your usual today?'

'A cappuccino, please, Aiden.'

Esther had been a regular there since she'd first moved to Earl's Court. Aiden had served her with a cappuccino on that first day and she had sunk into a chair on the back wall, people-watching while she yet again contemplated her future. She often came for breakfast now. Anything beat cooking in her grimy excuse for a kitchen. She'd been lucky not to catch food poisoning from the decades-old cooker, and the fridge was a death trap. The light in the freezer compartment flickered on and off at an alarming rate every time she opened the door.

'Off to work?' he asked, as she handed him the right change.

Esther nodded, even though she was lying. Why was everyone so friendly all the time?

She took a deep breath as he shouted down her order. It was going to be okay.

A shiver rippled through her. Who was she trying to fool?

Her coffee ready, she made her way to an empty table she had spotted on the side wall. She sat down so that she could see the entrance. If the police wanted to speak with her, she had to be able to move fast.

A flash of yellow caught her eye and she looked out on

to Earl's Court Road. Figure after figure, group after group, couple after couple rushed past the window, until they blended into one big mesh of colour.

Her eyes brimmed with tears when she thought of the trouble she was in, what she stood to lose if things were to get any more out of hand. She couldn't bargain with her freedom again, not so soon after the last time.

With a deep breath, she pushed her fears aside, and sat upright to appear confident. She was used to this kind of thing in her life. Bad things had happened before and she had got through them. It came with the territory. This had to be done too, before things got out of hand.

She lifted her cup to her mouth, blew on the hot liquid before taking a small sip, and checked the time on the clock. It was 9.25 a.m.

Five more minutes.

Tamara stepped off the tube on to the platform, willing her feet to move forward. It was going to be a long day; one she wasn't sure she would even get through. Dread and anxiety burrowed through her in equal measures, but she had to keep them both at bay. It was imperative to keep her wits about her while she was in Esther's company.

The day was warm, temperatures having finally reduced to a milder eighteen degrees with a slight chance of rain. Tamara made her way up the steps, almost being lifted by the throng of people. The large clock on the wall said it was two minutes after nine-thirty. It didn't matter if she was a few minutes late. It wasn't as if she was looking forward to the morning.

Her blouse felt sticky underneath her jacket, sweat patches revealing how nervous she was. It reminded her of happier times, when she had been pleased to have Esther around. Now she could curse herself for not being vigilant, for being too trusting, especially after what had happened with Michael.

A wave of nausea washed over her. Last night, she had tossed and turned in her bed, going over everything. Had she been tricked? *Could* Jack have died just like that?

In a matter of seconds, she came out into the open and turned left. Earl's Court wasn't an area she was familiar with. Now the hustle and bustle of so many small businesses, traffic and people crammed together overwhelmed her. The pavements were wide, like they were in Central London, but the clientele was a little livelier, a tad pushier. Petrol fumes hung in the air, the sounds of engines revving as they were at a standstill. The bleeps from the pedestrian crossing, a screeching of brakes, the odd peep of a horn.

The coffee shop where they had arranged to meet was right in front of her. Tamara knew instantly she wouldn't like it. She tried not to visit chains, instead choosing to use one of the many specialist coffee bars that were scattered across the city. There was something about their ambience that she loved, the aroma of baked cakes and coffee granules second to none.

She paused in the middle of the pavement, her feet finally unable to move forward.

'Watch out!'

She turned as a man slammed into the back of her. 'Sorry.'

Her voice came out as a whisper as she moved to one side, but he had already disappeared. She pressed her back into the wall of a building, almost suffocated by the crowds going past; like worker ants, all on a mission to get to their destinations as quickly as possible.

She wished she could turn around, go down the steps and travel back in time – to when she hadn't met Esther, or seen Jack Maitland again. Where her life was simple, and she only had herself to look after. Or look out for.

Tamara still didn't want to go into the coffee shop. Earlier she'd thought it would be best to go straight to the police, talk to the female detective again. But she wasn't certain anyone would believe her.

No, she had to sort this out first. No matter what the consequences. If her thoughts were right, her future could very much depend on it.

50

Esther's cappuccino had almost disappeared. She checked the clock on the wall and decided against getting another one. Too much caffeine on a day like today would make her more hyper.

The man and woman on the table next to her gathered their belongings. Almost immediately, a young woman squeezed past her and jumped in their place. Esther glanced at her surreptitiously. She looked late teens – a student from the amount of books Esther could see shoved inside her bag as she put it on the floor between her feet. As soon as she sat down, her phone was out and her fingertips were sliding back and forth across the screen. Esther wondered if she was sending messages to friends, family, a lover, maybe. Envy tore through her. She bet *her* life was simple.

She stifled a yawn. She had woken every hour last night and, by 4.00 a.m., had got out of bed and stayed up. Her mind wouldn't stop going over and over the details of Saturday afternoon. She closed her eyes momentarily, but the images that flashed before them made her open them abruptly again. A man upset, his face screwed up in anger, inches from hers. Then another: this time he was flat out on the floor, blood pouring from a wound, eyes dead. Despite how much she had hated Jack, it wasn't how she wanted to remember him either.

She turned back to the room. In a coffee shop like this one, she could blend into a crowd and yet still be part of life. More often than not, she could get away with a purse or two, maybe a bag but she didn't mess on her own doorstep, so the clientele in here were safe.

She looked through the window again, an army of people still marching by. And then she saw Tamara, taking slow steps towards the door, as if she didn't want to come inside. As if she didn't want to see her.

Esther had known, despite everything, that Tamara had always thought she was better than her. She'd often caught the odd glimpse of uncertainty; the seeds of doubt being formed in her mind.

But Tamara would do well to remember what part Esther had had in *her* success. It was she who had made people stand up and take notice of Tamara during the past few months. If it weren't for her, Parker-Brown PR would have sunk without trace.

She sat up straight, ready for the fight ahead. She knew one slip up from either of them and she would be in a lot of trouble. Yet, she didn't want to alert Tamara to how she was feeling right away.

Because the mask that she wore was beginning to slip. Even though she was extremely used to hiding her feelings, it was a fine line to balance acting normal for so long. Especially after what had happened on Saturday.

· · ·

Steeling herself, Tamara took a deep breath and entered the coffee shop. The steamer burst into life, making her visibly jump. Her eyes flicked around, but when they landed on one pair staring at her intently, there was no friendly greeting, no wave, no smile.

The coffee shop was busier than she was used to, even though the early morning rush had dissipated. There were a few groups of teenagers late for college, a couple of mums who had perhaps come in after dropping their children at school, and the odd person alone with their thoughts.

She wondered if her life would ever be that carefree again.

How she wished she could go back thirteen years to when she was at university, and live her life over. She wouldn't make the same mistakes, or the wrong choices.

As she waited to be served, she could almost feel Esther's eyes burrowing into the back of her. She held on to the counter as she gave her order, sweat building up on her brow and upper lip.

Had she been wrong? Esther was supposed to be her friend. Tamara had trusted her. She had confided in her, thinking she was a kindred spirit. Knowing that she too had been hurt in the past, she had told her things she hadn't told others, not even her own family. She thought she'd understood what Esther had been through, but now she wasn't sure. Had it all been lies about her past?

She turned as if to look out of the window, keeping Esther in her sight. But no, her head was down. She was tapping away on her phone. How could she sit there and act as if nothing had happened?

Her drink ready, she made her way to the table.

51

Esther stared at Tamara. She had quite enjoyed having a friend, someone to confide in, laugh with, share things with, even if it was for such a short time. But Tamara had to be collateral, didn't she realise that? If Esther stood to lose out, she would do anything to stop it.

Tamara had been a real find. Someone who was willing to pay her to get close to her target. It had been fun going with her to all the launch parties, PR receptions, get-togethers, and networking events they had attended.

But Tamara would be left bereft, with no friends again. No one would trust her; no one would want to work with her.

Still, that wasn't entirely Esther's fault. She had given her a good leg up with her business. Really, she should be grateful.

The young woman beside them gathered her belongings and made for the door.

'Esther, I'm worried about you,' Tamara began. 'How are you doing?'

'I'm fine.'

Tamara played with the handle on her cup. 'You're the only one who knows what really happened on Saturday.'

'It was an accident. I keep telling you that he fell.' Esther folded her arms. '*You* don't know because you weren't there.'

'That's the point I'm trying to make.'

Esther sighed. 'Do we have to go through all this again?'

'I only know what you're telling me.'

'What you *saw,* actually.' There was no disputing that. Tamara *had* seen the body.

'Don't be so melodramatic.' Esther sat back and folded her arms. 'We're going to the memorial together. It will look suspicious if we don't.'

Tamara put her head in her hands. 'I'm not sure I can face everyone.'

'You don't have to, but you won't like the alternative.' Esther glared at her, surprised by Tamara's hostility towards her. Tamara seemed more concerned about herself rather than how she was feeling. It wasn't on. And she shouldn't be questioning her. She needed to remember where her place was.

'I don't want to be questioned by the police again,' Tamara said.

Ah, she was only worried about being caught out lying. Esther reached across the table for Tamara's hand.

'It will be fine, as long as we stick together.'

Tamara snatched her hand away, almost knocking over her cup. She put it straight again before glaring back.

'No!' Tamara's voice rose again. People turned to stare for a second before looking away. 'Is there something you're not telling me?' she continued. 'Because looking back, it doesn't seem feasible that you would get me to lie to cover up your affair. Are you involved in his death?'

Esther ignored the question. 'He tripped, fell down the stairs, and hit his head twice.'

'You said you didn't see him.'

'I'm going by what the police told me. Why are you questioning me so much?'

There was a pause before Tamara spoke again. 'Because I don't believe you.'

'You don't have to believe me,' Esther snapped. 'You only have to keep quiet.'

'About what?'

'About what you think really happened.'

'What *did* happen?'

Esther was getting tired of the game now. She studied Tamara, wondering how she was feeling inside. She was visibly shaken up but it was time to start playing with her emotions, her weak side, her vulnerability.

'You wanted him dead, didn't you?' she said.

Tamara's eyes widened in horror. 'How can you say that?' she hissed. 'And what reasoning do you have for it?'

'It was your idea to cover it up.'

'No, it wasn't.'

'You're the one who's lying, so who will they believe?' Esther paused for a moment. 'When you came to help, you didn't stop to think about why I would have needed you there, did you?'

Tamara's brow furrowed.

'I wanted your fingerprints in the house as well as my own.'

'I came because you were upset,' Tamara said. 'You told me Jack was alive and concussed.'

'He was.'

'So there *is* no problem then?'

'Well, not if the police don't see us on any cameras.'

'You told me they were off at Jack's house.'

'They were, but they could still pick us up from the roadside. There's CCTV covering Holland Park.'

Tamara shook her head in dismay. 'What's going on, Esther? One minute you say that Jack fell down the stairs and the next you're trying to blame me – for what? If it was an accident, then you have nothing to worry about and you should have come clean straight away.'

'So should you.'

'He was dead when I got there ...'

'Yes, when you got there.'

Tamara's eyes widened again. 'What do you mean by that?'

Esther shook her head, a sly smile emerging. 'I don't appear to be the kind of woman he would have an affair with anyway.' She raised her eyebrows suggestively.

'What?'

'Oh, come on. You were sleeping with him, weren't you?'

'No, I wasn't.'

'Are you sure about that?'

'Of course, I'm sure. Why are you twisting everything?'

'I'm only looking at things from both points of view – you know, if I was Detective Carley.'

'I haven't done anything wrong.'

Esther sighed dramatically. 'Why do you keep saying that when all I'm trying to do is cover your back?'

It was no use. Esther was letting Tamara know what would happen if she went to the police. She would say that it was *her* having an affair with Jack. And once the police had gathered their evidence, plus the things Esther was lying about for her own benefit, Tamara knew she could be in terrible trouble. It could be her word against Esther's. She wasn't certain she would win.

But, for now, she needed to play the game. She had to get Esther to think she was in agreement with anything she was going to do or say.

'What do you really want?'

'Money.'

Tamara drew back her head.

'You've always thought you were superior to me because you were born into it. But that's worked out fine now. You have lots of it. You won't miss a few grand.'

'I hardly have any. You know that.'

'But you have Mummy and Daddy to help you.'

'I haven't had assistance from them either. I've been trying to keep afloat for months by myself.'

'Why?'

'Because I wanted to do this on my own.'

'Well, you'll have to ask them for a loan.' Esther folded her arms and glared at her. 'Because if you don't then I'm going to the police and I *will* say that you killed Jack.'

'The evidence won't stack up.'

'Want to chance it? You've already lied to the police.'

'Because you lied to them first!'

'Well, I think they'll have to work out which one of us did it for themselves.'

Tamara paled again as she tried not to be intimidated by Esther's glare, but she failed miserably.

'What do you mean?' she said, swallowing down her anxiety.

Esther folded her arms. 'Who will they believe, Tamara? Me, or you with your track record?'

52

Esther had thought it seemed a good idea last night to blackmail Tamara but now she wasn't so sure. Was it wise to make up more lies? It would always have to be an accident. She couldn't say it was anything else. And Tamara would have people to protect her, money for good lawyers to get her off with anything. Esther had no one.

Come on, Esther, she chastised herself, *get back into character.*

'I suppose we'd better be making a move to the memorial.' She popped her phone in her bag, watching as Tamara ran a hand over her hair before flopping it down to her side afterwards. Her eyes had blurred over, her shallow breathing making Esther wonder if she was about to pass out.

This was perfect, she thought. Tamara obviously knew she wasn't strong enough to overpower her.

Tamara stared at Esther. What the hell was wrong with her? She was warping everything to get herself out of trouble and to put the blame on her. And because she had already lied to the police, Esther had the upper hand.

She made to stand up, but Esther reached across the table and grabbed her wrist. Her stare sent a shiver up Tamara's spine. She pulled away to free her hand, pushed back her chair and got to her feet.

With trembling hands, she put on her jacket. She wasn't sure if she would get through the memorial service, but she had to go. Esther was right. It would look suspicious if they weren't there. And she did want to pay her respects.

Then she would go to the police.

Esther pushed past her and then turned back sharply.

'Remember, we both need to be on our best behaviour. And I think you should flag down a taxi. You don't want to be getting all flustered on the tube, do you? You look enough of a mess as it is.'

Tamara held in her shock at Esther's cruel tone. 'I need to use the bathroom first.' She walked to the back of the room, thankful her legs would carry her. To her dismay, the door to the ladies' led to two cubicles.

Once on her own, she glanced in the mirror. Her face was devoid of colour. She got out her phone and was about to go into a cubicle when the door opened, and Esther appeared. She knocked the mobile out of her hand and with one swift move, pushed her into the wall, her head connecting with the tiles.

'You think you can play with me?' Esther seethed, her face only an inch away. 'One false move from you and I will break every bone in your body. Do you hear?'

Tamara couldn't speak but she nodded her head. Esther's eyes were wild, pupils dilated.

'Good.' Esther smoothed down her dress. 'Now, out, where I can see you.'

Tamara walked with Esther close on her heel. With no evidence to back up her claims, she could end up in real trouble. She'd read about cases of injustice. Esther was clever enough to lie to pin it all on her.

Because Esther had fooled her. There had been no friendship on her behalf. Instead, there had been scheming and deceit, lies and misdirection. How could she not have seen through her act? She would never forgive herself for letting her guard down.

Yet, after all the months of being lonely, it had felt so good. Esther had brought brightness back to her life. She'd enjoyed working with her, socialising with her. Yes, she had seen the cracks appearing, but she had ignored them because she was having fun. She had found someone to trust.

How wrong she had been.

Over the past few days, she had learned more about Esther than she'd ever thought possible. She was so different than how she was perceived. She had most people thinking she was all sweet and innocent, that she was a shy soul, likeable but quiet. But she wasn't fooling her any more.

Tears pricked at her eyes. She had no one to turn to. No one to help her. She was stuck in this nightmare. She would look like a liar either way, trying to cover up what she had done, when in essence, she hadn't done anything at all.

One thing was clear, though; she had chosen the wrong person when she was in need of a friend.

53

St Bartholomew's Church was almost full by the time Esther and Tamara arrived. They managed to squeeze in at the end of a pew at the back, close to the aisle. There were people Esther recognised – Simone and her agent, Arabella, Tamara's parents, several of the book buyers and sales representatives she'd been liaising with over the past few weeks, as well as staff from Dulston Publishing. There were lots more that she didn't know too. How had he become so popular?

But she knew the answer to that. Even though she had hated his touch, he'd had charisma, a charm that made people warm to him. By far, Jack Maitland had been the most pleasant man she had ever set out to screw, in both senses of the word. She wasn't sure what would have happened if Jack had looked and acted like Oscar, or Ben.

She still would have gone through with everything though.

She craned her neck to look through the crowd. If she moved a little to her right, a photograph of Jack came into view. It stood proud on the easel that she suspected had also propped up the images of Simone and her book at the launch of *Something's Got to Give*. A warm, friendly image with the smile that used to light up any room ... the Jack that everyone knew.

Not the one who had let her down all those years ago.

Music came through the speakers. Esther heard mourners gasping as 'I Will Always Love You' filtered through. She wondered what songs would be played at her funeral, though she wouldn't be having a memorial like this. There would hardly be anyone attending to play music to anyway. Her mother might come, if she heard about it. She'd like that.

Everyone looked behind them when the family walked in. Natalie was first, her arms wrapped around her boys, standing on either side of her. They looked so much like their father it was a shame to see them crying. Esther had lost her father too; she knew only too well the pain they were going through.

She thought back to the last memory she had of him. They had been to the cinema, to see *Erin Brockovich*. It had been a rare treat to get all three of them together then. If she was in the house, she would be in her room, wanting to be on her own. But this night, they were a family and she'd had a glimmer of what the future might be like if she could get over her ordeal.

Two weeks later, he'd suffered the first of two strokes. It was then she knew she was being punished. To take her dad away after all she had been through wasn't right.

As the vicar addressed the crowd, she held her head high again, concentrating on the task in hand. He said a few words and then everyone stood up for the first hymn, allowing her time to look around again.

Usually she enjoyed watching people, but this time she was wondering if anyone was second-guessing what had happened. She could see the back of Oscar – was he wondering what had really gone on? She could see Ben next to him, a woman clinging on to his arm. Did he assume it was a tragic accident? Esther supposed no one there would be any the wiser really.

Tamara sniffed and Esther turned to face her, watched her wipe at her eyes. She could hear the shake in her voice as she tried to sing the hymn.

Tamara must have felt her stare, as she looked her way. Tears shimmered in her eyes. Excellent! Everyone would blame her when Esther was gone. She needed to finish what she'd started and then make a quick exit.

It was perfect really. Esther might have confided in Tamara about some of the secrets of her past, but she wouldn't be able to work out the truth from the lies. Tamara didn't know the half of her life. How far she would go to get her own way, ensure her safety and escape.

The service was over in half an hour. As they waited for the family to leave, Esther put down her head. When Natalie walked past again with her sons, a wild roar made her look up quickly. Natalie lurched at them, arms flying.

'How dare you show your faces here,' she bellowed, her hand catching the side of Tamara's face. As she was being pulled away by her father, Natalie continued. 'You know more than you're letting on! Why were you both at my house?'

Esther planted a look of shock on her face but inwardly she was smiling at the sight before her. She had brought Natalie to tears, her family ruined. Their tight-knit quartet had become a trio with a life-long gap of unfilled dreams and missed opportunities. It was better than nothing, she supposed.

As Natalie was led away, Gabrielle Maitland walked

behind. Reggie Maitland's arms were wrapped around her as she clung to him, an expression of disbelief. The veil on her black hat had fallen crooked slightly in the kerfuffle but Esther could see her eyes were puffy from crying, make-up blotchy.

Well, well, well, there was some justice at least. Everyone was feeling as much pain as she had felt all those years ago.

54

Tamara sat down on the pew and waited while everyone left the church. She wasn't sure she could face anyone who was hanging around outside. Everyone would be consoling Natalie and she didn't want her to make a scene again. It wouldn't be fair on either of them.

It didn't really matter in the grand scheme of things. Tamara knew she was ruined. No one would want to work with her now after this, even if it wasn't her fault. Natalie blamed her. Everyone had seen what she had done and said, and mud sticks.

And all those people she'd met recently, did they blame her too? Her cheek stung where Natalie had slapped it. She pressed her hand to it, feeling it burning. It wasn't the only thing – she was so humiliated.

Esther, who was sitting next to her, had her head down, looking at her phone. She was scrolling through something on her screen. Tamara spotted the Facebook logo.

'How can you pretend that nothing has happened?' she said.

Esther looked up with a frown, and then smiled. 'I'm

not. I'm looking to see what people are saying about Jack online.'

'I did say we would make things worse by coming here.'

'You did!' Esther smiled. 'And we have. You should have seen Reggie Maitland's face. Poor man.' She giggled again. 'And his stuck-up wife.'

'Please show some respect.' Tamara shook her head but Esther wasn't listening. She was back to her phone again, as if she hadn't a care in the world. Just how cold was she? After talking to her at the coffee shop, she wouldn't believe anything she said now.

She had to go to the police, even if she would be in trouble for lying. Maybe she would get a caution at the station, perhaps because the real truth would come out and then everyone would know she had nothing to do with it.

But what if Esther orchestrated it to seem as if she *had* done it? That Tamara pushed Jack down the stairs to his death. If she then lied, Tamara would be in even more trouble. She knew from experience how manipulative Esther could be. She wasn't sure if she trusted the police to believe her over Esther.

Her shoulders drooped. She didn't know what to do for the best.

Esther popped her phone into her bag and stood up. She stretched her arms over her head before looking down at her.

'I think it's safe to leave now, don't you?'

Tamara nodded. All she wanted was to get out of there.

Outside the church, there were still a few mourners but most were making their way to their cars. She kept her head down, avoiding anyone's eye as they hurried past a few groups of people.

Needing some space, she verged off to the left and

walked to the back of the church. Hidden behind the building, away from any prying eyes, she rested her hand on the wall and bent over. Vomit poured from her as it all became too much.

Images of being locked in her room every night began to crowd her again, trying to convince professionals that everything was fine. It had taken a whole six months before anyone had believed she was well enough to leave.

She couldn't trust the police yet. She couldn't trust anyone; she had no one to turn to. But she had to find a way to clear her name before all this came down on her.

She turned to see Esther behind her. 'Leave me alone.'

'What's up now?' Esther was by her side. She rested a hand on her back. 'Got a case of the nerves?'

Tamara shrugged it off and took a step away from her. 'Can't you see how much damage you've done?' She glanced up at Esther, a look of innocence on her face, but she recognised it now for what it was. She'd seen it so many times over the past few weeks, but had thought it was a stubborn streak she had. Only now was she realising just how clever Esther was at playing the lying game.

'You need to keep your wits about you.' Esther spoke quietly but with menace. 'There are eyes and ears everywhere. Remember that.'

Tamara didn't reply but watched as Esther turned and walked away.

'Maybe you'd better remember that too,' she said quietly.

She decided there and then that she wasn't going to go down without a fight. She would use that drive and spirit she'd found again during the past few months. She would believe in herself enough to take on Esther.

This was her reputation and livelihood at stake. She had to find some way of getting the truth out of Esther, to make sure of her own innocence. Then she would go to the police.

She hated to even think about it but there was only one person she could turn to right now.

Carley's desk phone went off.

'DC Evans.'

'Are you dealing with the death of Jack Maitland, Carley?' a voice asked.

'Yes, in between everything else. I might be sweeping the floor soon as well.' Her voice was light. Everyone was multi-tasking. 'What's up?'

'There's someone in reception that wants to see you. Mrs Williams. Says it's urgent.'

'On my way.'

The woman sitting in the interview room appeared to be in her mid-fifties. She was sitting upright, hands clasped on the desk in front of her. Carley knew the look, a talker who needed to get something off her chest.

She had blonde hair that had thinned out with age, and bitten-down nails. Her expression was one of concern but that wasn't unusual. A lot of people were nervous in police stations, even if they hadn't broken the law. She peered at her again, wondering why she looked familiar.

'Mrs Williams?' Carley sat down across from her and

smiled. 'I'm Detective Constable Carley Evans. I believe you might have some information for us with regards to Jack Maitland?'

'Well, yes, but more about my daughter too. I haven't seen her in years until yesterday.' She rummaged in her bag, pulled out a newspaper and pointed to a photograph.

Carley studied it. It was a small feature on Jack Maitland's death. The woman was pointing at a photograph. There were a number of people with him. Carley had seen it yesterday. It was a photo from the recent launch of the book *Something's Got to Give*. She wondered what its significance was.

'She knows Jack Maitland,' the woman said.

Carley's eyes snapped back to her.

'Who does?'

'Bethany.' She tapped a finger on the image of a woman.

Carley looked again. 'We know her as Esther Smedley.'

'No, that's my daughter, Bethany. I'm telling you, it's her.'

A prickle of excitement rose up Carley's back, the hairs on her arms standing up. Where had she seen the name Bethany Williams recently?

'Mrs Williams,' Carley found herself holding her breath, 'are you saying that Bethany could be Esther?'

There was a small pause from Mrs Williams. A tear rolled down her cheek and she wiped it away quickly. 'Bethany was raped when she was barely fifteen.'

Carley's shoulders drooped. What a tragedy at such a young and impressionable age. At least Esther, as they knew her, had managed to sort her life out. Having completed a spate on the domestic violence team before moving to CID, Carley knew so many women who hadn't been able to get over their attacks.

'Are you able to tell me about it?' she asked gently.

After a moment, Mrs Williams nodded. 'Bethany was crazy about horses from a young age. She used to spend as much time as she could at the stables down the road.'

'Down the road at?'

'Ascot. I live a few minutes from the racecourse. Been there all my married life. Bethany was raised there too. She got a job as a stable girl when she was fourteen, for Reggie Maitland. It was only supposed to be the odd hour after school but she would spend as much time as she could there. Horses were her life then. They had twelve and she got attached to so many of them. She was a quiet teenager, always on her own, so I guess she took solace in it. She said she was going to be a trainer – until the day her life changed forever.'

Carley took notes as the woman gathered a second wind. Her words tumbled out, as if she didn't want to bring the memories to light again.

'Bethany came home one Saturday afternoon and she wasn't her usual self. I asked her what was wrong and she said she didn't feel too well. She didn't want to go to the stables on Sunday and begged me to keep her from school on Monday, saying she wasn't well.

'It took me four days to get out of her what had happened. She had been raped, in one of the stables. I had to listen to all the details while she cried. My poor baby had been violated by that ... that bastard and your lot didn't believe her.' Mrs Williams's tone became accusatory. 'The family were well-to-do. Of course, he denied everything, but I knew my daughter. She would *never* make anything up like that.'

Carley put down her pen and frowned. 'Are you saying your daughter knew who it was that raped her?'

56

Esther rushed back to her flat. Things were happening way too quickly. She needed to get away and then come back to sort everything else out once the heat was off her.

In the bedroom, she pulled down a holdall from the top of the wardrobe and threw it on to the unmade bed. She raced round opening drawers and pulling clothes out. She'd have to leave some behind. She certainly didn't need all the fancy dresses, shoes, and bags she'd bought recently, only essentials. T-shirts, jumpers, and trousers. Underwear, pumps, and a jacket.

At the chest of drawers that doubled as her dressing table, she pushed off its contents with her arm and dropped them straight into a cheap toiletry bag.

In the bathroom, she retrieved the tin from behind the bath panel. She removed the passport and money she had saved, plus the gun, and shoved them in the holdall too. At the bottom, underneath everything, there was an envelope. Family photos were the only things she had left of her past now, but she couldn't bear to look at them too often for that reason.

There was one of her mum and dad, standing proud on their wedding day. Underneath that, one of her and her mum. Another of her at the seaside on a donkey, head back as she had roared with laughter. Happier times. She'd had such a loving childhood.

Her dad popped into her thoughts and her eyes brimmed with tears. She wondered if she'd have taken a different path if he had still been alive. He would have been so ashamed of her now, and that hurt more each day.

Her mum said she had her dad's eyes, most of his features and that it comforted her to see him looking back from her. But she knew that would have turned to hate eventually, when she realised she was never going to see him again, and that it was her fault.

She had let her parents down by allowing that monster to attack her. She should have fought to stop him but she was too afraid.

The best thing she'd been able to do at the time was leave. And that was when her life had really gone rotten.

Next, she opened up her laptop and located a cheap holidays website. Within minutes, she had found a flight that left early the next morning. There was a desk at the airport where she could pay for it in cash.

And then she'd probably have to change her appearance again.

She flopped down on the bed. What was she going to do about Danny? If the police came there, they'd find him in the garage and know what she had done.

And Tamara was innocent. She was the closest Esther had ever had to a friend. Someone she could have learned to trust in different circumstances. Someone she could have seen herself knowing for many years to come.

Tamara was such a lovely person, always put everyone

before herself. She must have gone through some trauma for her to have a breakdown. Esther didn't know why she had let that jerk Michael Foster do that to her. She was stronger than that.

And had things been different in Esther's life, perhaps she would have had children, like Jack had, and a husband with a good job, a large house and a nice life. But now she'd never know because everything had been taken from her when she was fifteen.

She still remembered every bit of it: the hurt, the humiliation, the pain. And then the anger. It never stopped, and had got worse over the years.

And here she was again, taking her fears and frustrations out on innocent people.

But Tamara's downfall had to be to Esther's advantage. *She* would be believed over her because no one knew who she really was.

57

Carley listened attentively, adrenaline pumping through her.

'Oh, yes, she knew who raped her.' Mrs Williams nodded, wringing the handkerchief in her hand. 'But he denied it all, said she had made it up because he was going to fire her. He said he'd caught her messing around with one of the stable boys. We found out the boy in question had been given money to say Bethany was his girlfriend and that they regularly had sex in the stables. The boy denied that when we challenged him, though. But it became *their* word against Bethany's.'

'Whose word?'

'The Maitlands.'

Carley frowned, wondering if she was thinking along the right lines. 'Are you saying the man who raped your daughter was Jack Maitland?'

'No!' Mrs Williams shook her head. 'It was his father. It was Reggie Maitland who took my little girl's innocence.'

Carley tried her best not to give away the shock that was

running through her mind. Keeping her facial expression straight, she continued.

'And you say you haven't seen Bethany since she was seventeen?'

'No. My husband suffered a stroke shortly after it happened, and then another one four months later. The first took his speech and mobility: the second took his life.'

'And Bethany blamed herself?'

'Yes. I'm sure it was nothing to do with it. She thought the stress had killed him because she'd overheard the doctor say it could be a factor. And because no one believed her, once it got out at school, she became a victim of bullying. She was called names, in particular a liar and a slut.'

Carley passed a fresh tissue to her, waiting patiently until she began again. It must be raking up such terrible memories for her.

'I can't tell you how many times I had to go into the school to talk to her teachers about it. Even I was accosted by some of the neighbours. It's a small community and everyone knows everyone. News travelled fast and Bethany lost all her friends. She was fifteen, dealing with a rape and no one believed her, except us.'

Carley looked back at her notes. 'But you said you reported it to the police?'

Mrs Williams wiped at her face. 'They dropped the case through lack of evidence. Bethany went completely off the rails then. She got into trouble for vandalising Maitland's car, and breaking into his stables as she wanted to see the horses. When her father died, I couldn't keep her in school. I tried to get her into college but she didn't want to leave the house. I felt such a failure as her mother but she wouldn't let me help her at all. I think she blamed me for no one believing her.'

'That can't be true,' Carley soothed.

'She wrote a note saying not to look for her. It broke my heart, and of course I did eventually go in search of her. I found her in some squat and she broke my heart again when she wouldn't come back. She was such a mess. She was dirty, smelled a bit, if I'm honest. She looked underweight and her hair was matted.' Her voice caught in her throat. 'I tried to be there for her but it wasn't enough. I haven't seen her since I found her in the squat. No letters, no phone calls, nothing. Until yesterday when I noticed her in the newspaper.'

Carley couldn't give details out but also knew that she had to tell her something. 'We believe she might have had something to do with the death of Jack Maitland.'

'I know, but it doesn't make sense. Jack was only a few years older than Bethany. She wouldn't have known him that well. He would have been at some university like Cambridge or Oxford when she was working at the stables.'

Carley thought back to when she had met Esther. Although first impressions counted for nothing in this job, she had seemed extremely upset by Jack's death. Was there more to her tears than grief?

It was time to dig into her past and see what she could find out. The things her mother was saying could have given Esther a perfect motive if it was Reggie Maitland that had died. Something didn't add up.

Mrs Williams left and Carley almost tripped over her feet in her haste to get to see Max.

'Esther Smedley is really Bethany Williams,' she cried, breathless as she walked into his office. She updated him with what she had found out. 'I'm going to check if she's on our system.'

Max's eyes widened as Carley took a breath. He pressed

a few keys to bring up a new screen on his computer and the image of a young woman came up. They both peered at it. The hair was blonde rather than auburn, but it was definitely Smedley.

'Her charges range from shoplifting, prostitution, and the odd drug bust.' He stopped. 'She got three years for GBH – served eighteen months and was released six months ago.'

'That's not the address she gave to us,' Carley said, pointing at the screen. 'There's a number for her probation officer, Amy Farmer. I can try her?'

A knock on the door. 'You're wanted for the briefing, sir,' a young PC told them.

Max nodded. 'On my way. Carley, get on to forensics, see if anything is ready yet on the Maitland case. And then get on to Probation Services too.'

Carley went back to her desk, picked up her phone and dialled Amy Farmer's direct line.

Tamara took a deep breath as she opened the door to Foster Security Systems. Michael had owned his company since he had left university. She held her head high as she marched across to the reception desk of the plush building.

'I'd like to see Michael Foster, please,' she told the young woman behind the desk.

'Is he expecting you?' she asked, with a welcoming smile.

Tamara shook her head.

'Who should I say would like to see him?'

'Ms Parker-Brown.'

'One moment, please.'

Tamara sat down in a swish chair. The decor seemed more suited to an interior design company, or a hip marketing department, rather than a place where you could buy cameras and security equipment. Pale settees, light oak flooring, bright chrome lighting. A magazine left out on a whitewashed, wooden coffee table made the place look less formal, but inviting at the same time.

The receptionist put down the phone and stood up. 'I'll take you to him.' She smiled again.

Tamara breathed a sigh of relief as she followed her into a lift. At least Michael had agreed to see her. She wasn't sure what she would have done if he had said no. She clasped her hands together in front of her to stop them from shaking so much.

The lift doors opened onto a bright corridor with blue carpeting, and cream walls below a row of frosted glass windows. They stopped at the second door on the right.

The woman knocked and went right in. 'Your visitor, Mike,' she said.

'Tamara.' Michael stood up and came towards her. 'What a surprise.'

Michael was in his late thirties, tall and slim, with receding blond hair. She noticed a pair of glasses next to the desk phone, a few more wrinkles around his eyes. She wondered how he would see her now. Tired, wrung out, anxious.

His smile seemed so genuine as he pointed to a seat that she almost burst into tears.

The office was the same one she remembered he'd been in before but the decor was different, following on from the colours in the corridor. Michael had a large wooden desk that looked out of place but she knew it had been passed down from his father, who had died when he was in his early twenties. It was good to see that he hadn't wanted to dispose of it.

She glanced around, spotting a photo of him and another woman. She didn't bear any grudges now – how could she after what she had done – but it did make her sad to think of what might have been between them if she hadn't had a breakdown.

'So, how're things?' he asked, sitting forward. 'I'm not going to patronise you and say you look well. What's brought you here?'

'I'm in so much trouble.' This time she let her tears fall. He moved to sit next to her while she explained what had happened.

'You know how ill I was when I last saw you?' she looked at him sheepishly, 'but I am better now and I don't want anything to happen to make me feel the way I did before. I was getting on my feet, doing well, and I trusted Esther but she played on my loneliness. I don't know what to do for the best.'

'Don't you think you'd be better going to the police?' Michael asked.

Tamara shook her head. 'I had to drag myself here as you're the last person I want to talk to but I'm desperate. And you, more than anyone, would know that.'

Michael touched her hand but she moved it out of his reach. She didn't want his pity. She needed his help.

'I think Esther had something to do with Jack's death and is manipulating the truth to her own advantage. She's trying to put the blame on me. I need to get her to admit what she did. Can you set me up with something to record a conversation?'

'Of course.' Michael nodded. 'You can use your phone too.' He stood up. 'You'll need her to come to your flat. Can you do that?'

Tamara balked. 'I don't think I dare.'

'Then you will have to go to the police.'

'But I've lied to them already, and with my record—'

'You were ill.' Michael shook his head. 'And if she's framing you, you could end up in prison.'

Tamara shuddered involuntarily. Images of her room at

the hospital crowded her mind. Staff observing her every minute of the day. She herself having to watch patients for fear of being attacked. Her freedom gone, doors with locks. She couldn't go back to that.

But could she trust herself to do this? Could she go up against Esther? If she did, she could go to the police with solid evidence and then all this would be over.

She nodded. 'Tell me what I need to do.'

59

Back at home, Tamara had been amazed at the array of tiny devices Michael had shown her that could be used to record video and audio discreetly.

'Are you sure that will be enough?' she asked, as she watched him slip a wire behind the sideboard.

Michael nodded. 'It's very simple to use too.'

He tucked everything out of sight behind a photo of her and her siblings at her youngest brother's wedding in 2012. Tamara had been happy then. Her cheeks reddened as she realised that Michael was in the frame. It had been one of her favourite photos and despite throwing away lots of relationship mementoes, she hadn't wanted to lose this one.

She was still amazed at how quickly Michael had come to her aid. For all she knew, he might not have wanted to see her. She had caused him emotional stress as well as damage to his property and she didn't deserve his help. But she didn't know the first things about surveillance and had to get this right.

From where she was sitting on the settee, she couldn't see the red light that symbolised the camera was recording.

She got up and moved along a seat, tried again but still it wasn't visible.

'Are you certain she won't spot it?' she asked, still unconvinced.

'It doesn't really matter if you don't catch her on the screen,' he explained. 'It will still record what you both say.'

'And you think that will be good enough?'

Michael stood up, stretching his back. 'I don't know, but this must be better than nothing. Then you can take it to the police.'

Tamara nodded at him. Only three months ago, she hadn't known Esther. And in a few short weeks, her life had changed beyond recognition. Much of it was for the better, but this could be the undoing of everything if no one believed her.

Michael touched her arm and it was only then she realised he must have spoken to her and she hadn't replied.

'It's set up.' He handed her a fob. 'All you need to do before she arrives is press this button here and you're away.'

'Thanks so much for your help. I know I don't deserve it after—'

He placed a finger on her lips. 'I don't want to hear it. I'm happy to help. You can contact her now, if you're ready.'

Tamara knew she wasn't ever going to be prepared enough, but she nodded all the same. She was determined to clear her name, before it was tarnished for good.

She picked up her phone.

Esther was sitting in a pub when her phone beeped with an incoming message. She'd been drinking most of the after-noon and had taken the rest of the speed to tide her over.

I have some money. Come to my flat. 7.30 p.m. Tx

She laughed out loud. This couldn't be more perfect.

60

Carley had been out with uniformed officers to visit Esther Smedley's address but there had been no one home. Neighbours, when questioned, had either not seen her for a while or had seen her that morning. She hadn't answered her phone either.

She was leaving a contact card asking for her to call the station when her phone rang. It was her colleague, Dan.

'Natalie Maitland wants to see someone in CID. Said she's found something missing from her home.'

When Natalie opened the door, Carley saw immediately how striking she would be when grief hadn't overtaken her features. Her eye lids were swollen, her skin blotchy from crying and she was dressed in a black blouse and dark trousers, a sombre thing for such a beautiful woman. Her blonde hair was tied back and she wore no make-up, except a sheer lipstick, perhaps to give her a bit of colour.

She was shown into the living room, remembering the last time she was there and Jack Maitland had been lying at the bottom of the stairs in the hall. Identical twin boys were playing with remote control monster trucks at the far end of the room.

'Ethan, Henry. Can you take those out into the garden for a moment, please?' Natalie asked. 'There's chocolate ice cream in the freezer, too.'

At the mention of ice cream, the frowns that were forming turned to smiles and they raced off. Natalie held it together until they were out of the room and then her tears fell.

'It's hard not to get upset in front of them.' She wiped at her eyes. 'But I wanted to tell you something. I held a memorial for Jack this morning. I came back not long afterwards. I didn't even want my parents to stay and look after the boys.' Natalie played with the tissue. 'I was sitting at the breakfast bar with a coffee when it struck me. There's a marble paperweight missing from the worktop. We use it when we're working out in the garden and it's windy. It's in the shape of an apple. I've done a thorough search around but I can't locate it.'

Carley's heartbeat quickened.

'I knew it wasn't an accident,' Natalie continued. 'It's too much of a coincidence. I take the boys away and he meets those women without telling me?' She shook her head. 'He would have said something to me, especially if he was preparing lunch. I'm fine with Jack meeting the women but he wouldn't have done it at the house. He would have met them in a restaurant. They are lying.'

'What makes you think that?' Carley wanted to know why she seemed so venomous. Was it only the grief that was making her accusatory or was it something else? 'Is there anything you can tell me about Tamara Parker-Brown or Esther Smedley?'

'The security camera wasn't on and I know that Jack wouldn't switch it off. It's the women themselves that I don't trust,' Natalie went on. 'One of them had a mental breakdown when her fiancé left her. The other is someone I wouldn't trust as a friend. She seems so snippy to me.'

Carley wasn't sure that she was hearing anything that was justified. These were the ramblings of someone who was coming to terms with the death of a loved one. Natalie needed someone to blame. But she would follow up on the paperweight when she got back to the office.

'When can I bring him home to bury him?' Natalie asked next.

'When we've finished with our enquiries.' Carley gave her a faint smile of understanding. 'These things take time to put together. Policing is nothing like it's portrayed on the television, where forensics is done in an hour or so. We have to take our turn along with everyone else, and things take time to analyse too.'

'You don't have any news yet?'

Carley shook her head. 'We have to look into everything first, and then we can release the body. Jack took quite a fall down those stairs. We need to ensure it was an accident. And for that we need to wait for the forensic evidence. But Jack did take two blows to his head so I'll be straight on to that now that there is an object missing.'

'It's one of those women, I'm telling you.' Natalie nodded vehemently.

'Your husband could have fallen and hit his head,' stressed Carley. 'It would explain why his fall to the floor was so hard if he'd then been unconscious.'

'She still could have pushed him. I knew there was something about her.'

'Who?'

'That Tamara. Everyone knows what happened with her and her ex-fiancé, Michael Foster. She's clearly unhinged. I want her arrested for perverting the course of justice. She knows more than she is saying. I bet she's got that Esther girl to cover up for her.'

'The fact we may be able to prove someone is lying doesn't necessarily mean we have enough to convict them of a crime,' Carley reiterated. 'We need tangible evidence to back that up. Some suspects deny they are on CCTV footage, even though the images confirm it's obviously them. And prosecutors not only have to prove there's no mistaken identity, but that the suspect didn't have an innocent reason for being at the scene. For that alone, we always make sure we have the evidence in place.'

'Then please get it!'

'I know it's hard, Mrs Maitland, but let us do our job.'

Carley stood up and pocketed her notebook. Once out of the house, the doubt planted itself on her. Something was happening here. Forensics would piece together so much but she was determined to do the rest.

A paperweight in the shape of an apple could be just the right object to have made the mark on the side of Jack Maitland's head. Yet unless they could find it, it didn't prove anything.

But she had remembered where she had seen the name Bethany Williams.

Back at the station, Carley flicked through the files on her desk. She located the sheet of paper she was looking for, ran her finger down a list of names and then tapped the tip of it twice.

Bethany Williams. Why would that name be on this list? What was the connection?

She rang Terry to see where they were up to with forensics. He was able to send her emails over of the information she required. Everything fit into place. It was time to chat to Max.

'Sir, I've spoken to the Maitland's nanny who was there during the working week, the cleaner and the gardener who visit twice weekly. They all had keys to the property, but they all had alibis for where they were at the time Jack Maitland was pronounced dead. But—' she paused for effect '—because we know that Esther is Bethany, her prints are on the list that came up at Ewan Smith's address.'

Max beckoned for her to sit down. 'You think she's involved with Danny Bristol and his mob?'

'It doesn't necessarily mean that she was involved in Smith's murder, but something is definitely not right. Esther's fingerprints, as Bethany, are at our victim's flat, and she is also one of the last two people to see Jack Maitland alive. She could definitely be involved in his death because of the connection to his father and what he did to her.'

Max ran a hand over his chin. 'The name isn't familiar to me. She wasn't known on our patch, even though she has previous.'

'I also caught up with Amy Farmer,' Carley added, looking at her notebook before continuing. 'The GBH was in relation to an assault on a man who Esther met at a nightclub. According to her, he tried to rape her. According to him, everything was going well until she gave him a good beating because he'd held her hands above her head. Then she took a knife to him. Luckily, he only had cuts to his arms where he tried to fend her off. But she did break his jaw.'

She paused. 'Oh, and another thing. Williams hasn't turned up for her last probation meeting.'

'Have uniform found her yet?'

She shook her head. 'We've been to her flat but she isn't there.'

'Get them back there again. We'll break in or get a warrant if necessary. We need to bring her in.'

61

Esther jogged up the steps and let herself in to the main building, pressing the buzzer to alert Tamara that she was on her way up to her.

Tamara was waiting at her door and beckoned her into the office. Esther noted the weary look, the teary eyes, the resigned drop of her shoulders.

When Tamara disappeared to make coffee, Esther sat down in her favourite chair to undermine her. She could look out on to the street from there. A man with a dog jogged past. Traffic sounded in the distance. She had liked this place since the moment she had stepped inside. It was such a shame her time here was to end soon.

'I need to talk to you about our conversation this morning.' Tamara came in with a tray, which she slid on to the coffee table.

Esther could feel her tense vibes emanating across the room. 'You have some money for me?' She got straight to the point, wanting to be out of here and on her way as soon as possible.

'Yes, but I wanted to let you know that the police have questioned me again.'

Esther's eyes snapped from the window back to Tamara. 'Here or at the station?'

'They came here.'

'What did they want?'

'They were still quizzing me about exactly what happened.'

'Jack fell,' Esther snapped. 'I've told you how many times but you don't believe me. I had nothing to do with his death. It's my word against yours at the moment and I like that. The police are veering towards you anyway as they haven't been to see me.'

'Oh.' Tamara looked on in surprise. 'I assumed they would have. They said they had lots to talk to you about.'

'What did you tell them?'

'That I wasn't there.'

'You did what?' Esther's skin prickled.

'If Jack fell down those stairs and it was an accident, then I don't see why I need to take the blame for anything.' Tamara's tone was more cautious now. 'No one can be held accountable if he fell, don't you see? But by talking about putting liability on me, you've made out that you are very guilty of something. It's only a matter of time before the police realise that. So I had to come clean.'

'But I told you not to.' Esther spoke through clenched teeth. 'I won't go back to prison.'

'Prison?' Tamara gasped. 'You never said—'

'Chill out. I was innocent. Some bastard attacked me so I laid into him good and proper. It was self-defence.'

Esther watched as Tamara's eyes filled with fear. What had she to be scared about? It was all right for her. She had told the police things she shouldn't. Her anger beginning to build, she clenched her fists as she tried to control it.

'What really happened to you, Esther?' Tamara asked. 'Why do you have such an anger towards Jack?'

Esther shrugged, not lowering her guard for a moment. She wasn't sure how to tackle this now that Tamara had spoken to the police. All of a sudden, she had doubts that her plan would work.

Had she underestimated Tamara?

62

'I don't have an anger towards Jack,' Esther scoffed. 'I think all men are quite stupid actually.'

'Not all of them.'

'The ones I've met are. Especially the men who work at Dulston Publishing. Your pathetic Oscar—'

'He's not my—'

'And Ben, he's a leech. Did he tell you he made a pass at me and I brushed him off? He's been harassing me ever since,' she lied, 'but I've stayed silent about it.'

'Ben?' Tamara frowned. 'I don't believe you.'

'Well, you wouldn't, because you think that I pushed Jack down the stairs.'

'Did you do that?'

Esther looked underneath her fringe, hard eyes staring. 'I really think you should give up on this now.'

'What, the truth?'

Esther laughed. 'The truth is that you pushed him. I've been covering up for you.'

'Stop lying,' Tamara cried. 'It's all going to come

tumbling down around you soon if you're not careful.' She paused. 'Let me help you to get out of this mess.'

'How can you do that when you're the one in trouble?'

'*I'm* not.' She shook her head. 'Why don't you tell me what really happened? Maybe I can figure out what to do, if it was an accident.'

'What do you mean if it—' Esther spotted a beam of red light and stood up quickly. She rushed over to the sideboard and lifted up the framed photograph.

'You've planted a camera?'

Tamara froze.

Esther pulled at the wire she could see behind the machine. It came loose in her hand and the connection to the camera was gone. She threw it onto the floor and held out her hand.

'Give me your phone.'

'No! I –'

'You're working with the police to get me to confess.' She slapped the palm of her hand on her forehead. 'Of course. Why didn't I work this out earlier? Stupid Esther.'

She grabbed Tamara's arm and pulled her to her feet.

'Where is your phone?' she roared at her, feeling around Tamara's torso.

'Get off me,' Tamara demanded.

'Are you wired?'

'Of course not!'

'Then give me your phone.' Esther tried to slip her fingers into the back pocket of Tamara's trousers. But Tamara moved out of the way.

'Give me your phone.'

'No!' Tamara had it in her hands now but Esther pulled it from her. She could see the record button activated.

'You bitch.' She slapped Tamara across the face. 'How could you betray me like that?'

'I had to! I need to know the truth. You can't blame me for something I haven't done.'

'I won't if you give me the money.'

'Esther, you're scaring me.' Tamara held up her arms in surrender, her voice cracking with emotion. 'I know you're grieving over Jack and are very emotional.'

'I'm not grieving,' Esther sniggered. 'I lost my temper and lashed out. I should have stayed in control.' She pulled out a knife from her jacket pocket. Flicking out the blade, she held it out in front of her.

'Esther, please,' Tamara cried.

'It's all right for you. *You* would have been fine in your little fancy room with your group hugs and therapy sessions. I was in prison for eighteen months, with murderers and filth. I was treated like scum.' She pointed to her temple. 'It messes with your head. You never forget things like that. I had it so hard and you—' she pressed forward with the knife again '—you had it so fucking easy.'

'Esther, stop!' Tamara was crying now.

Esther had her cornered. There was nowhere for her to go.

But Tamara wouldn't stop talking.

'Let me help you through your grief,' she said. 'We can talk about Jack and your feelings for him and—'

'You think I'm grieving for Jack?' Esther's laughter cackled. 'I hate that bastard for what he did.'

Tamara's brow furrowed. 'I don't understand. I – I thought you loved him?'

'He hurt me and he paid for it,' Esther continued. 'He wasn't supposed to die though. I was only going to wreck his marriage but he made me so angry. After all I did, he wouldn't sleep with me. He bottled out at the last minute. I was fed up of being rejected, but rebuffed by him? It was the lowest form of insult.'

'But you asked me to cover so that it wouldn't come out about your affair.'

'There was no affair. I lied about that too.'

Tamara sobbed. 'Have you told me the truth about anything?'

Esther shook her head, a manic grin. 'All those work references, they were made up. I learned all about social media and marketing in prison. I took some classes to get me through, alleviate the boredom. It was the only thing I'm grateful for. I've never lived in Shoreditch either. Oh, and I used to live in Ascot.'

Tamara's face had gone a deathly shade of white.

Esther prodded herself hard in the chest. 'My name was Bethany Williams but I couldn't bear to be her after what happened. Bethany is who I was before that bastard took away my innocence.'

'You mean, Jack ...' Tamara stood up quickly.

'SIT DOWN!' Esther roared. 'You want to know about my life? Well, now you're going to listen.'

Tamara's face crumpled and she made a run for the door.

63

Tamara raced into the hall, Esther close behind her. She almost had her fingers on the front door handle, when Esther placed a hand on her shoulder.

'Leave me alone,' Tamara cried.

Esther turned her round and thrust the knife deep into her abdomen.

Tamara groaned, her eyes widening as Esther then pulled the knife out. She pressed her hands to the wound, blood seeping through her fingers.

'You were always collateral,' Esther shouted. 'Constantly in the way. But I liked you.'

Tamara gasped; red-hot pain coursing through her where the knife had been removed. She steadied herself with a hand on the wall.

'I thought you were my friend,' she whispered.

'Where is my money?'

Tamara looked at her.

'Where is it?' Esther repeated, this time through gritted teeth.

'I don't have it,' she admitted.

Esther punched her in the face. She followed it with another and another. Fist after fist rained down until Tamara fell to her knees, hoping to avoid anything further.

'You betrayed me!' Esther screamed. 'I won't stand for that.'

With as much strength as she could muster, Tamara pushed herself back to standing and staggered through into the kitchen. She needed to get a tea towel to press on the wound but she dropped to the floor as dizziness washed over her. She reached up to the worktop, trying to pull herself to standing again but she cried out in pain. She slumped with her back to the unit, both hands cradling the wound.

Esther put the knife out of her reach. Then she pulled out a chair and sat down at the table, crossing her legs.

Tamara pressed a hand to her nose, thankfully not feeling any more blood. Her lip was split though. Most of the punches had gone to her head, its ringing incessant in the quiet of the room. But it was the wound to her abdomen that she was concerned with. She screwed up her eyes. She had never experienced anything like it, spasms of pain as a bit more of her blood dripped out every second.

'Help me.' A shaky hand went out to Esther. 'Please, call an ambulance.'

'But you wanted to know what happened to me.' Esther's voice was quiet. 'So I have to tell you that first. Then you will understand. It won't be pleasant to hear but, then again, you don't care about anyone but yourself, do you?'

'I thought I was a good friend to you.'

'Friends don't try to record confessions for the police, do they?'

Even if she had the strength Tamara wouldn't have said what she was thinking – that friends wouldn't want to blame another for something they had done. Pain engulfed her again. As more blood came out, she coughed.

But Esther wasn't even looking at her. 'I first met Jack in ninety-nine. He was at Cambridge when I was working for his father. I was fifteen; he was nineteen. We only met briefly a few times, whenever he would come home for a weekend or holiday. The first thing he would do was to check out the horses, take one out for a ride. I got to know him quite well, but I was always Bethany the stable girl. Not that I minded. I didn't want a boyfriend or anything. But he didn't take any notice of me anyway.

'His father, however ... I never liked him. None of the stable hands did. He was cruel and I heard rumours about him being rough with some of the girls. I wasn't much to look at. My hair was short and I hadn't really grown into my body. So I don't understand why he—' Esther paused to look at her. 'Then again, I wasn't special to him so he could do what he wanted and get away with it.'

Tamara couldn't understand Esther because she was mumbling. 'What do you mean?'

'Reggie Maitland raped me,' Esther said, eyes full of anger. 'But someone watched it happen. I saw a shadow and put up a hand to show them that I needed their help, but whoever it was disappeared. When I went outside afterwards, there was Jack. He even said I looked a little peaky.'

Tamara couldn't speak as Esther went on.

'I went straight home. I washed my clothes and cried while I took a bath to rid me of his touch, his smell, but I didn't confide in anyone. I was so ashamed, and bruised inside and out.

'It was my mum who finally got it all out of me because she couldn't understand why I didn't want to go to the stables. I was a virgin before then.' Esther nodded vehemently. 'I'd never had a boyfriend. I was quiet and preferred to be with the horses. But from that moment, people treated me like I was a slut, like I had made it all up and I hadn't, I swear. No one believed me but my parents and they couldn't get Reggie charged.

'My dad threatened him, you know. Apparently, he laughed in his face. Called me a liar. Then Reggie threatened him, said he would ruin our family if he pursued the matter. My mum told me this when I last saw her.'

Tamara tried to work through the fog of pain. Was Esther telling the truth this time or was this another lie? She wasn't sure she could trust anything she said.

Esther stabbed a finger in the air. 'As that bastard raped me, Jack was standing in the doorway watching. He heard my screams, and watched his father slap me into submission.'

Tamara was struggling to take everything in. She couldn't ask if Esther was sure because it would seem patronising. She couldn't speak through the pain anyway. And it wouldn't have helped because Esther seemed in some kind of trance.

It couldn't be true ... Could it?

Esther was struggling to get her breath too. As if the memories were crashing back into her, making it hard for her to cope. If she wasn't so injured Tamara might have felt sorry for her. All she needed was a friend. But it wasn't going to be her. If Esther didn't do something soon, Tamara might die sitting there beside her.

She tried to sit up, the pain in her abdomen making her feel sick in an instant. The blood was sticky on her blouse, and she wondered if the bleeding had stopped or if there was unseen damage being done. Was she bleeding internally, or perhaps only superficially?

'It was their fault I ended up in prison,' Esther said. 'I became so mixed up, so *angry*. I found it hard to get close to anyone after the attack. One night, I met a man and we ended up back at his place and I – I tried to be all loving with him, I really did. But he wanted it rough and it reminded me of what had happened and I flipped.' Esther pointed at Tamara's stomach. 'I got three years for GBH – served eighteen months.

'I didn't like prison. It's horrible being the odd ball inside. Once those women smell fear, they latch on to you and they hunt you down. For the first month, I was a punch bag. And then I went to the gym, toughened myself up and fought back. No one messed with me then.'

The room continued to spin but Esther ignored Tamara's protests, so intent was she in telling her story. She prayed she would get out of this.

But as pain engulfed her once more, she passed out.

64

Esther had removed her dress and slipped on one of Tamara's black jumpers and a pair of her dark trousers. At least if Tamara bled when she was about to move her, no one would see it.

She had moved her twice to clean up around her. The blood wouldn't come out of the cracks in the kitchen tiles but it would have to do for now. Then she'd used the bathroom and washed her hands.

When she went back into the kitchen and saw her friend slumped on the floor, guilt swamped her. She ran her hands through her hair, grabbing handfuls in her fists and pulling at it with all her might.

Not Tamara. She liked Tamara.

But Tamara had let her down too. And she had lied about the money. Now the only choice Esther had was to go to search it out elsewhere.

Although she didn't really want Tamara to die, Esther didn't know if she had any choice. But suddenly there was a groan. She turned sharply. Tamara's head moved slightly.

She's alive!

But that altered things completely. She would have to take her with her.

Esther stooped down in front of Tamara. 'Hey.' She slapped her gently on each cheek. 'Wake up, sleepy head.'

When she didn't move, she slapped her harder this time.

Tamara's head reared up and she groaned in pain. Her eyes flickered open.

'Help me,' she whispered, her chin hanging down then. 'Pain.'

'Come on.' Esther pulled her up to her knees and then to her feet. She thought Tamara might pass out on her again but she didn't. She placed an arm around her neck.

'Can you manage to walk?' she asked her.

Tamara opened her eyes briefly before her head fell to the side. 'Pain,' she repeated.

'I know. I'm sorry but what can I do? Now, one foot in front of the other and we'll soon be out of here. Hold on to me.'

It took them a few minutes to get to the front door and out into the hall. Esther wasn't sure what she would say if she saw anyone but she would cross that bridge when she came to it. There would be cameras but once she was out of there, no one would be able to stop her.

Out on the pavement, the road was quiet. Tamara groaned as she missed her footing on the step and they both stumbled to the ground.

'Watch what you're doing, will you?' Esther snapped, as she pulled her to her feet again.

They made the last few metres to the car and she pressed the key fob to open the driver's door. Holding Tamara up, she leaned inside and pressed the button to open the boot. Then she walked with her to the back of the car.

'Come on, let's get you sorted,' Esther told her. 'It won't be long now.'

She pulled her fist back and punched Tamara in the stomach. As she doubled over, Esther pushed her into the boot.

'Now be quiet,' she said. But Tamara was unconscious again anyway. Esther hoped she didn't suffocate in the boot. *Could* you even suffocate in a boot?

A door opened further down the street, laughter boomed out. Esther pulled down the boot lid quietly. She stooped down out of the way, not wanting to bring attention to herself.

A couple were saying goodnight to friends. She waited until their car had pulled away from the kerb and the neighbour's door was closed before standing tall again. Quickly, she climbed into the driver's seat. Within seconds, she was out of the street.

Tamara's car was sheer luxury to drive, and an automatic so she didn't have much to do. Esther's phone went off again, but she ignored it. She wasn't going to answer it until she was ready.

Within minutes, she was heading to her final stop. It was nearing 10.00 p.m. The pavements were full of people, the roads busy with cars. She snarled. Look at everyone, out enjoying themselves with family and friends and who did she have? No one.

What did she have to look forward to? Nothing.

Did anyone care about her? No.

Except for the woman you've left bleeding in the boot of her car.

Esther tried to push that thought aside. Tamara had been good to her over the past few weeks. She had made mistakes, of course, but she had made amends too.

What kind of a friend was she? Esther didn't know if Tamara was alive or dead.

She thought back to when they had met. Tamara had always been pleasant to her. She had treated her well, she had taken a chance on her, and yes, perhaps she had been gullible by believing everything she had said but it had worked out fine until now.

She remembered doing the pitch with her. It had been fun, even taking over at the right time to ensure they got the job. The dress that Tamara brought her from Mario's. How understanding she was after she had thumped Oscar, and the mood she'd been in at the book launch.

Tamara had ample times when she could have let her go and yet she hadn't. Because Tamara was a nice person. And what had she done in return? She'd tried to shift the blame to her for Jack's murder.

But it was his stupid family that had got her into this predicament.

Why couldn't she have settled down with someone kind and sincere, and forgotten about her past? She had a right to be happy, not Jack. He deserved what he got. Someone had to pay for how her life had turned out. She would see to it. Revenge was going to be hers.

She couldn't bottle out now, not after getting this far. Tamara shouldn't have tried to trick her. She should never have set up equipment to record her. She was only inter-ested in getting off herself. The police had no evidence, but if they listened to what she'd told Tamara, she would be for it. She wasn't going back to prison until she had justice.

Tears poured down her face as she argued with herself. She was close to her destination now. All she had to do was finish what she'd started and then perhaps she could take

Tamara to the hospital. She could say she had been mugged. No one would know she had made the story up.

'Stop being so weak and get on with things,' she chastised herself as she put her foot down on the pedal.

She pressed on, determined to finish what she had started. She heard a beep and a red light started flashing on the dashboard.

'Tamara!' Her hand made a fist and she banged it on the steering wheel. 'You let it run low on fuel. You idiot.'

Esther got out her phone and typed the address she knew so well into Google maps. There was a petrol station nearby. She could fill up on the way.

65

Being bumped around in the back of the car was utter agony. The confined space hurt Tamara's limbs, but at least the wound in her stomach didn't have room to bleed much more as its opening was clamped together in the tight space.

How could Esther have put her in the boot of her own car? Her chest tightened: please don't let me die in this confined space.

She tried to move around in the back, see if there was anything she could put her hand on to attack Esther with when she opened the boot again. But she knew there hadn't been much in there to start, and anything there was, Esther must have left on the roadside. She was stuck.

However she had one saving grace. She had known Esther was taking her to the car. She had known she had put her in the boot, and she could clearly remember the punch in the stomach.

But Esther thought she was more injured than she was. Of course she was hurting, except she was putting some of it on too. She just needed to keep her cool, stop the blood from escaping too much and get out of this mess.

What she also knew was she couldn't get away because of her injury, so it meant playing the game until she could.

She had no idea where Esther was taking her. It wasn't to a hospital or else she would have put her in the back seat. Yet, Esther would assume that she wouldn't be able to attack her. But she had her feet.

She tried to manoeuvre herself around so that she could kick out when the boot lid was opened again. But it was no use; there wasn't enough room. She hurt too much.

Every now and then when they stopped, she could hear noise outside. Traffic, music, lights beeping at crossings. Where was Esther heading?

Now she knew about the rape she could understand more, and it had been her downfall to doubt that Jack had anything to do with it. But she wasn't sure whether that was another lie. The Jack she knew wouldn't do that, would he?

Yet maybe he had been frightened of his father. When Tamara had met Reggie Maitland, he seemed someone who exerted his authority. Perhaps Jack did as he was told. Having said that, although Tamara's father was strict there was no way she would cover up anything like that for him.

But she didn't know what Jack had been through as a child. She hadn't known what trauma Esther had suffered until two hours earlier.

She wondered why Esther had changed her name; perhaps to leave her past behind. She had been stupid not to check her references but at the time she had no reason not to believe her. Esther had been very good at her job, no matter how she'd turned out. And who hadn't told the odd white lie on a reference to get a job? She had, more than once or twice.

But Tamara still couldn't believe she had fallen for all her lies. Esther was so nice to her face: behind her back she was scheming, using her to get to Jack and his family. She must have had this planned for some time. How could she have been so stupid?

If she got out of this alive, she was going to make this her own PR campaign. She was coming back from this.

Tamara groaned as the car swerved around a corner, pain slicing through her abdomen. She pressed her hand to it. It was still bleeding but it had eased off slightly.

The car came to a stop. Tamara sniffed, her remaining senses on full alert as she couldn't see.

She could smell petrol.

She could hear noises, a car door opening and closing. It was quiet for a few seconds but then nothing. She wondered, if she banged on the inside of the boot, would anyone hear her? She had to try.

She raised her fists and shouted. 'Help!'

Please, someone hear me!

66

Esther had stopped at a station to fill up with fuel. Her phone rang as she got back to the car. It was the same number that had been calling for the past few hours. As she approached the boot of the car, she heard banging and rolled her eyes. Stupid Tamara.

'Yes?' she answered the call this time, ignoring the noise.

'DC Evans, Esther. You remember me from the police station?'

'Yes.'

'Where are you?'

'Out for a drive. It's a nice evening.'

'I know it's late, but I need to talk to you.'

'About what?'

'Things in general. Nothing to worry about. Can you meet me somewhere?'

'Not at the moment. I can call at the station tomorrow, if you like?'

'First thing? Around nine?'

'A bit early. Can we make it ten?'

'Okay.'

Esther disconnected the phone. They were on to her, she was sure of it. But she had the night to do what she wanted. She would be gone in the morning. As long as Tamara kept her mouth shut. She released the boot lid, all the time muttering to herself.

'Will you shut—'

Tamara launched at her. Taken by surprise, her fist connected with Esther's chin. Esther staggered back for a moment and then came to her senses. She hit out, punching Tamara a few times in quick succession. Then she slammed the boot lid shut, trapping Tamara inside again, and got into the car. She banged her hands on the steering wheel.

'Damn you, Jack Maitland,' she wailed. 'This is all your fault.'

As she drove away, Esther didn't spot the man talking on his phone.

Tamara didn't know which part of her hurt the most after Esther's assault but, as the car pulled off, in a way she was glad she could feel it. It meant she was still alive.

It was maybe two hours since she had been attacked, so perhaps her stab wound was more superficial than she had originally thought. She prayed she could keep going long enough. She didn't want to die in the boot of her own car.

The car veered to the right and she clung on for dear life. She wondered where Esther was going now, where they had just stopped and why? She hadn't been able to make out where they were. She could still hear cars in the distance, but nothing nearby so she decided to save her energy for when she would need it.

Because as soon as Esther opened the boot, she was

going to go for her again. She had to try and get away somehow.

For now, she tried to think happy thoughts when her doubts of getting out alive began to resurface. Maybe this was the chance she had to prove herself again. She was not going to let Esther win.

It was only now that she realised how much she had going for her. She had her own business, her own flat, her own everything. She couldn't die.

Please let me live.

Her head caught the side of the boot as Esther took another corner with speed. She cried out as the car mounted the kerb and went back down to road level. She prayed her wound wouldn't get any wider, cause her problems before she could get out.

I don't want to die in there.

She banged the palm of her hands against the inside of the boot lid.

The car stopped.

'Let me out,' Tamara sobbed, banging again. 'Please, let me out.'

67

Esther had pulled up on the road outside the house for a moment, to gather herself. She had one chance at this and she wasn't going to mess up.

There was a light on at the downstairs window, the one she had stared into so many times while she'd watched them unnoticed. At the side of the house was the large double garage with a room over the top, where she had often stood behind. She was glad he had moved from Ascot so that she didn't have the memories rushing back at her.

There were no gates to this house, so she started the engine and drove right in, parking next to a Toyota Land Cruiser. The holdall was on the passenger seat so she reached inside it and removed the gun from its towelling wrapper. She shoved it into the waistband at the back of the trousers she was wearing and pulled the jumper over it.

Next, she took out the knife, wiped clean of Tamara's blood, flicked it closed and pushed that deep into a pocket. Reggie Maitland might be older now, but he was still a big man.

She got out and stood by the side of the car, listening.

The outside lights were flooding over her, but she could hear nothing coming from the boot of the car. Instead she saw a figure appear in the bay window of the house.

She made her way to the front door.

It was thrown open before she got to it. Reggie Maitland stood on the doorstep.

'Yes?'

Esther pulled out the gun and, without a shake in her hand, aimed it at him. 'Get inside,' she said.

He raised his hands in the air. 'Please, whatever you want, I can get. Just don't harm us.'

She stepped into the hall as he moved backwards into another room.

She followed him and stood in the doorway of a lounge. It was far too old-fashioned for her liking. Set up like an old gentleman's club, it had thick red carpet and dark velvet curtains to match. A family portrait hung over the fireplace, a gilded frame the only brightness in the room.

Gabrielle Maitland was sitting in the chair nearest to her. When she saw Esther, she stood up quickly, putting her drink on the coffee table.

'What's going on?' she asked, moving to her husband's side. 'Reggie?'

'It's okay, Gabrielle.' He looked at Esther. 'What do you want?'

'As much money as you have.'

'We don't keep a lot at home.'

'You'll have to get some from somewhere. You owe me.'

His eyes narrowed as he stared at her.

'You don't recognise me?' She sniggered. 'How many girls did you attack in the stables?'

That did the trick. Esther took great delight in the recognition on his face.

'You were that stable girl? Bethany?'

She nodded slowly.

'Get out of my house,' Gabrielle demanded. 'You have no right to be here. I want you to leave, or I'm calling the police.'

'I don't think you're in any position to tell me what to do.' Esther held the gun a little higher. She aimed it at Gabrielle, enjoying the fearful look on her face. Then she looked to Reggie.

He still had his hands in the air. 'Bethany, let me explain.'

'My name is Esther!' she screamed.

He took a step back. Gabrielle covered her ears with her hands.

'I left Bethany behind a long time ago, because I couldn't bear what had happened to her, and what *you* turned me into.' She pointed at Reggie with the gun. 'You ruined me, my childhood, my life! And then you lied. You denied doing anything. How could you do that to me?'

Reggie averted his eyes from her stare. Esther turned to Gabrielle.

'When I was fifteen, your husband raped me.'

'Yes, I remember the fuss you caused over a little misunderstanding.' Gabrielle nodded. 'You tarnished our reputation. It took us a long time to recover from it.'

'*I* ruined *your* reputation?' Esther's voice trailed off at the audacity. 'It was him, the dirty bastard. He took advantage of me and then he tried to deny it.'

'I'm sorry,' Reggie said, taking both of them by surprise. 'I was younger then, and not a nice man at times.'

'You don't have to explain yourself,' Gabrielle insisted. 'What's done is done and all in the past.'

'I suppose so.' Esther grinned. 'But at least I got you back for it.'

Gabrielle paled and her hand went to her mouth. 'Does this have anything to do with Jack's death?'

'What do you think?' Esther snapped. 'I wanted revenge on all your family. I was coming after you next, and he shouldn't have died, but I wanted to deal with him first.'

'But this had nothing to do with our son,' Reggie said, his face perplexed.

'Of course it did.' Esther rolled her eyes. 'I know he was in on it too.'

68

'I saw him,' Esther yelled. 'I saw him standing in the doorway, watching as you—'

'He didn't do anything!' Gabrielle almost shouted as loud as her. 'Did you kill Jack because of what Reggie did?'

'No, that was an accident. I wanted to embarrass him, ruin his family. I was going to take some photos of me with him and then show them to Natalie.'

'You were going to blackmail him?' asked Reggie.

'Yes, but now he's gone, I want money from you instead.'

'My son wouldn't go with the likes of you,' Gabrielle scoffed.

'Really? I have so many photos of us, except the ones I thought I was going to get when I went to his house. I was wondering whether to get them printed out anyway and send them to Natalie at home or at work.'

Gabrielle glared at her; her brow furrowed as she tried to work out what Esther meant. Then her eyes widened. 'You were going to break up his marriage?'

Esther nodded, a childish grin spreading across her lips.

'What on earth for?'

'Because I've never had the chance to love and to be happy, to marry and have a family, so why should he? And because he stood by and watched. He could have stopped it from happening.'

Reggie was pacing now.

'I was going to get money from him and then come after you for the same,' Esther continued. 'But he made me angry and—'

'What did you do?'

Esther watched his fists clench and unclench. She had her back to the door; knew she could get out first if necessary.

'That's not important now,' she replied.

'It matters to me!'

Esther faltered for a moment as flashes of that afternoon came back to her. But then she smiled when she saw the looks going between Jack's parents. They were scared of her.

'You stupid, stupid girl,' Gabrielle cried. 'Don't you see? You killed our son for nothing.'

'Don't you call me that.' Esther scowled.

'It's true because you got it all wrong. It wasn't Jack who was watching by the door.'

Esther couldn't take in what she was saying. If it wasn't Jack who was watching, then ...

'You?' Esther shook her head in disbelief.

Gabrielle nodded.

'How could you stand there and watch while he – he violated me? Have you no heart?'

'I made sure it never happened again by hiring stable boys to be with the horses full-time, rather than girls.' Gabrielle scoffed. 'But I wasn't going to let a schoolgirl wreck my family and what it stood for.'

'Have you any idea what I went through because of

that?' Esther said. 'No one believed me; they all called me a liar. And then my dad died – because of the shame that you brought on *our* family. But you ... you stood and watched and you never came to help. How many times did you do that?'

'I told you. There were no others.'

'That doesn't make it any better. He ruined my life! I was fifteen, and everyone thought *I* was lying.'

'We kept it as quiet as we could. Of course, some people found out because you were working with a large team of people and news travelled fast. But I kept it under wraps. I told the police that Reggie was with me at the time he was alleged to have attacked you.'

You gave him an alibi?'

'Of course I did. I wasn't about to lose everything I had built up for one silly mistake.'

'He – he raped me! And if you saw him, why didn't you stop him?'

'Because it would have tarnished our reputation, our livelihood.'

But Esther wasn't listening. 'I remember the bruises he left behind on my body. I remember the dreams he took from me, the embarrassment he forced upon me and the hatred I received from people I knew who thought I was lying. And you – you defend all of that?'

Gabrielle snorted. 'It wasn't that bad. I know he can get a little bit rough every now and then.'

'He told me I'd been asking for it, that no one would believe me if I said what had happened. That I'd never get to work with horses again.' She glanced at him. 'He said he'd do more than that if I told anyone what had happened.'

'Wait.' Reggie put his hands down a little. 'What has this got to do with Jack?'

Jack.

Esther had killed him for nothing. Vomit came up in her throat and she pushed it back. These despicable people standing in front of her were good for the punishment, but Jack had been an innocent in all this.

'Why did you kill him?' Reggie went on.

'Keep up, will you? I thought he was watching us!' Esther slapped at her head, as if to rid herself of the images she'd created over the years. 'I thought he'd enjoyed it, and then I thought he had been lying about what happened too. I wasn't to know it was *her*!'

'You stupid bitch!' Gabrielle screamed.

Esther pointed at Reggie. 'It was his fault!'

'I knew there was something about you from the minute I set eyes on you again.' Gabrielle lunged towards her. 'You're going to pay for this.'

'Stay away from me,' Esther warned, bringing the gun in line with her. 'Get me some money and I'll go, but I'm not leaving without any.'

Gabrielle's hands were up in the air, coming at her. 'I'm calling the police.'

'Don't come any closer.'

As Gabrielle continued, Esther stepped back, her foot hitting the doorframe. When she came too close, Esther had no choice.

She pulled the trigger.

69

Esther stood, frozen to the spot, as she watched Gabrielle fall. She almost let go of the gun as Reggie dropped to the floor next to his wife.

'Gabrielle?' he cried, pulling her into his arms. 'Gabrielle, can you hear me? Speak to me.'

Esther watched the woman who had caused her so much pain throughout her life gasping for breath. Her eyes began to glaze over in the same way that Jack's had.

With an animal like roar, Reggie launched himself at Esther. His hand sliced across her face before she had time to move and he grabbed for the gun.

'No!' she shouted, keeping a grip on its handle. He prized her fingers away. Even though she resisted, he was too strong for her. She had to let the gun go. It dropped to the floor and he kicked it away.

Reggie pushed her against the wall and his hands went around her neck. Squeezing her this time, she grappled with him. She dug her nails into the back of his hands as he pressed harder, restricting her breathing. Flashes appeared before her eyes.

Esther gasped for air, her hands grappling around for anything she could hit out with but there was nothing this time. She was going to die in Reggie Maitland's house.

'You've taken away everything I have,' he seethed.

She tried to get to the knife in her pocket, but her eyes were blurring over. She pushed at his face with the heel of her hand. His head went back but still his hands kept squeezing. The room was fading out.

There was a commotion and shouting. Reggie was pulled away from her and she was turned to face the wall by the detective who was dealing with Jack's case.

'He came at me with a gun,' she cried. 'It was self-defence.'

'Stay still.' Carley placed a cuff around one of Esther's wrists, pulled her other arm down and did the same.

'I tried to run but she got in the way,' Esther tried again to be heard. 'He shot her, not me. He did it!'

Behind her, Max was handcuffing Reggie Maitland, and reading him his rights.

Reggie tried to drop to his knees next to his wife. 'Gaby? Gaby, darling, wake up.' He looked up at Max. 'Please, take off these cuffs. I want to comfort her.'

'The emergency services will be here soon.' Max called the incident in, requesting an ambulance. At his feet, Reggie roared in pain.

'You got what you deserved,' Esther told Reggie quietly. 'All this was your fault.'

'I – I—'

'All your fault! Do you hear me?' she yelled.

'Esther Smedley – also known as Bethany Williams – I'm arresting you for the murder of Jack Maitland.' Carley walked her out into the hallway. 'You do not have to say anything. But it may harm your defence if you do not mention when questioned something which you later rely on in court. Anything you do say may be given in evidence. Do you understand?'

'It wasn't me.' Esther cried. 'Tamara did it. It was her. You can't arrest me. She did it!'

70

TWO WEEKS LATER

Tamara woke with a start and sat up. She listened but there was no noise.

The clock by the side of the bed told her it was 8.35 a.m. The sleeping tablets she'd been prescribed were helping in one respect, but only every now and then. She hadn't wanted to take them straightaway. She was more opposed to interrupting her sleeping pattern than not sleeping at all.

And even when she did go to sleep, images of that day came rushing back to her. Being trapped in the boot of her own car, fearing for her life while she was with some mad woman.

It had been a huge relief when she'd heard a voice outside her car. At least the police officer had been spared a punch in the face because he'd shouted out to her before getting the keys and opening the boot. He had helped her

out on to the driveway where she had lain until the ambulance arrived.

She'd been straight into surgery after having numerous
tests and had stayed in hospital for two days. Her parents
had insisted she went home with them afterwards, while the
flat was cleaned of her blood.

A week later it had been time to face the music and start
her life again. She knew she needed to get over the firsts.
First time driving in her car which Esther had driven to the
Maitland's home, where Esther had shot dead Gabrielle
Maitland.

The first time going into her flat and seeing blood everywhere, even though it had been removed.

The first time being alone since that day. She'd had to do
it all again. It was the only way to get on with her life.

She pulled back the bed covers and padded over to the
window. Outside, the weather was dry but overcast. She
wondered what the day would bring. Maybe she would go
out today. She had so much to catch up on.

She showered and dressed, all the time wary of her
wound. The dressing was off now; the stitches dissolved a
few days ago. The bruising from her face and body was
mostly gone; what was left of it a fading yellow-green. She
had been lucky, she'd been told, the knife having missed
vital organs and arteries. She would make a full recovery in
time. Her mind, however, would take a lot longer to get over
the trauma.

She was still shocked that Esther had changed so much
in the time that she'd known her. Yes, she said causing Jack's
death was an accident, not like when she attacked her, but
Esther was the one who had lost her temper. She did it.
Plain and simple.

The intercom buzzed. Tamara was expecting DC Evans. When she opened the door, Carley was holding a bunch of flowers.

'I'm not supposed to buy gifts for members of the public but I was on my way to work and saw these at the petrol station.' She smiled apologetically. 'I'm not sure which looks more exhausted. Me or these, but it's the thought, I guess.'

Tamara smiled as she took them from her and closed the door. She clicked the double lock into place, something she had never done until now. She had always felt safe in her home. Not anymore.

'How are you doing?' Carley asked when they were both in the sitting room.

'I haven't felt much like eating. Even I jumped at the reflection staring back at me from the mirror this morning.'

They chatted about the case in general before Carley sat forward, putting down her coffee.

'As you know, we went to Bethany's flat when all the evidence came in and we wanted to question her. When she wasn't there, a warrant was put out for her arrest. With the call from your neighbour, Raj, who had seen you being dragged outside, plus the call from the petrol station, we put two and two together once we had a description of your car, and it was so close to the Maitland's home.'

As Tamara had suspected, Jack hadn't been pushed down the stairs. Forensics had revealed that his body had been moved from the kitchen to the hallway. Esther had admitted to hitting Jack with a marble paperweight she'd found on the worktop. It was still missing. Esther hadn't told anyone its whereabouts.

'We've since found out that she has been travelling the country using a few names but always coming back to

Shoreditch. If she was caught doing anything and bailed, she would move on.'

'Esther mentioned she'd been in prison,' Tamara said. 'Was that true?'

Carley nodded. 'Amy Farmer told us—'

'Amy Farmer?' Tamara bristled.

'She was Esther's probation officer.'

'Esther told me Amy was a friend who had been raped and then killed herself.' Tamara shuddered. 'Just how many lies did she tell me?'

'Esther is very damaged and mentally unstable. She's also extremely calculating. You aren't the first victim of hers. Did she ever mention a Danny Bristol to you?'

Tamara thought for a moment, then shook her head. 'She didn't very often open up about her past.' She smiled weakly. 'I know why now.'

'We found his body in the back garden of the house where Esther was staying.'

Tamara almost dropped her mug.

'She had beaten him with a bat and then buried him in a compost container in an old garage that no one was using.'

'When was this?' Tamara hoped it wouldn't be while she had known her, but in the back of her mind knew it was going to be.

'He was murdered approximately a month ago. According to Amy, he was someone who caused Esther a lot of pain. It seems she came out of prison and went after some members of the gang she hung around with. We think she might have been involved in the murder of another man, Jamie Kerrigan, too but we can't be positive, and she won't admit to it. He was lured into an entry where he was beaten and then shot.

'Because she handled the same gun that had been used for that crime to then kill Gabrielle Maitland, we can't be certain her fingerprints are on it because of that alone, or if she pulled the trigger on both occasions. It's very complicated to prove and, as you know, she was very good at manipulation.'

Tamara's hand covered her mouth.

'We also found her fingerprints at another murder victim's flat, Ewan Smith. Until we knew her as Bethany Williams, she wasn't linked. We can't ever be certain she was involved in his death though. When we questioned Danny Bristol earlier in the year, he gave Williams's name as an alibi, saying he was with her, but we could never find her to corroborate this. She may have been going under both Esther and Bethany then. We were only able to shed any light on things after her mum came forward.'

'You didn't take prints when you interviewed her after Jack died?'

'It isn't necessary at that time in the enquiry. We thought his death was an accident. She wasn't under arrest then, nor under suspicion so we had no reason to request it.'

'But you had mine.'

'Yes, you were already on the system.'

'Wow, how stupid was I for not checking her out.' Tamara shook her head in embarrassment.

'You mustn't blame yourself,' Carley said. 'I think you should be thankful that you came away with your life.'

She nodded. 'I won't let her win.'

And she wouldn't. Later she would start looking over her shoulder for Esther. But for now, Tamara felt safe knowing she was locked up in prison.

. . .

Esther lay on the thin mattress in a room where plans were made but often never realised. The room where everything was taken away.

The lights were out, the doors locked, but the voices were still loud and vulgar. Women shouting things to each other – declarations of love, hateful slanging matches. Banging as soon as the lights went out. She covered her ears as she curled up on her side.

At least she had a cell to herself for now. And even though she'd been bullied before, she'd become stronger since then. She hadn't done what she'd set out to do, but she had got revenge.

No one would get the better of her inside again. Not now everyone knew she was on remand for the murder of three people. Esther had got wise this time. She'd already set out her stall by confronting one of the main ringleaders as soon as she got there. Mandy Dixon was in for three years for attacking her partner and leaving him with no sight in one eye. Killing Danny Bristol had made Esther realise that standing up to bullies was the way to earn respect.

It was incredible how quickly Mandy backed down after she'd laid into her. She was always smiling at her now. Overnight, Esther had become someone to look up to. Being a murderer does that for you, she surmised. She knew things could change whenever a new inmate came along, but, for now, it seemed easier in there than last time. Which is just as well considering the sentence she was going to get.

Killing Gabrielle Maitland with the gun had set her up good and proper. Esther's prints had been found in Ewan's flat. The police linked the bullets in the gun used to kill him to the murder of Jamie Kerrigan too. There had been a warrant issued for Danny's arrest. He'd stayed on the run for quite some time before turning up at her flat.

Still, no one would have seen him since that night she'd found him waiting for her when she'd arrived home. The police must have had quite a shock when they found him in the rear garden.

And now she was in here for so many crimes, no one would believe she'd acted in self-defence when she'd killed Danny, fearing for her life, would they?

She supposed she could plead insanity, cite hearing voices inside her head. She could even say, 'it wasn't me. She did it.'

Now that would be something to work on while she was planning her revenge on Tamara.

A NOTE FROM MEL

First of all, I want to say a huge thank you for choosing to read THE LIES YOU TELL. I hope you enjoyed getting to know Esther and Tamara as much as I did.

If you did enjoy The Lies You Tell, I would be extremely grateful if you'd write a short review. I'd love to hear what you think, and it can also help other readers discover one of my books for the first time. Or maybe you can recommend it to your friends and family.

Many thanks to anyone who has emailed me, messaged me, chatted to me on Facebook or Twitter and told me how much they have enjoyed reading my books. I've been genuinely blown away with all kinds of niceness and support from you all. A writer's job is often a lonely one but I feel I truly have friends everywhere.

Why not join my book club? I keep you up to date with when the next book will be out, run regular competitions to win books and goodies, and talk about other books I've read and enjoyed. You can also download a catalogue to find out more about me writing as Mel Sherratt and writing advice, Start Write Now.

Keep in touch,
Mel

ABOUT THE AUTHOR

Ever since I can remember, I've been a meddler of words. My novels take you to the heart of the crime. I write police procedurals, psychological suspense and crime dramas - fiction with a punch. Shortlisted for the prestigious CWA (Crime Writer's Association) Dagger in Library Award 2014, my inspiration comes from authors such as Martina Cole, Lynda la Plante, Mandasue Heller and Elizabeth Haynes.

I live in Stoke-on-Trent, Staffordshire, with my husband and terrier, Dexter (named after the TV serial killer) and make liberal use of my hometown as a backdrop for some of my books.

I also write women's fiction as Marcie Steele. You can find out more at my website .

OTHER BOOKS BY MEL SHERRATT

Click here for details about all my books on one page

ACKNOWLEDGMENTS

I can hardly believe that The Lies You Tell is my eleventh crime novel—it feels like it was only yesterday when I was tentatively publishing Taunting the Dead and hoping that one or two people might like it. To say that I am grateful to the hundreds of thousands of readers who have invested their time and money in my books would be an enormous understatement. Your faith and support has meant so much to me over these last few years—thank you all so very much.

Particular thanks must go to the friends I am very lucky to have – and who are nothing like Esther Smedley! Alison Niebiezczanski, Caroline Mitchell, Talli Roland, Louise Ross and Sharon Sant. Also to my fabulous agent, Madeleine Milburn, and her ever growing team. Thank you all for coffee, cake, Pimms, chats, laughs, pick-me-ups and general cheerleading.

I want to say a huge thank you to anyone who has read my books, sent me emails, messages, engaged with me on social media or come to see me at various events over the country. Without you behind me, this wouldn't be half as much fun. I love what I do and hope you continue to enjoy my books. Likewise, my thanks go out to all the wonderful book bloggers and enthusiasts who have read my stories and taken the time out of their busy lives to write such beautiful reviews, I am grateful to all of you!

Thank you to Martin Tideswell and everyone at The Sentinel, Stoke-on-Trent. Thank you for taking this Stokie under your wing. The support you give me is amazing! #localandproud

Finally, to Chris. Without your support I know I wouldn't have got this far. One million books sold! Love you to bits, fella.

❀ Created with Vellum

Printed in Great Britain
by Amazon